CW00820308

MAKE YOURSELF AT HOME

BOOKS BY WENDY CLARKE

What She Saw

We Were Sisters

The Bride

His Hidden Wife

Blind Date

Childhood Sweetheart

The Night Out

The Garden Party

MAKE YOURSELF AT HOME

WENDY CLARKE

bookouture

Published by Bookouture in 2025

An imprint of Storyfire Ltd.
Carmelite House
50 Victoria Embankment
London EC4Y 0DZ

The authorised representative in the EEA is Hachette Ireland
8 Castlecourt Centre
Dublin 15 D15 XTP3
Ireland
(email: info@hbgi.ie)

ISBN: 978-1-83618-607-6
eBook ISBN: 978-1-83618-608-3

For Emma and every other teacher who has made a difference

PROLOGUE

The orange flames draw upwards, teasing the ends of the curtains. Licking up their seams until they, too, start to smoulder. The fire began in the wastepaper basket stuffed with administration forms, yesterday's unmarked class assignments and worksheets scribbled on by teenage hands, but now it's spreading fast. The grey smoke that fills the classroom thickening to black.

A man, returning from his night shift at a nearby warehouse, puts down his bag in front of his home and pulls his door key out of his pocket. But, instead of putting it in the lock, he lets his hand drop to his side again, his attention caught by the flickering, orange glow behind the windows of the building at the end of his road.

Inside the classroom, the fire has climbed the legs of the teacher's desk. The filing tray has started to melt in the intense heat. The pot of Biros and rulers too – the plastic twisting. Popping. The tongues of the flames tasting their way through the detritus of the day before. Their appetite growing. Hunger turning their attention to the carpet. The students' tables. To anything that will satisfy them.

A window shatters. The fresh supply of oxygen causing dark smoke to billow into the night, chased by angry yellow flames.

'Yeah, it's the school,' the man shouts into his phone. He's in the street now. Standing in the middle of the road to get a better look. 'Anyone in there? It's the middle of the bloody night. Why would there be? Anyway, how the hell should I know? Just get here!'

He runs to the gate, grabs hold of one of the railings, the mobile pressed to his ear. Wondering why there's no fire alarm.

'I'm still here, yes.' He can hear it now, the roar of the fire as it consumes everything in its path. 'You'll be how long? Five minutes... thank God. My son goes to that school.'

Behind him in the road, curtains are twitching. A couple have come out in their dressing gowns. A dog barks. A front gate opens, then another.

'What's happening?'

'Did you hear that bang?'

'Is it the school?'

The man is shielding his eyes to see better. The smoke reaching him now, making him cough.

'What did you say? No, I can't see anyone. Oh, wait. Wait.' The wind has changed direction, sending the smoke on a different path. He looks again. Thinks he sees something at the window.

'There's someone in there. Oh, Jesus, yes, there's someone there.' His voice is choked. 'Is it a woman? Is it a child? Why are you asking? What does it matter?'

Because it's already too late. No one could get out of that burning classroom alive and the desperate hand he'd seen pressed against the glass has already gone.

ONE

Can you love someone too much? It's a question Catherine has asked herself many times since she and Gary tied the knot ten years ago. She looks at him now, long legs propped up on the coffee table, feet crossed at the ankle, frowning at whatever the newsreader has just said – something about another train strike. Or maybe that scowl is simply that her husband doesn't like the man's tie.

The question had elicited smirks and a press of hands to red faces in her GCSE English class that week. Because no one wants to discuss love with someone old enough to be their mother. Even if they don't look bad for their age. But it's an important question, nonetheless. How can anyone love their partner *too* much when just the sight of them at the end of a bad day can make everything feel a hundred times better? When being with them is better than being without them.

Yet, there's something she doesn't like about that phrase, the words *too much* bringing with them more than a hint of the obsessive. Invoking the sense of something suffocating. Unhealthy. What had made her think of that? Why is she still mulling it over, even now?

She steals another glance at her husband. There's nothing unhealthy or obsessive about her love for Gary. Is there?

Gary looks up at her now, aware she's staring at him.

'What?' He rubs at his cheek as though she's seen something he doesn't know about: a mark or a patch of stubble he missed when he shaved that morning.

'Nothing.'

'No, really. What? You've been staring at me for the last five minutes. I can feel your eyes burning into my skin.'

Leaning forward, Catherine puts her Diet Coke onto the coffee table, then, worried Gary will kick it over, slides it away from his socked foot.

'Eyes can't burn,' she says.

'Don't be pedantic. You know what I mean.'

Forced to acknowledge she's carried her teacher hat into their home, she grants him a smile. So what if she was looking at him? He is, after all, as her mother likes to put it, easy on the eye. Olive skin that tans as soon as he looks at the sun. Dark eyes, the brows that arch above them just the right side of heavy – enough to make him look as though he's thinking hard about something important when he draws them towards each other. Lips that when pressed together lend a certain irony to his smile.

She has a sudden urge to kiss him but resists.

Gary pulls a face at her. 'You're still doing it. What's got into you tonight?' He points at the open folder on her lap. 'Can't you leave that?'

'You know I can't. I owe it to the kids to come in tomorrow properly prepared.'

'Even if it means I go to bed without you?'

It's said as a joke, but Catherine hears the note of truth in his voice. Ignores it.

'Yes.'

He huffs out his derision. 'Back when I was teaching, we

did our next day's prep in class after the kids had gone home and anything we didn't get done, we made up. It's called winging it, Cath. Though you probably wouldn't understand that word. Adds a bit of creativity.'

The pillow she throws lands with a satisfying thud against his chest. 'Oh, shut up. That's not true and you know it. Anyway, you're a fine one to lecture me on the ins and outs of teaching.' She looks down at the page of notes she's made.

'You work too hard.'

'It must be hard going through life as a cynical bastard.'

'Actually, I find it quite easy.' He grins. 'Now put that folder away and come here.'

Reaching out a hand, he grabs her wrist and pulls her over to him. 'Perhaps I can help you forget about that bloody school for five minutes.'

'Only five?'

'Well,' he says, drawing a finger down the side of her neck, making her shiver. 'Maybe ten.'

He kisses her hard, the way she likes it, taking her breath away. And, when he draws away again, she's disappointed. Not that she'll let him see. It's something he does on occasion, this leaving her wanting as though his love is something to be earned, and she wonders whether it's intentional. A subtle way of highlighting the imbalance between them. A reminder that when he could have chosen anyone, he'd chosen her.

She pushes him away. Brushes the hair from her face. 'Idiot!'

Gary picks up the TV remote and points it at the screen. 'Now why would that guy think a red striped tie would go with that suit? Bloody newsreaders, they should get themselves a stylist. Or, better still, bring back that Ronda what's her name... the one with the pout and the tight dresses.'

'Ronda's the weather presenter.'

'Whatever. They all look the same to me.'

He presses a button and the screen blanks, just their reflections left on it. His thumb strokes the centimetre of bare flesh at her waist. 'How about we go upstairs... finish what we started? I'm fed up talking about school stuff.'

'It doesn't just disappear once the bell's rung, Gaz. Less than twenty per cent of the kids at Greenfield will leave the school with five decent GCSEs. If I can make it twenty-one, then it's progress.'

Gary groans. 'With the best will in the world there are some kids you can't help.' He stops and it comes to her suddenly that he's referring to her brother, Aled. 'It's just that sometimes, just sometimes, I wish you wouldn't take your job home with you. Hearing about it day in, day out, can get pretty boring, if I'm honest.'

Catherine moves away from him, surprised at what he's just said. She'd been happy that evening, despite the prospect of a new school week, but now she's filled with unease. 'You're saying you're bored of *me*?'

He looks at her. Frowns. 'That's not what I said. It's just that sometimes...'

'What?'

Catherine's stomach twists and she waits, her eyes fixed on Gary's face, for what will come next. Wondering if she should be worried. Scared even.

But instead of finishing what he was going to say, he leans across to her and kisses the side of her head. 'Forget it. Of course I'm not bored of you. You're my wife.'

'Maybe you're bored of me *because* I'm your wife. Maybe you wish I was more like Ronda the weather girl, who, dare I point out, is young enough to be your daughter.'

'What?' He looks at her, perplexed, then away again. Runs a hand through his hair. Making the ends stick up. 'You're making too much of this and, anyway, how could I ever be bored of someone who leaves crazy love notes for me to find?' He widens his eyes and twists an imaginary curl around his finger. '*I lerve you, sexy husband.*'

'Shut up, Gary!' But Catherine can't help smiling and the yelp Gary gives when she pokes her finger into his side, dulls the thin blade of pain that had lodged in her chest a second earlier. She tucks her folder under her arm, then picks up her empty glass with the other hand. Stands. 'It won't take me long to finish this. I don't want the Year 11s to run riot.'

'Which is why I don't know why you carry on at that rough school. Maybe you should think about doing something else.'

'What? Like payroll administrator? You forget I majored in English, not maths and, anyway, I like what I do. I'm challenged by it.'

'Okay, I admit working for the council isn't the most exciting job in the world but give me a good financial spread-sheet over a classful of feral kids any day of the week. No wonder you...'

Gary stops, a worried look on his face, and Catherine knows what he was going to say. Is glad he didn't. No good will come from dwelling on it; it was a long time ago. She looks at the glass of wine he's holding. Eyes the half-empty bottle on the side. She won't relapse... too many years have gone by.

'All I'm saying is you don't need to work there, or work at all if you don't want to. I make enough to support us both.' He watches her appreciatively as she walks across the room. 'No hot sex tonight then?'

She stops and turns. ''Fraid not. Oh, and I forgot to tell you. That new girl's really struggling.'

'What new girl?' he asks, but the question can't disguise his lack of interest.

She knows she should leave it, but she can't. She wants him to understand.

'The new ECT that Ross is mentoring. Remember I told you?' An image comes to her of the girl. Long dark hair pushed behind her ears. Wide doe eyes framed by the overlarge glasses she wears. 'I'm not sure if she's ever going to make Qualified Teacher Status.'

'Maybe she's too busy in bed with her boyfriend.'

Catherine freezes, wondering if he'll comment further, compare Lisa to the girl Catherine was when he first met her. She laughs. Tries to pretend he hasn't hurt her.

In the kitchen, she slides the drawer of the dishwasher out and puts in her glass. Hears it rattle as she closes the door on it. She's done it again – turned the conversation around to teaching. What's the matter with her?

She sees the calendar on the wall. Tomorrow's date circled in red. *That's* what's the matter.

From the silver frame on the side, Gary's face smiles out at her from their wedding photograph. Blinking back tears she doesn't want Gary to see, she picks it up and studies it. Presses the cold frame against her forehead. The question she'd posed earlier, whether you could love someone too much, is back in her head.

Catherine listens to the sound of her husband walking upstairs, and as she returns the photograph to its place, a new question forms.

What happens when your husband doesn't love you enough?

TWO

It's seven fifteen in the morning, the world still edging towards monochrome, but Catherine likes to arrive at school when the classroom windows are still dark and blank – reflecting the clouds or the security light, depending on the season. The corridors hushed. The pound of school shoes and the slam of locker doors just a memory.

She drives into the staff parking area and gets out of her car. As she shuts the door and locks it, something makes her turn her head. It's darker than usual, the few other cars that are parked there just dark shapes. She's lost count of how many times she's asked for the security light to be fixed, but nothing has been done about it. She adds it to her mental to-do list.

She stands by her car, looking across the tarmacked area. It's the same spot she's parked in since she started teaching here, so why have the small hairs on the nape of her neck inextricably started to prickle? Putting it down to lack of sleep, she ignores the feeling. Bends and slides the plastic box full of folders from the back seat, using her hip to slam the car door shut.

Catherine walks towards the school, the high fence that encloses the site rising in front of her, bringing back memories of the fort her brother played with when he was just a little kid. The thought stops her in her tracks... Aled would have been thirty now... not a child. Yet the image of him as he'd been in happier times is the one she tries to cling on to. An image that could only be a reality if what happened fifteen years ago had never happened. She thought things would get easier with each passing year... but her guilt and grief still linger.

She's reached the locked gate, but, somewhere off to her right, a shadow edges across the green metal uprights. She turns, straining her eyes to see, her heart pounding, but there's nothing. For a second, she'd thought it was Aled moving silently along the fence line, but of course it isn't. How could it be? It's just a flap of loosened tarpaulin agitated by the wind. Nothing more.

Stop it, Catherine, she tells herself. *Get a grip.*

Her brother is in her head again and it takes a supreme effort to push the image of him away, even though she knows she has to if she's to function normally. Because Aled's dead – a truth she has to remind herself of, even now after all these years. Nothing is going to bring him back.

But there it is again. That same shifting movement she'd seen before. Pressing the box to her chest, Catherine braces herself.

'Who's there?'

The shape moves, grows bigger. But then slips away unseen.

Lifting the lanyard that's round her neck, Catherine quickly presses the card bearing her name to the keypad next to the gate. She waits for it to open, her eyes on the large sign welcoming visitors to Greenfield Comprehensive, then crosses the playground, the light from the reception area drawing her towards it. As she walks, her eyes scan the windows where only a few rooms have their lights on. The rest are just blank squares against the red-brick.

She reaches the main door and lets herself in, craving

normality. And, once she's over the threshold, the walls with their motivational quotes and the warmth coming from the radiators, quickly calm her. Today is the anniversary of Aled's death and it's made her jittery.

'Morning, Lynne.'

The receptionist looks up. Smiles. 'Ah, Catherine. Just the person. I've had a call from Mia Cooper's mum. Something to do with her homework.'

'Already?'

''Fraid so.'

Catherine purses her lips. 'What was it this time? Please don't tell me she blamed the dog again.'

'No, a death in the family.'

'Not the most original.'

'Anyway, you're early, Cath. Bad night?' Lynne puts her head on one side. Studies her. 'You look awfully pale.'

Catherine forces herself to smile. 'You know me, Lynne. I like having time to get my thoughts in order before the mob arrive. It turns me into happy, kind Mrs Ashworth rather than the alternative. Snappy and miserable.'

'In all the years you've been with us, I've yet to see *that*.'

'Then I'd better get to my class to ensure that you don't!'

It's said lightly, but, as she unbuttons her coat, Catherine can't help wondering what on earth made her say it. She's always been careful to avoid saying anything that might give the suggestion there could be a different version of herself. One that no one's seen. Not at this school anyway.

Catherine stares through the window at the dark playground. She loves her job, but now, with the anniversary of her brother's death in her head, it feels a little less bright, a little less enjoyable. More like something she needs to get through to prove to herself she can do it. For what Lynne, or anyone else for that matter, doesn't know, is that the second person she'd described is the one she once was. Not recently, but way back in the early days of her teaching career, in the weeks after Aled's death. A time when dealing with difficult kids and a heap of marking and paperwork threatened to unhinge her.

Before Gary had come along and saved her.

'Who else is in?' she asks quickly, cross with herself for having allowed these thoughts to get into her head. 'Lisa?'

Lynne screws up her eyes and taps at the screen of her computer with her pen. 'No, not yet. In fact, no one from your department's in except for the head honcho.'

'Hmm, what mood is she in?'

Lynne laughs. 'The usual.'

'Great.' Not that she has a problem with Ellen. Quite the opposite in fact. She's a good head teacher. It was she, after all, who had dragged Greenfield Comprehensive kicking and screaming out of special measures when she took over the school three years ago and thank God she did, or who knows where they might be now. Catherine has a lot of respect for her and, as far as she can tell, it's reciprocated.

Lynne is flapping a hand at her to get her attention. 'Sorry, Cath. I made a mistake. Ross is in.'

'Ross? Oh, bugger.' She'd failed to see his car in the dark car park.

'That's a bit strong. I thought you two were like this.' Lynne crosses her middle finger over her first. 'Haven't had a falling-out, have you?'

'What? No, of course not.' She and Ross have been friends and colleagues for as long as she's been at Greenfield Comprehensive, acquaintances before that, and she knows he'll be waiting for her in the staffroom, a mug of coffee in his hand and a smug look on his face. *What took you so long? Gary fancied a quickie this morning, did he?*

Catherine chuckles to herself, her mood improving again. 'First into school' is a childish game, she knows, but one that amuses them both. Last week he'd beaten her three days out of five, despite her having taken a shortcut through the housing estate to avoid the lights in town. She'll need to do better if she's to regain her crown.

'I'll see you later, Lynne.'

After signing in, Catherine presses her name card to the pad next to the door and lets herself into the main school building. The corridor is eerily quiet, her footsteps echoing as she walks, the rows of grey lockers she passes locked shut.

She pushes through the door that leads into the hall where the year groups have their assemblies, then climbs the stairs to the first floor. After dropping the box off in her classroom, she walks back down the corridor, heading for the door marked *Staffroom*. As she'd expected, Ross is there, sitting on the faux leather settee, a pile of Year 8 workbooks in front of him. When he sees her, he closes the book he's marking and folds his arms.

'What kept you?'

'Some of us need our beauty sleep, you know.' Catherine takes off her coat. 'Not all of us can survive on five hours and a hangover.'

It's a cheap dig, but he takes it well. Looks her up and down and grins. 'You can say that again.'

'Fuck off, Walker. Anyway, where's my coffee?'

'In the jar.'

With a shake of her head, Catherine goes over to the small kitchen area. She unscrews the jar of coffee and spoons some into the mug she's taken from her bag. *Awesome Teacher* printed on its side. 'Who have you got first?'

'Year 8. You?'

'Double period with the class from hell, then Year 9.'

Ross laughs. 'Class from hell? I presume you're talking about Year 11. I hate the lot of them.'

'Yeah. Who else?' She glances at the door. 'But you need to be careful what you say, Ross. Ellen's in and if she catches you talking like that, she'll have you out on your ear before you can say Ofsted.'

Ross shrugs. 'I say it because it's true and anyone who tells you they like all their classes equally is a liar.'

Catherine leans back against the counter and takes a sip of her coffee. She's not going to argue with him as it's an argument she'll never win. Year 11 is difficult, there's no getting around it.

Ross looks at his watch. 'You know this is the best job in the world until the kids arrive.' He scoops up his books and puts them in the plastic box that's on the floor beside him. 'Anyway, gonna love ya and leave ya. I've still got some prep to do for first period.'

'Me too. I'll catch you later.'

'If you get out of your first class alive.' Ross stands, picks up the box and walks over to the door with it. 'Oops. Might need another pair of hands.'

'And a few more brain cells.' Catherine opens the door for him. Waves him through. 'Lead on, Macduff.'

Ross stands with the red box in his hands, fingers whitening under the weight. 'You know that's a misquote, don't you? Shakespeare never wrote it.'

'I'm going for Head of English, Ross. I'd be pretty worried if I didn't know it.'

''Suppose not. Damn, this box is heavy.' He puts the box down, his expression turning serious. 'What are your chances, do you reckon?'

Catherine looks away from him. Turning her attention to the Year 11 artwork that's displayed on the wall – abstract portraits of well-known people – as she thinks how to answer him. 'I think I've got a pretty good chance, if I'm honest.'

'You know they've got some externals going for it too.' He draws quote marks in the air. 'To ensure a fair and competitive selection process.'

'I had heard.'

Ross rubs his hand up and down the back of his neck. 'Does Gary know? About you applying? He hasn't said anything to me.'

'Not yet,' she replies, not liking that he presumes he would.

She forgets sometimes that Ross had been her husband's friend before he was hers. Forgets that the two of them are still close. And thank goodness for that as it was Ross who'd found her the job at Greenfield Comprehensive at a time when she was beginning to think she'd never find another teaching position. He who'd put in a good word for her with the old head in the days before Ellen took over the running of the school.

Catherine looks at her friend, assessing him. Now, having taught with the man for many years, she believes the balance of friendship has tipped in her favour and she's pretty certain he'd choose her over Gary any day.

'Promise me you won't say anything to Gary about this, Ross. Not until the interview anyway. I have this *thing* about it... call it superstition.'

'Like saying *Macbeth* in a theatre will curse the production?'

She laughs. 'Something like that. Anyway, no one knows except you.'

If she'd expected him to comment, to say he's honoured or something like that, he disappoints her. Instead, he changes the subject.

'So, what are your thoughts on my mentee? From what you've seen of her so far, how do you reckon she's doing?'

'Lisa?'

'Yeh.' Ross glances down the corridor in the direction of her classroom. 'I know Ellen's worried about her. Just wondered what *you* thought.'

Catherine thinks back to the conversation she'd had with Gary last night. 'I suppose, if I'm honest, I'm worried too. Lisa's young, lacks backbone, and the kids can sense it. They smell weakness as keenly as a shark with a drop of blood in the ocean and run rings round her. You should spend some time going over strategies with her.'

Ross grimaces. 'I'm paid to teach not babysit. I don't know what they teach them at uni these days, but it sure ain't classroom management. The way she's going, she'll be lucky to meet the Teachers' Standards.'

It's nice to be able to talk to Ross about these things – if only Gary was more interested in her career. But last night he'd said he found the subject boring and she still can't help wondering if that makes *her* boring? Less appealing to him? Her mind turns back to Lisa, and she has a sudden urge to ask Ross if he finds the girl attractive. Thinks better of it.

'Don't be too hard on her.' It's not as if she doesn't know what it feels like to struggle. 'She'll learn.'

'The hard way most probably... like we all had to. Anyway, I need to get on. I'll see you at lunch.' He picks up the box and starts to walk away but is stopped in his tracks by a voice.

'Morning you two. Putting the world to rights?'

They'd been so busy chatting neither of them had seen Ellen Swanson approach.

Catherine smiles. 'Morning, Ellen. Something like that.' She doesn't mention Lisa, and neither does Ross. Despite everything they'd said, they both know the last thing the girl needs is for the head teacher to be breathing down her neck.

Ellen folds her arms and leans against the radiator. 'Just wanted to give you a heads-up. Dean Gibbs's father is on the warpath again. Says his son's being picked on and that the last three-day suspension was unjust and uncalled for.'

Ross raises his eyebrows. 'He used those words?'

'Well not exactly, they were punctuated by a lot of colourful language, but that was the gist of it. Anyway, security have been notified and Mr Gibbs won't be allowed on the premises unless by direct invitation from me. I'm presuming you and the rest of the staff will be okay with that.'

'Fine by me. The man's a thug.' Ross juts his chin at the box he's holding. 'Look, I really do have to go before I drop this bloody thing.'

'Of course.' Ellen waits for him to leave, then turns to Catherine. 'What about you, Cath?'

'It's fine with me too. That family needs to be sent a strong message.' She thinks of the incident that had led to Dean's suspension. The chair he'd raised above his head in anger after she'd told him to move to a table away from the friends who had helped him disrupt the lesson. A chair that Catherine had wrestled out of his grasp to the accompaniment of cheers from students who'd grown tired of him and his hangers-on. Once upon a time, an incident like that would have thrown her into a panic, but now, after years of experience with difficult teenagers, she'd dealt with it calmly. Efficiently.

Only once she'd got home, had she been overcome by an uncontrollable shaking. She hadn't told Gary, or Ross even, and she knows why. Acknowledging the event had shaken her would be the same as admitting to some weakness.

And that's something she will never do.

Not if she can help it.

THREE

'I'd better be getting to my classroom. Time has a habit of running away with me in this place.'

'Doesn't it just.'

Ellen walks away, but Catherine stands a moment, her eyes drawn to the fire extinguisher on the wall – a laminated poster on the noticeboard next to it explaining what to do in the event of a fire. The words come into focus: *Sound the alarm, leave the building by the nearest available exit*, and as the same old question repeats itself in her head, her heart starts to pound. They have regular fire drills, but, if a real fire was to break out on their floor, would she be able to get the children out in time?

Catherine looks back at Ellen, the fight or flight instinct strong.

The head teacher has reached her blue office door and, seeing Catherine still standing in the corridor, she stops. Lifts a finger.

'Oh, actually there *was* something else I wanted to talk to you about, Cath. Lisa Prescott... I know Ross was supposed to be her mentor, but she's requested a transfer.'

'A transfer? Really? To who?'

'To you, Catherine. I know it's a bit sudden, and I didn't want to say anything to Ross before I checked with you first, but I think it's a good idea. You have a proven knowledge of classroom management, and I'm certain you'll do a good job. We should probably have assigned her to you in the first place.'

'Do you know why she wanted to move?'

'Let's just say that Ross, for all his experience, is a bit laissez-faire when it comes to discipline and Lisa wasn't convinced he could pass on the required skills in that area.'

'I see.' She can't help feeling rather pleased.

'So you're happy to do it?'

Thoughts of the upcoming interview for Head of English come into her head. This could be a very good thing. 'Yes, of course. It's nice she felt me worthy.'

'We all do, Catherine. Good classroom skills are worth their weight in gold in a school like Greenfield and not everyone has them. If anyone can help her, you can.'

Catherine nods and tucks her hair behind her ears, hoping Ellen hasn't noticed the heat that has come into her cheeks. Praise isn't something the head teacher gives out easily, or without good cause, and she's flattered by it.

'I'll go and see her as soon as she comes in.'

'Please do.'

With a parting smile, Catherine leaves her and walks back down the corridor to her room, her eyes drawn to the windows of the other classrooms in the English department. Some are still in darkness, but, in the room next to hers, the light is on.

She stops, surprised to see Lisa at her desk marking books; she hadn't thought she was in yet. As she watches, Lisa takes off her glasses and slumps back in her chair, the heels of her hands pressed to her eyes.

Concerned, Catherine gives a light knock on the door. Puts her head around it.

'Morning, Lisa. You're in early again. All okay?'

Lisa straightens and Catherine's shocked to see the bruise-like shadows beneath the girl's eyes and how pale the skin of her face is beneath the harsh strip light. Usually, Lisa wears her long dark hair loose, but, this morning, she's scragged it back into a careless ponytail.

As though aware of what Catherine is thinking, Lisa picks up her glasses and puts them back on. Smooths a hand from her pale forehead to the scrunchie that traps her hair.

She gives a watery smile. 'I'm fine.'

'Are you sure? You look done in.'

Catherine goes into the classroom, closes the door behind her and makes her way between the tables. She leans back against the one opposite Lisa's desk.

'Ellen's just told me you'd like me to be your mentor instead of Ross.'

'If you'll have me.'

'I'd be glad to, but, if I do, it's important you know you can talk to me about anything that's bothering you. It's what I'm here for.'

'I know that, but, really, I'm fine.' She sounds weary, defeated, and it worries Catherine. Should she press her?

'Is it Year 11 you're concerned about?' It's a stab in the dark but an obvious one. Lisa is their form tutor and it can't be easy. 'You know that everyone finds them difficult, don't you? Even me. You wouldn't be the first to let them get under your skin and you definitely won't be the last. I've got half of them for my first lesson and by the end of it, I'll look like a wrung-out dishrag, I can guarantee you.'

It's meant as a joke, but Lisa doesn't laugh. 'You have them so under control. You make it look so easy.'

So she was right. It *is* what's bothering her.

'It wasn't always like that.' Unsure of why she's said it, she hurries on. 'Please don't be downhearted. It takes a lot of practice, but you'll get there.'

Lisa's eyes widen slightly. 'Really? You struggled too? What happened?'

It's the first time Catherine has admitted it to anyone. It should be a relief, but it isn't. Already, she's wishing she hadn't said anything. But it's not fair of her to expect Lisa to open up if she can't do the same.

'It was nothing in particular. I was young, inexperienced like you. Let's just say I had a bit of a wobble, and it took a while to get back on track.' She pushes herself away from the desk not wanting to say anything more. 'Now, we need to make a timetable for your progress meetings, and when we've agreed on a date for your first one, we can discuss classroom strategies. Good idea?'

Lisa gives a weak smile and picks up her pen. 'Thank you. Yes, that would be good.'

'Excellent. And I'll be just next door if you need anything.'

She nods. 'I know.'

Leaving Lisa, Catherine goes into her own classroom and shuts the door. Usually, she enjoys this time before the children arrive, but, today, she feels unsettled. She puts a pile of worksheets on the side ready to give out later. Finds the right file on her computer and makes sure the interactive whiteboard is working properly. With nothing more to do before the kids arrive, she sits at her desk.

Then, as if it has a life of its own, her hand moves to the top drawer of her desk and pulls it open. Her fingers reaching. Feeling the shape of the vodka bottle wrapped inside the Tesco carrier bag.

FOUR

The bell's gone and Catherine breathes a sigh of relief. It's been a hard day, the kids pushing at boundaries, and she's getting a headache.

In her bag, her phone pings a message and she bends and rummages for it, pleased when she sees it's Gary who's messaged her. *Got out of the meeting early and it looks like I'll make the 4.50 train. Was going to walk from the station, but it's pissing down with rain so thought I'd cadge a lift home with you instead. OK?*

Catherine smiles to herself. Glad that Gary will be coming home with her. She replies. It's exactly what she needs today.

She's just putting her phone back in her bag when there's a knock on the door. It's Lisa, a folder of work clutched to her chest. She looks shattered – as though she hasn't slept for a week. Or maybe worry has caused the shadows beneath her eyes.

'Are you all right, Lisa? Bad day?' She tries to keep the concern out of her voice, but it's there all the same.

Lisa rubs at the sleeves of her blouse. The thin material wrinkling under her hands. 'I'm fine.'

But if that's true, why is the girl here?

'You don't look fine. Sit here and I'll go and make you a coffee. If it's Year 11, I can help you—'

'It's not them.' It's said quickly, her eyes on the door.

'Then what is it? If there's anything I can do to make things better, I promise I'll try.'

'There's nothing you can do.' Lisa's eyes are still on the door as though she's expecting someone to walk in. 'I just needed to tell you. To explain. It's... well, it's my mum.'

'Oh?' Catherine hadn't been expecting that. Lisa's never talked that much about her parents. 'Is she okay? Has something happened?'

'No, not really. It's just...' To Catherine's surprise, a tear slips down the side of Lisa's nose and she watches as the girl wipes it away.

'Go on.'

The way Lisa stands there in front of her, the folder she's clutching turning her knuckles white, you'd think she was one of the sixth form, not a teacher. Her fine features pinched. Her slight frame childlike beneath her blouse. But then at twenty-two, to Catherine, she *is* still a child. On the first rung of her career. Scared to make mistakes for fear that others might see it as failing. Scared to reach out for help for the same reason. Until now.

Catherine stretches out a hand to her. 'Talk to me.'

'She and Dad,' she says miserably. 'They don't want me at home.'

Catherine's shocked. 'I'm sure that's not true.'

'It *is* true. They've made it quite clear.' She covers her face with her hands. 'Dad said that at twenty-two I was too old to still be living at home. That I wasn't a kid and needed to find somewhere else to stay.'

'And your mum?' Catherine draws in a breath. 'What did *she* say?'

Another tear follows the first. 'She didn't.'

Catherine looks at the girl, assessing her, then gets up and pulls out a chair from behind one of the desks. 'Sit down and tell me when all this happened.'

Lisa does as she's told. 'Last weekend.'

'I see. And have you thought what you're going to do?' On an ECT's salary she'd be lucky to find a house share she could afford.

'I'll find something.' She leans forward, fingers trapped between her thighs. 'But it's the reason why I have to make it work at Greenfield. Why I can't fail. I need to save for a deposit.'

Catherine's heart goes out to her. 'You won't fail, love. I'll make sure of that.' She shakes her head. 'It's a tough world out there. An unfair world. Things happen when you least expect them to and that's why you must learn to rely on yourself not on others. Training to be a teacher and getting this job was the first step. You just need to be brave and take the next. I'll ask around, see if anyone's heard of a place that's going at a reasonable rate. I won't mention your name.'

The smile Lisa gives her is edged with relief. 'Thank you, Cath. I'm so glad I told you. I've been a bit, you know, flaky, unable to cope, and I thought it only fair to explain why.'

'And I'm glad you did.' Catherine leans forward. Gives Lisa's hands a squeeze, then releases them. 'I'm here for you, Lisa. You know that.'

Lisa nods. Gets a tissue out of her pocket and blows her nose. 'I know. Thank you, and I'm sorry.'

'For what?'

She gives a half-hearted smile. 'For being like this.'

'Honestly, there's nothing to apologise for. I told you before... we've all been there. *I've* been there. Now come on.' Forcing a smile, Catherine gets up. 'I'll go and make that drink, and when I get back, we'll go over your lesson plans for tomorrow. Make sure you're happy with what you'll be doing. Sound okay?'

Lisa nods. 'More than okay.'

'Great. I won't be long.'

With a reassuring smile, Catherine leaves Lisa and walks down the corridor in the direction of the staffroom. On the way, she passes Lisa's classroom and stops, seeing that the white-board is filled with Shakespearean quotes written in black dry-erase marker.

'Oh, Ross.'

Last lesson, when Lisa had a free period, Ross had used her room for a revision class. Trust him not to have bothered to clean off the board.

'Lazy bugger.' Lisa had enough on her plate without having to clean off his mess.

Catherine steps into the classroom. Looks for a cloth with which to wipe the board. When she doesn't see one, she opens the cupboard behind Lisa's desk where the classroom equip-ment is kept.

She stares, then frowns. Not because the cloth isn't there, but because shoved into the space under the shelves containing stationery supplies and rolled-up posters is a sleeping bag and a pillow. The zipped holdall next to them, bulging at the seams.

Catherine knows she shouldn't look, but the worry she'd felt when Lisa had told her about her living arrangements is grow-ing. If she's right in what she suspects, isn't it better that she knows for sure?

With a quick glance at the door, Catherine squats down and unzips the bag, her fears confirmed. The holdall is full of clothes... ones she's seen Lisa wear.

She shakes her head. *Oh Lisa.*

'What are you doing?' Catherine's head shoots up. Lisa is standing behind her, her face white.

Catherine stands. 'I'm sorry. I didn't mean to pry, but I was

looking for something to use to wipe the board and saw this.'
She points to the sleeping bag. 'What's going on, Lisa?'

The girl crosses her arms. Looks out of the window into the playground where the last of the stragglers are milling by the gate. 'I told you they didn't want me. They left me no choice but to leave.'

'And when was this?'

Her eyes don't leave the window. 'Last Thursday.'

'Thursday? But that's four days ago. Where on earth have you been staying?' God forbid she's been sleeping rough. 'Please, tell me you've been at a friend's place?'

'I don't have any friends.'

'Then where...?'

But she doesn't need to ask. It's obvious. Lisa being so early into school isn't because she's keen, it's because she'd never left.

'You've been sleeping here? In the classroom? But how?'

'It's not difficult. I sign out at the end of the day, then slip back inside when Lynne's attention is elsewhere. I used to come to school by train, so there's no car left in the car park to give me away and it was easy to avoid the cleaners. I know which class-rooms they do first.'

'But what about the CCTV?'

'All the kids know the dead spots. Sometimes, it pays to listen to their gossip.'

Catherine looks around her. 'Jesus, Lisa. You've been sleeping on the floor, then trying to do a day's teaching? No wonder you've been looking so tired. Why didn't you tell me? Why didn't you say anything?'

Lisa looks down. 'Because I was ashamed. I didn't want anyone to feel sorry for me. I didn't want *you* to feel sorry for me.'

'Oh, love.' Catherine puts her arm around her. 'That's not what I'd think.' But she's lying. She's never felt more sorry for anyone in her life. She looks at the classroom floor trying to imagine what it must be like to be there at night. The hard carpet tiles chosen for their noise reduction not as a surface to sleep on, the large windows with nothing but the playground and the staff car park to look out onto. The empty corridors.

She shudders. 'What are you going to do?'

'I'll find something.' Lisa's eyes fill with tears. 'You don't need to worry. I just wanted to explain why I was a bit...' She rubs at the side of her cheek. 'You know.'

'Come into the staffroom with me and I'll make that coffee. Lord knows we could both do with one.'

'Okay.'

Catherine leads the way to the staffroom and opens the door. Thankful that no one else is in there – a rare thing at this time of day. She spoons coffee into mugs and pours in water from the urn. When she brings them over, Lisa is already sitting on one of the chairs, her folder open in front of her.

The table is ringed with coffee stains, and Catherine puts the mugs down, not worrying that there are no mats. 'There you are. Now let's take a look at what you've planned for tomorrow.'

They spend the next half hour talking about themes and objectives and are so absorbed in what they're doing that they don't see Gary through the bank of glass windows. Head bent. Walking purposefully down the corridor towards them.

When he reaches the open staffroom door, he rests his bent elbow on the door frame. Smiles.

'I don't want to break up the party, but I was wondering how much longer you were likely to be. Ross has already pissed off home and I didn't fancy helping Ellen set out the chairs for tomorrow's assembly.'

Catherine laughs. 'Oh hi, Gaz. We're almost done.' She gestures to Lisa with her hand. 'This is Lisa our new ECT. Lisa, this is my husband Gary.'

Lisa looks up and, seeing Gary, her face freezes.

Catherine frowns. 'Lisa?'

Lisa's standing now. Squinting at him from behind her glasses. 'I can't believe it. Is that you?'

'You know each other?' Now it's Catherine's turn to be surprised.

Dropping the folder she's holding onto the table, Lisa takes a step forward and, for a moment, Catherine wonders if she's going to embrace her husband. But then she sees Gary's face, the shock on it, and knows it's not going to happen.

'Yes.' Her eyes are fixed on his. 'Gary is my brother.'

FIVE

Catherine looks from Lisa to Gary, unsure of what to say, but before she can think more about it, Ellen's voice carries through to her from the corridor.

'Catherine, can I have a word with you before you leave? It won't take a moment.'

'Yes, of course.'

She gets up, leaving her husband standing stunned in front of Lisa. Why does Ellen need her right now? She wishes she could have waited a minute. She meets Ellen in the corridor but can't help glancing behind her.

Her stomach churns. 'Is it about Lisa?'

'No. If you could come to my office, I'll explain everything.'

'Maybe it can wait until tomorrow.' She turns her head again. Wonders at her husband's tense expression. 'Gary's here and we're in the middle of something important.'

Lisa's and Gary's voices are urgent but muted. It's frustrating she can't hear what they're saying. Why had Gary not told her he had a sister and that the same sister had been working under the same roof as her all these weeks?

'Need I remind you you're still in school, Cath?' Ellen says no more and, realising her error, Catherine moves away from the door. What she's just said to the head was unprofessional.

'Yes, I'm sorry. I know that, of course.' She follows Ellen to her office and takes the seat offered to her. Tries to focus. 'What did you want to speak to me about?'

Ellen puts on her glasses and squints at the computer screen in front of her. 'Actually, it's about a new boy who'll be joining us tomorrow. His name is Jake Lloyd and he'll be in Year 13.'

'Really?' They didn't normally have students joining them so late in the school year. 'Have his family moved house?'

'No. He was a student at Westley Academy, but it seems he didn't get on well there. He'll be in your A Level English class.'

Catherine sighs. 'So it's a case of inheriting another school's problem.'

'That's not like you, Cath.' There's a sharpness to Ellen's tone. 'You're usually one to embrace a challenge.'

'I know. It's just that...' But what can she say? She can hardly tell Ellen that all she can think about at the moment are the two people who are sitting in the staffroom – her husband, Gary, and Lisa the sister he'd never told her about.

Not able to stand it any longer she pushes her chair back and gets up. 'Rest assured, I'll do everything I can to help Jake achieve his goals, Ellen, but I really need to go. Was there anything else?'

Ellen takes off her glasses. Frowns. 'No. I'll make sure you get all the information on him as soon as it comes over from his old school. I just wanted to give you the heads-up before tomorrow.'

'Thank you.'

Catherine leaves Ellen's office and, when she knows she can no longer be seen, runs down the corridor in the direction of the staffroom. When she gets there, she finds Lisa back in her seat. Gary is at the window, his hands behind his back. The tips of his ears pink.

When he hears her, he turns and smiles, but there's something off about him.

'I can hardly believe Lisa's here. I knew Dad remarried and had another child, but the only time I met Lisa was at my gran's funeral years ago. I'd never have recognised her.'

Lisa smiles. 'I'd have only been a child, maybe nine or ten, but Gary looks just the same. I'd have known him anywhere.'

'Jesus.' Cath takes a seat opposite her. 'This is weird.'

Gary's face is grim. 'You said it.'

He shoots a look at Lisa, says nothing more, and Catherine knows why. He hasn't spoken to his father in years. The sudden appearance of his half-sister wouldn't have been something he'd wish for. It must bring back so much pain. But it's happened and they need to make the best of it... for his sake and for hers.

'But a sister, Gary. That's pretty awesome.' Catherine had always wanted a sister, but she keeps that thought to herself. It would be too disloyal to Aled to voice it. Especially today. Instead, she turns to Lisa.

'Tell Gary about what happened. About them chucking you out.' She looks up at him. 'She's been sleeping on the floor of the classroom, Gaz. Can you believe it?'

His eyes flick to her, distracted. 'What?'

'The classroom floor, Gary. That's where Lisa slept because she had nowhere else to go.'

She'd expected him to be sympathetic, but he merely looks annoyed. Angry even. 'Well, there you go.'

'And that's all you have to say?'

'What do you want me to say?'

'That it's a bloody shame,' she says, exasperated. 'A travesty. That your dad and stepmum should be ashamed of themselves. What's the matter with you, Gary?'

She looks at Lisa who's sitting with her head bent, her cheeks pink with embarrassment, unable to understand her husband's behaviour, however hard she tries.

'Do you know where you'll go tonight? Do you have anywhere to stay?'

Lisa looks up at her from under wet lashes. 'I don't suppose you and Gary...'

'Stay at ours, you mean?' It's not a question she'd expected her to ask. 'Oh, I don't know, Lisa.'

'I wouldn't have asked, but Gary *is* family.' Lisa glances out into the corridor. Shudders. 'It's just that I don't feel safe here alone at night. I think I hear things, see things, and keep imagining what could happen. A break-in. A fire.'

'A fire?' Catherine's heart stops. 'Why would you think that?'

Gary's staring at her and Catherine knows what he's thinking – that she's being drawn back to the past – and he'd be right. Already, images of her burnt-out classroom are pressing into her head.

She can't leave Lisa to sleep here. Alone.

'Then it's agreed. Come home with us tonight and I'll make up the bed in the spare room.'

Lisa reaches across the table and grabs Catherine's hands. 'I'll pay you rent. I promise. And I'll find somewhere else as soon as I can.' For the first time in weeks, she looks almost happy. 'I can't thank you enough. It's so kind.'

Catherine laughs. 'You might not be saying that when you have to put up with Gary's smelly feet. Or his heavy metal.'

'Believe me, it will be worth it.' Her eyes slide over to Gary. 'And it will be good to get to know my brother after all this time.'

'Half-brother.' He says the word as though it pains him.

Lisa's smile drops. 'Yes, half-brother.'

'Ignore him. As long as he gets his dinner on time and watches what he likes on the telly, I could have a whole bunch of people living with us and he wouldn't care. He just doesn't like change, that's all. We'd be delighted to have you.'

Catherine gives Lisa a reassuring smile, but behind it, she's concerned. Gary's face is sullen, and although he hasn't said no, he's clearly unhappy with the idea. There's no getting away from the fact that having Lisa in their house will upset the status quo. Maybe she should have asked him first. Made sure he was all right with it.

She'd said they'd be delighted to have her. How she wishes she could be as sure as she'd sounded.

But this is fate... it has to be.

Catherine thinks of Aled and how she'd let him down. A new family member living in their house, might be just the thing to solve their problems. Help her atone for the mistakes she's made in the past.

Gary might not be keen now, but she'll work on him and in time he'll see this was the right thing to do. The best thing.

SIX

'This will be your room, Lisa. I know it's not that big, but it should have everything you need. A chest of drawers to put your clothes in, a chair, a bed...' Catherine laughs self-consciously. 'Well, of course it's got a bed. Anyway, I hope you'll be comfortable here.' She hands Lisa the towels she's holding. 'These are for you. I didn't think you would—'

'No.' Lisa takes them from her. 'I didn't take anything much from Dad's house except a few clothes. And the room's really nice. I don't need much space.'

'I'll leave you to settle in then.' She looks at her watch. 'I'll make supper for seven thirty if that suits you.'

'Whatever you like. I don't want to be any trouble.'

'That's a plan then. I'll see you later.'

Catherine goes out of the room and closes the door, trying to assess how she's feeling. Apart from Ross staying over on the odd occasion he's had one too many, they don't have overnight guests. And this isn't going to be just one night. Who knows how long Lisa will be with them?

On the drive home, the atmosphere had been odd, tense

even. She'd expected a reunion of sorts: shared memories of Gary's father, Gary showing an interest in what Lisa has been up to since the funeral. But they'd both stayed oddly silent. She'd tried to break the silence a few times with chat about her day: the kids who'd played up, the occasion when she'd overheard Lauren Granger saying her mum's favourite coffee was an *expresso* rather than an espresso or when Ross had caught one of the Year 9 boys sneaking into the girls' toilets.

Each had met with little more than a half-hearted chuckle from Lisa whilst, in the passenger seat, Gary had remained tight-lipped. His head turned to the window.

She hurries down the stairs knowing this might be her only chance for a while to catch Gary on his own. There are questions she needs to ask him. Quite a few. He's in the kitchen, a glass of scotch in front of him, his fingers pressing against the glass as though trying to break it.

Catherine closes the kitchen door behind her and points to the ceiling, her voice an urgent whisper. 'I think you have a lot of explaining to do.'

He lifts his glass. Takes a gulp of his drink. 'You think I *knew*? Jesus, Cath, I had no idea she was teaching at the school.'

Catherine goes to the fridge. Her eyes lingering a little too long on the bottle of white wine that's in the door before fishing out a can of Diet Coke and pouring herself a glass.

'And you expect me to believe that?'

'You can believe what you want. It's true.' He drains his glass and puts it down on the table with a dull thud. 'You know I don't have anything to do with my dad. He was the one who wanted to shack up with the slut—'

'Gary!' Catherine glances up at the ceiling. 'Keep your voice down. It's Lisa's mother you're talking about.'

He looks at her as though he's about to say something, then changes his mind.

'You can't blame the girl for her parentage.' Catherine pulls out a chair next to him and sits down. 'And it sounds to me like her dad's treated her as shoddily as he treated you and your mum. If anything, that should make you closer. Give you empathy.'

'Empathy?' He spits out the word. 'You're having a laugh.'

'Then what? I'm trying to understand. Why did you never mention her? Why did you never say your dad had another child?'

'Because... because that girl, that *girl* is nothing to me. As far as I'm concerned they can all rot in hell.'

'Gary!' She's never heard him speak like this before and it shocks her to the core. 'Whatever you think about them, they're your flesh and blood. Whatever your dad did had nothing to do with Lisa, and you should be ashamed of what you said. The girl's here now and you have two choices... make the best of it, or act like a sulky child.' She reaches over and puts a hand on his knee. 'Look, I know your dad let you down, but this isn't about him. It's about Lisa and me, and it's also about being a decent human being. You said she could stay, so won't you please try to make the best of it? For me?'

He looks at her and she sees the resignation in his eyes. In the slump of his shoulders.

'Okay, I'll try but don't expect me to pretend to be anything more than a landlord.' He pinches at his bottom lip, turning it white. 'She might be my half-sister, but I don't know her. She's virtually a stranger and that's how I'm happy to keep it.'

Knowing it's better than nothing, Catherine gives his knee a squeeze. 'Thanks, Gaz. She'll be gone before you know it. I'm sure of it.'

'She'd better.'

The weak smile he gives her back tells her she's won and it makes her happy.

'Now we'd better get on with the dinner if we're to eat tonight. My stomach's rumbling.'

Catherine puts the flat of her hand to it knowing hunger's not the reason it's churning. It's because she's caught sight of the calendar on the wall. Ideally, she would have offloaded to Gary about Aled – her guilt and grief over the anniversary. But Gary hasn't mentioned it and she doubts now he will. It isn't as though he really understands. To him, there's no such thing as blood being thicker than water, and her desire to help Lisa seems greater than his.

She gets up and starts the dinner, waving away Lisa's offer of help when she comes downstairs, hair tied back in a scrunchie Catherine recognises as the one she left on the shelf of the bathroom cabinet the previous night.

Catherine had hoped that the meal she'd cooked would help break the ice, but instead, it's a sombre affair. Each of them picking their words carefully. Her neck aching with the tension of trying not to show her frustration at Gary's lack of effort.

She pushes back her chair and takes their plates to the sink to rinse. As she passes Gary, she raises her eyebrows at him. *Make an effort* she mouths.

Reluctantly, Gary clears his throat.

'So, Lisa,' he says, her name on his lips sounding as though it's been pulled out of him by force. 'Isn't it a temporary contract you're on? Where are you planning on going next?'

Although it's said lightly, Catherine knows exactly what he's doing. And if *she* knows, then so does Lisa. How could he be so rude to her on her first evening?

'She probably doesn't know yet,' she says hastily, but Lisa raises her hand, stopping her.

'No, it's all right, Cath. It's a reasonable question.' She holds Gary with her stare. 'I'm thinking that if a permanent position comes up at Greenfield, then I'll apply for it.'

'Even though you can't keep your class under control?

That's what you told me, wasn't it, Cath? *They run rings round her.*'

'I didn't tell you that.' It's true. She's never said those exact words to Gary, but she'd said them to Ross. Trust him to have repeated them.

She looks over at Lisa, not knowing how she'll react to what's just happened, relieved when she sees her nodding sagely.

'It's all right. It's no secret it's taking me a while to find my feet, but I know that, with your help, Cath, I'll get there. Maybe one day I'll even be as good a teacher as you.'

Catherine raises her hand to her neck, feeling the warmth that's creeping there. 'You don't have to say nice things to me because I've cooked you dinner.'

'I know I don't.' Lisa smiles at Catherine across the table. 'I mean it. You're one in a million.'

'Well, that's very sweet of you.'

She looks across at Gary, hoping he'll agree with her, but he's pushing back his chair. Patting his trouser pocket to check for his wallet. 'I'm going to the pub.'

Catherine looks at her watch. 'What now? I thought we'd...' But what had she thought? That they'd all play happy families? 'Okay but please don't be late.' Her eyes narrow a fraction. 'I presume Ross will be there.'

'Maybe.'

But they both know he will be... and what if he is? A drink and a whinge with his best friend will probably do Gary a power of good. Maybe Ross will even talk some sense into him.

'I'll see you later then. I won't wait up.'

Gary doesn't answer. She hears him take his keys from the bowl on the table, then hears them drop back again as he thinks better of driving. The security light outside the window clicks on as he walks down the front path, and a few minutes later as she clears the rest of their meal away, it clicks off again.

'I hope I haven't caused any problems between the two of you?' Lisa's voice is full of concern. 'I didn't think it through. Of course Gary would resent me being here. I was stupid not to realise it.'

'Oh, love. It's not that. It's just that it's been a shock for him, his half-sister appearing like this after all this time. For me too, if I'm honest.'

'And me. When Gary was younger...' She trails off. Looks down at her hands.

'Yes?' Catherine wonders what Lisa was going to say.

There's a hint of pink in the girl's cheeks. 'Oh, nothing. It's just that I really do want to get to know him. *Really* know him. The only trouble is, I'm not sure he's ready.'

'I think you're right. Gary's never been good with change, but I'll work on him, I promise. He's estranged from his father, yes, I get that, but knowing you better isn't a show of weakness. It's a show of strength... proof that he can rise above it. He'll come round.'

'I hope so.'

'Leave it with me. I'll make sure he does.'

Lisa gets up. Gestures at the pans that are waiting to go in the dishwasher. 'Can I help with that?'

'No, you're all right. It will be quicker if I do it.'

'Then I'll go up to bed, if you don't mind.' She yawns into her hand. 'It's been a pretty mind-blowing day and the thought of a real bed is blissful.'

'I hope you sleep well.'

'I'm sure I will.' She goes to the door. 'Night, Cath.'

'Night, Lisa, and welcome to our home.'

Catherine waits until the door closes behind the girl, then presses her hands heavily onto the worktop. She thinks of Ross and Gary at the bar, a few pints inside them. Wishing she could join them. Knowing it would be unwise if she did.

Above her head, she can hear Lisa moving around her

bedroom and she tips her head to the ceiling, a frown creasing her brow.

She thinks of the long corridor of the English department, of Lisa's classroom next to hers, and the image leaves her strangely puzzled. Not because Gary's half-sister has appeared in their lives so suddenly... but because Lisa getting a job in the same school as her feels like more than a coincidence.

SEVEN

'Bloody hell, Ross. You look like something the cat dragged in. Look at the state of those eyes... bloodshot doesn't come close to it. And I can still smell the beer on you.'

Catherine shifts away from him, surprised at how triggering it is, even after all these years.

Ross gets up and goes to the mirror at the back of the staffroom and studies his face. 'Shit, I forgot to shave.' He breathes into his hand and sniffs. 'You don't think Ellen will notice anything, do you?'

Catherine folds her arms. Studies him from across the room. 'Not if she's got a cold to end all colds and lost her eyesight overnight, she won't. Jesus, Ross. It was a Monday night. What were you both thinking?'

'It was Gary, he—'

She holds up her hand. 'You can stop it right there. Don't you go blaming my husband for your inability to say no to another pint. You're a grown man, not a kid.'

'Thanks for your sympathy.' Ross rubs at his cheeks and turns away from the mirror. 'I hope you gave Gaz as much of a hard time as you're giving me.'

'Too right I did.' Though it's not entirely true. She'd been asleep when her husband had come home and hadn't woken when he'd got into bed beside her. This morning, he'd seemed as right as rain, and she hadn't wanted to rock the boat further.

'Anyway, what was up with old Gazza last night?'

Catherine stiffens. 'How do you mean?'

'I dunno. He had a face on him like a wet weekend. Couldn't get more than a couple of decent sentences out of him. Things all right at home?'

'Of course.' Wishing to change the subject, Catherine points to the clock above the photocopier. 'Anyway, the upside of your mini bender is I beat you in today so that makes one all. Maybe it will be you buying the drinks on Friday, after all.'

'Fuck that.' Ross massages his forehead. 'The way I feel, I doubt I'll even make it to Friday. What the hell did I think I was doing getting in so early just for the chance of a sodding free pint!'

Catherine laughs. Whoever wins 'first into school' out of the two of them buys the drinks at the Angel on a Friday lunchtime. She counts each win as a badge of honour, but it's also a test of her resolve... proof, as Ross slides her Coke towards her, that she can do without alcohol. Not that anyone at Greenfield knows except her.

'It's because you just can't bear to see me win,' she says with a grin. Lifting her bag onto her knees, she rummages inside for the foil strip of paracetamol she knows is in there, pops a couple from their bubble and hands them to him. 'Get these down you.'

'Ta.' Ross tips back his head, swallowing them without water. 'Don't want Ellen on the warpath.' He picks up his battered briefcase. 'I'll see you later.'

'Yeah. See you.'

Her eyes follow Ross through the window as he walks along the corridor back to his classroom. It's clear Gary hadn't said anything to him about Lisa coming to stay with them, or that she was his half-sister. If he had, Ross would have taken advantage of the choice piece of gossip. Poked fun at the fact Gary and Lisa were related.

Wondering why he hadn't, Catherine picks up her bag and makes for the door. Should she keep it to herself too? Is that what Gary would want?

When Catherine reaches her classroom, she turns on the lights and puts down her bag. If anyone had asked her what had made her look towards the window as she'd pulled out her chair and sat down, she wouldn't be able to tell them. Maybe it was some instinct. Some form of preservation. Whatever the reason, as she looks towards the glass, there's something about the light outside that feels wrong. Not as it should be. The side of the school, where her classroom is, faces west, and the strange yellow light she can see suggests a sunset. But at seven in the morning, that's impossible.

Confused, she gets up from her desk and walks to the window. The sight opening up before her causing her to press the palms of both hands against the glass in shock.

'Jesus Christ!'

To her left the sky is still dark, but over to her right, where the staff car park is, there's a strange orange and yellow glow. Throwing open the window, Catherine leans out, not wanting to believe what she's seeing. The eerie light is coming from the staff car park and now she can see what's causing it. A car is on fire. Flames licking at the bonnet and the roof.

But the car isn't any old car. It's *her* car.

The stench of acrid smoke mingles with the cool early morning air and, even from where she's standing, on the first floor of the school building, Catherine can hear the crackling of burning metal as the fire grows. The shatter of glass as one of the windows blows.

She knows she should sound the alarm, do something, do anything, but the shock of what she's seeing has frozen her.

Stolen all feeling from her arms. From her legs. Then, as she watches, a figure runs across the open space below her and the spell is broken. Blood returns to her veins.

Leaving the window, Catherine runs out of her classroom, along the corridor and down the stairs. Not stopping to alert anyone else. Not bothering to answer Lynne's query as she throws herself through the front door and onto the playground.

From out here, the smell is much stronger – a mixture of burning rubber and upholstery. Catherine runs to the gate, only realising as she gets to it that she's left her lanyard with its key card on her desk, but as she gets closer, she can see through the smoke that the gate is open. Someone has got there before her.

She runs across the tarmac but stops when the heat becomes too intense. Stands with the back of her hand pressed to her brow, transfixed by the flames that are engulfing her beloved car. Her eyes sting with smoke and tears. The roaring flames around her car have grown hungrier. Twisting the metal carcass. Consuming everything in their reach.

She sinks to her haunches, her hands clasped behind her head. 'Please God. Not again.'

'Catherine!' A rough hand grabs at her shoulder. Pulls her up. It's Ross who's shouting at her over the roar of the flames. His shirt untucked. His eyes manic. 'Get back. It's too danger-ous! I've called the fire service, but you need to go and tell Ellen what's happened.'

But Catherine's not listening. Instead, she's staring at the unforgiving flames.

Remembering.

Remembering.

'Catherine.' Ross gives her shoulder a shake. Shouts louder. 'Did you hear what I said? It's not safe here.' Seeing she's not listening, he picks up the fire extinguisher he'd put down next to him and runs closer to the car. Aiming the hose at the flames and directing a blast of fine powder at their centre. He looks behind, his jaw stiffening as he sees she's still there.

'For fuck's sake, Cath. I said go!'

Catherine starts. Feels the searing heat on her face, on her bare hands, and registers the danger.

'Stand back.' Ross is shouting at a group of early arrivals. 'Get into school.'

Reluctantly, they move away, and, knowing there's nothing she can do to help Ross, Catherine follows them across the playground.

Lynne is at the door, her mobile in her hand. She directs the children into the school building. Shouting to make herself heard over their excited voices. 'Go into the hall and wait until Mrs Swanson decides what to do with you. With any luck you'll get an extra day's holiday.'

She waits until they're out of earshot, then turns to Catherine, wide-eyed. 'Your car! Why the hell would anyone want to do that?'

Catherine's starting to shake. The enormity of what's happened only now sinking in. 'I don't know.'

In the distance, the wail of a fire engine can be heard. Getting louder. Closer.

Lynne puts an arm around Catherine's shoulder. Ushers her inside. 'Are you okay, Cath? You're shaking like a leaf. Sit here and I'll make you some tea. I can even put a bit of something stronger in it if you like. No one will know.'

'No.' It comes out sharper than Catherine meant. 'I mean, I'm fine. Just give me a moment.'

Lynne looks doubtful. 'If you're sure.' She leads Catherine to the chair. 'Take the weight off and I'll ring through to the boss. Let her know what's going on... that's if she hasn't already seen.'

Catherine takes the blanket Lynne hands her and sits on one of the chairs assigned to parents waiting to attend meetings with the head teacher or heads of department. Closing her eyes, she leans her head against the noticeboard, images of the dancing flames and the twisted, blistered chassis of her car, playing out across the back of her eyelids. She opens them again when she hears the double doors swing and sees Ellen bustle through.

'Can you please tell me what on earth is going on? Is it true someone tried to set fire to your car, Cath?'

'They didn't just try. They succeeded.' Ross pushes in through the front door, his face red, circles of sweat under the arms of his shirt. He puts the extinguisher down and wipes his brow with his sleeve. 'I'm sorry, Cath. I did all I could, put it out before the fire service got here, but I wasn't quick enough. The fire had already taken hold.'

Ellen frowns. 'Has anyone phoned the police?'

'Yeah.' He coughs into his arm. A deep smoke-induced cough. 'I did. They're on their way now and someone from the fire service will be wanting a word as well.'

'I think you need medical attention too, Ross. Who knows how much smoke you inhaled.'

'I'm fine. Really. Thank God I saw it. I've never run so bloody fast down those stairs.' He wipes his arm across his sweaty forehead. 'I'm too old for this.'

'Well, if you're sure.' Ellen turns to the receptionist. 'Lynne, I'm going to need you to email as many of the parents as you can, letting them know the school will be closed today. And if you could put something vague on the website, I'd be much obliged... no details, we don't want to freak them out. Catherine, can you run along to breakfast club and let the children there know they can go home? The ones in the hall too.' She leans her elbows on the counter. Massages her forehead with her finger-tips. 'We can't have the kids coming into school today with an arsonist on the loose.'

'I'll do it.' Ross runs a hand around the back of his neck. 'Cath's in no fit state. She's had a shock.'

Ellen looks at the state of him. At the smoke stains on his shirt and the grime on his face. 'I don't think so, Ross. Do you? We still have standards to keep.'

'It's all right. I'll catch the rest of the kids as they come in.'

Lisa's standing in the doorway, her coat already on. Catherine had given her a lift in and, in all the excitement, had forgotten about her. Now, though, she's glad to see her. Glad she's stepped up, for the responsibility will do her good.

'Very well.' Ellen holds open one of the double doors to the main school. 'In that case, Catherine, I'd like you to come to my office. The police will want to talk to you, I'm sure. Seeing as it's your car that was targeted.' She folds her arms. 'Can you think of anyone who might do such a thing?'

Catherine pulls the blanket tighter. Shakes her head.

'No.'

But a shiver runs through her, nonetheless. Although she's kept it a secret for fifteen years, the memories the fire brought back to her makes her terrified someone knows the truth of what happened back then.

The question is who?

EIGHT

The male police officer who is sitting in front of Catherine is one she knows from his community visits to the school. The other, a female officer with a delicate face and intelligent dark eyes, she's not seen before. They're sitting on grey plastic chairs like the ones in the school hall, and Catherine forces her voice to sound conversational despite the blood that's racing in her ears.

'Not the most comfortable, I'm afraid.'

'We've sat on worse.' PC Dawson shifts on his seat. 'Now you say you've had the car, a Fiat Panda, for around eight years.'

'About that, yes.'

'And you're the only one who drives it? Never your husband?'

Catherine shakes her head, trying to picture Gary inside the compact space. 'He has his own car and wouldn't be seen dead in mine. Would be scared someone might see him.'

It's said as a joke, but it's true. Gary's street cred is as important to him as his football matches. A wave of sadness crashes over her at the realisation she'll never drive in it again. She'd loved that car.

'And do you always park in the same place in the car park? We Brits are creatures of habit, after all. Same seats on the train. On the bus.' PC Dawson gives a laugh. 'My missus even likes to book the same row at the cinema, if you can believe it.'

'I suppose I do park in the same place, yes. I like it because it's near the security light.'

PC Dawson looks at his notes. 'The one that doesn't work.'

Feeling foolish, Catherine glances at Ellen, who's studying her nails. 'Yes, that one.'

'It's on the site manager's list of things to do.' Ellen's tone is defensive. She's proud of what she's done with the school and doesn't like it criticised. Even with good cause.

PC Olds, the female officer, turns to her. 'And CCTV? Any in the car park?'

'It's something we're working on. At the moment, the school is our priority, not the staff car park. We're making plans to extend the areas covered by our cameras.'

Catherine bristles. What if the person who did this had been lying in wait for her? What if the car had been set alight while she was still in it? The idea of it is horrific, the image it conjures setting her heart racing again. No one would do that, surely? No one could be that evil. Not even someone with a grudge against her. It must have been some sort of accident.

PC Olds has obviously been thinking the same thing. 'Maybe I could suggest you make it a priority, Miss Swanson. Without teachers, you have no school. If anything had happened to one of your staff because of faulty equipment, I can only imagine what the parents and governors would say. Not to mention the court.'

Beside her, Ellen stiffens. 'Of course, I'll get our site manager on to it straight away.'

'I think that would be a good idea. Also, what do you have in place security-wise regarding the school site?'

Ellen's face is stony. 'We follow good practice here. We lock our secondary gates during the school day but keep the main gate closed but unlocked during the early part of the day.'

'Why's that?'

'It's to allow the children to come into school.' Her face shows her impatience with the question. 'After that, the gates are locked. Each member of staff has an electronic key card system that allows them to enter freely.'

PC Olds makes a note. 'And visitors?'

'They must use a buzzer at the main gate and Lynne in reception will let them in.'

'Could you tell me what provision you've made in the case of a fire on the premises... if, say, the key card system fails or you need quick access?'

'We have an emergency master key that's kept in reception. I have access to it of course, along with Lynne and our designated emergency coordinator, Karen.' She sits forward. Frown lines deepening. 'You're not thinking the person who set fire to Cath's car might try to enter the school, are you?'

Suddenly, the room feels too hot. The space too small for the four of them. Catherine's fingers grip the sides of her chair, but she says nothing. A deep-rooted fear taking hold.

Ellen has seen. 'Catherine. Are you feeling unwell?'

She pulls herself together. 'No, I'm fine. It's just a bit hot in here, that's all.'

PC Dawson looks at her. Gives a sympathetic smile. 'We'll not be too much longer, but there's some boring stuff I need to ask. I'll need you to give me a rundown of your movements, and their approximate times, starting from when you left the house this morning. It could be useful.'

Catherine thinks. 'I left around seven and got into school around seven fifteen.'

'And you were the first here?'

'No, Ellen was here. Then there was Lynne on reception, my department colleagues Ross and Lisa and a few others.'

'Like I said before, staff have to sign in with their cards.' Ellen lifts the lanyard with her photograph on it. 'Lynne will have a record of those who were here and the times they arrived.'

PC Dawson makes a note. 'That's very helpful. I'll make sure I get her to print me off a copy. And did you notice anything unusual when you parked, Catherine? Any cars you didn't recognise? Any people loitering in the vicinity?'

Catherine shakes her head. 'It was dark and, to be honest, I just wanted to get into school. Start getting things ready for my day.'

Ellen smiles. 'Catherine is the most organised of our teachers. A credit to the school, I'm happy to say. If only all the staff were as conscientious.'

Catherine wonders if she's referring to Ross. In the years they've been working together, she's noticed how his enthusiasm, his motivation for the job, has waned. But the kids like him, if only because he's lenient.

'That's good to know.' PC Olds' dark eyes are on Catherine. 'My eldest is about to start secondary and I know how important structure is.' Her phone buzzes and she lifts it from her jacket and looks at it. 'Excuse me. I won't be a moment.'

Pushing back her chair, she steps into the corridor, closing the door behind her, and Catherine watches her through the window of Ellen's office. Sees how she listens and then replies, turning her eyes to Catherine before looking away again. Catherine looks down at her hands, wondering what she's been told. What she's said in return.

PC Dawson is talking and she realises she's been asked a question.

'I'm sorry. Could you say that again?'

'I was asking whether you had any enemies, Catherine? Anyone with a grudge against you. A disgruntled ex-student. An unhappy parent, maybe.'

Ellen answers for her. 'Catherine is one of our most experienced teachers. The children like her. Respect her. Ask them yourself.'

'I will do.' PC Dawson closes his notebook. 'That's probably all for now, but if there's anything else you can think of that might help us, Catherine, please do call us. We will, of course, be in touch again once forensics have taken a look at your car. But hopefully this was just some silly prank by a student that went wrong.'

The door to Ellen's office opens and PC Olds comes back in, her face serious. She looks at Ellen but remains standing. 'Might we have a word with Catherine in private?'

Ellen looks surprised. 'Of course. I need to be getting on anyway. Even without kids here, a school needs to be managed.'

She goes out and PC Olds sits again in the seat she'd earlier vacated. 'There's something I'd like to ask you, Catherine... with regard to some information that has come in. It's thrown up a few things we need to follow up on.'

'Of course.' She swallows, unsure as to what will come next. 'What would you like to know?'

PC Olds is looking at her. Her dark eyes studying her face as though trying to read her. 'The school you were at before this, Dane Street Comprehensive...'

'Yes?' The air in Ellen's office feels a little thinner.

She pauses. 'There's something you didn't tell us when you reported your car as having been set alight. A clear case of arson.'

'It wasn't me who reported it, it was Ross.'

'Be that as it may, there was still something you neglected to tell us. This isn't the first time there has been an arson attack at a school where you've been teaching, is it?'

Catherine stares at the floor. She feels sick.

'No, it's not.' There's no point in lying. 'But that was different. It happened in the night. Someone set fire to one of the classrooms.'

'They set fire to *your* classroom, Catherine. And, looking at it statistically, I'd say that was a big coincidence, wouldn't you?'

Catherine had been studying her hands, but now her head shoots up. 'What are you saying? That I set fire to my own car? To my own classroom?'

'I'm not saying that at all.'

'Look, they think a rough sleeper had broken in. Tried to light a fire in a wastepaper bin.' Catherine's throat constricts. 'They found his...' She chokes on the words, her eyes swimming. 'His remains, but he was so badly burnt it was impossible to identify him even from dental records.'

PC Olds nods. 'Yes, that's the information I was given. Though there's no way of knowing the circumstances that led to it. Accident or arson... it's unlikely we'll ever know. It's just a mercy it happened at night when no one was in the building. But that was nearly sixteen years ago and we need to get back to today. A classroom, a car in a staff car park... a fire is a fire.'

'What happened to my car this morning... Look, I was nowhere near the staff car park. I was in my classroom.' She stares with desperate eyes at the young policewoman, needing her to understand. 'Anyone will tell you. Ross, Lisa, Ellen even.'

PC Dawson puts a steadying hand on her arm.

'My colleague's not saying that you were the one who caused the fire, Catherine. All she's doing is pointing out that there is something linking these two fires on two separate school grounds.'

He stops, not needing to say any more, because it's clear what they're implying.

The link between the two fires, the common denominator, is Catherine and they all know it.

NINE

Gary paces the room. He hasn't yet changed out of his suit, and it makes Catherine feel uncomfortable.

'Your car? What the fuck!' He stops in the middle of the living room. Folds his arms as though he's a barrister in court. 'You could have been killed, Cath. Burnt alive! What type of school is this? I bloody rue the day Ross got you the job in that cesspit. Why couldn't you have chosen a nice public school?'

'Like the one you taught at? Like Newland High?' she says wearily. She's glad that Lisa has gone to the shop to get some milk and wonders whether she'd done it deliberately to give them space to talk.

'Exactly. A place where kids can properly learn. Where teachers can be heard and actually do what they're paid for rather than act as law enforcement.'

Catherine puts down her cup of tea. 'Yet *you* left... so it couldn't have been all that great. Why did you leave, Gary? You've never said.'

He rubs his fingers and thumb together. 'You know why. They didn't pay me enough. And I'm glad I got out when I did.

The education system is a fucking joke. I think you should consider leaving too.'

Catherine looks up at him. She'd been hoping for his support, for his sympathy, but she's not certain his anger is about her. More about him.

'I can't leave. I love working there and anyway, I've applied for the post of Head of English.'

His face slackens. 'You've what?'

She hadn't meant to tell him this way. Had meant to wait until she'd actually got the position. 'I wanted it to be a surprise. I've got a really good chance of getting this.'

He sinks down onto the settee opposite her. 'Jesus. What is it with you and these schools? You'd have thought after what happened before...'

She knows what he's talking about: her lack of control in the classroom, her inability to function properly unless she'd had a drink – things she'd confessed to when they'd first got together and that he'd helped her get through. But there are also things she's kept from him.

They don't argue much, she makes sure of that, and she doesn't want to now. She just wants this to stop.

'I was going through a difficult time, Gaz. You know that. That business with Aled... I didn't know how to deal with it. Then, when he died, I had to live with the guilt of not having helped him.'

Gary raises his hands in despair. 'The guy was unhinged. You did your best for him, but it was never enough. You couldn't keep on doing it... giving him money to sustain his little drug habit. Everyone knew the truth, though he preferred to tell them he needed it for rehab. What in God's name made him think you'd let him live with you?'

'Because I'm his sister. *Was* his sister.' Catherine sinks her head into her hands. Drags her fingers back through her hair. 'I should have had more faith.'

Gary gets up. He crosses over to her and she feels the settee cushion give as he sits beside her and puts his arm around her shoulders. Protective. Comforting. 'You know that isn't true, Cath.'

'But you didn't know him.' She turns wet eyes to him. 'If you'd seen him as a little boy. So vulnerable, so desperate to be loved, you'd understand.'

Aled's there in her head, the child her parents had never wanted. He must have been around seven or eight, sitting cross-legged under the apple tree in their garden. His head bent to his task, sunlight bringing out the natural highlights in his fair hair. Catherine feels again her love for him, her fierce need to protect him. She walks across to her younger brother, her school shoes flattening the grass. Sees the burnt patch of ground in front of his pavement-grazed knees. The lighter he's taken from their father's jacket pocket beside him. She holds out her hand.

Give it to me, Aled. Don't worry, I won't tell Mum. I'll put it back and no one will know.

Covering for him as always. Enabling him. Something that had not changed with time.

'You didn't know him,' she says again, a tear dropping from her lashes, darkening the fabric of her jeans.

'I didn't need to know him to understand what he was like.'

They sit in silence and it occurs to Catherine that this is how their conversations about Aled always end – why Gary doesn't like to have them in the first place. Forever worrying that it might set her off again. Drive her off the rails to that dark place where she couldn't cope. Where he'd found her all those years ago.

But she won't forget her brother. She mustn't.

Because when the begging phone calls had stopped, the knocks on the front door too, she'd been shocked to find she missed them in the way she'd once dreaded them. She was all

Aled had, the only one who cared, and she knows that she needed him as much as he'd needed her.

Catherine had given Lisa her spare key and now she hears it in the lock. 'Only me,' she calls, even though it's unlikely it would be anyone else.

If they hadn't been talking about Aled, Gary would have been annoyed, but he actually looks relieved. He gets up.

'I'm going to take a shower. Don't worry about food for me, I'm eating at The Crown tonight.'

Catherine stares at him. 'That's two nights in a row you've been there. You never said.'

'I did, Cath. I told you this morning, but I could tell you weren't listening. Most of the guys from the Seasoned Strikers will be there and it wouldn't go down well if I baled.'

Catherine thinks back. Gary had got up early, left the house before Lisa had even emerged from her room. She's sure she'd have remembered if he'd said.

'I'm presuming Ross with be there again too.' She's not sure why this bothers her so much. He had, after all, been Gary's friend before he'd ever met her. Recently, though, she's found herself becoming more than a little possessive of her own friendship with him. Hating the thought that the two of them might discuss her when they're out together. When the beer is flowing. Sharing anecdotes of the things she's said and done at school and at home.

They wouldn't do that, would they?

With no warning, Catherine's stomach twists and she puts a hand to it. Gary had promised her he'd never tell Ross what happened at her last school and there's no reason to doubt him. But what if one day he did? After a few pints. Heads together at the bar. Lads together. Forgetting they're no longer young men but steaming towards middle age.

She shakes her head to get rid of the thought. No, he'd never do that to her. She'd made him swear on his life. Gary is the only one who knows the real reason she sticks to soft drinks. The real reason she left her last school halfway through a term.

Lisa opens the bag she'd taken with her for the milk and pulls out a family-sized bag of Doritos and a large bar of fruit and nut chocolate. She places them onto the coffee table.

'I thought we could all watch a film tonight... but it doesn't matter.'

Immediately, Catherine feels bad for her. It's only her second evening here and Gary hasn't made a single attempt to get to know her. She looks at Lisa's dejected face. Maybe they're better off without him here. And it could, after all, be her chance to find out a little more about Gary's past.

'You go and play with the big boys then, Gary, and me and Lisa can have a girls' night in.' She smiles at the girl. 'We can have a proper heart-to-heart.'

Gary's face changes as though he's just thought of something.

'I don't have to go. I could tell them that—'

But Catherine's warming to the idea of it being just her and Lisa tonight.

'Don't be silly. I don't mind, honestly.'

'If you're sure.' He sounds uncertain now but stands, picks up his coat from the back of the settee and puts it on over his hoodie. 'I won't be late. Just a couple of pints.'

Catherine smiles. With Gary, it's never just a couple of pints. She points to the window. 'Take an umbrella. It's pissing it down outside.'

'Really? Damn... where is it?'

'In the hall cupboard where it always is.' Catherine gets up too. Kisses him. 'And keep an eye on how much Ross drinks. Remind him it's a school night. You two might think Tuesday is the new Friday, but tell that to the kids in Year 11... or their parents.'

Despite himself, Gary laughs. 'What am I, his mum?'

'He could do with one... or a wife.'

'Well, I'll do my best, but you know what the lads from the football club can be like. It might not be easy.'

He's right, from the size of the girths of one or two of the guys from the Seasoned Strikers, it's no secret they're fond a drink. It's one of the many reasons Catherine never joins Gary at their local.

'I'll see you then.'

Gary lets himself out the front door and Catherine turns a bright smile to Lisa. 'How about I chuck a pizza in the oven? We can have a chat while it cooks, then watch the film. Does that sound like a good plan?'

Lisa nods. 'It does.'

'Great. I'll put the oven on then.' She takes the carrier bag from Lisa's hand and carries it into the kitchen, but when she gets to the fridge, she realises the bottle of milk isn't the only thing in there.

'Oh, I bought some wine.' As if she'd been reading her thoughts, Lisa's voice floats to her from the living room. 'It's a thank you for letting me stay. I thought we could have it when we watch the film.'

'You have a glass,' Catherine calls back. 'I'm not much of a drinker and, to be honest, I'd prefer a Coke. It was a lovely thought, though.'

Once the pizza's in the oven, Catherine pours their drinks, then goes back into the living room. She hands Lisa her wine and raises her own glass.

'Here's to you, Lisa. I hope you enjoy your stay with us.'

'Thank you.' Lisa points to her glass. 'I'm sorry I bought the wrong thing. I should have checked.'

'Why would you? Honestly, it's fine. You and Gary can finish it tomorrow. It's just that...'

She'd been going to lie, say that alcohol disagreed with her, but what's the harm in telling her the truth? She doesn't need to know the rest. What the drink had done to her.

She sits beside Lisa. Pulls open a bag of peanuts and puts them on the coffee table in front of them. 'I don't drink because when I was a lot younger, I had a bit of a problem with it. I've been dry for years, but that was only because of your brother. He showed me that it wasn't the best way to live my life. I couldn't have done it without him.'

Lisa raises her eyebrows. 'Really?'

'Yes, he was my knight in shining armour.'

Lisa points to the kitchen. 'Would you prefer it if I—'

'No, you're all right. It takes time, but you have to learn to live with other people drinking. Gary still does, as you can see. You can't avoid it forever.'

Bringing the glass of wine to her lips, Lisa takes a delicate sip. 'Was it hard, after what happened today at school, not to...' She taps at her glass, leaving the rest unspoken.

'A little but I viewed it as a test... one I passed with flying colours.'

'I so admire you.'

Not knowing how to answer, Catherine points the controller at the TV. 'Let's choose a film. The pizza will be done soon.'

She flicks through the films, but it's hard to concentrate now that Lisa has put the memory of her burnt-out car in her head.

'So, do they have any suspects?' Lisa leans forward, shakes some peanuts into her hand. 'Do they think it might be one of the kids?'

'I don't know. They haven't said.'

'I was just wondering...' – Lisa studies the peanuts in her hand – 'how often Gary comes by the school.'

'Gary? That's an odd question... Why do you ask?'

'It sounds a bit silly, but I thought I saw him outside the school today.'

Catherine puts down the TV controller. 'You must have been mistaken. Gary catches the train and the station's in the opposite direction.'

Lisa laughs. Adjusts her glasses. 'You're right. I really need to make another appointment at the optician.' She tips the peanuts into her mouth. Points to the TV screen. 'What have you chosen for us to watch?'

'Wait and see.' Catherine picks up the controller again and points it at the screen.

But somewhere deep inside her something is niggling. What if Lisa was right and Gary had been there? What would have been his reason?

TEN

Lisa has gone to bed, but Catherine isn't tired. Despite the light-hearted film the two of them had watched, it's as if her brain is hard-wired to be forever flashing images of that morning's fire onto the back of her eyes.

Feeling at a loose end and knowing Gary won't be home for a while yet, she flicks mindlessly through the TV channels until she finds what she's looking for. For five minutes or so, she watches Ross and Rachel pretend they no longer have feelings for each other. Listens to Chandler's ironic jokes. Usually, it would be the perfect antidote to a difficult day, but this evening, with Gary out, the house feels too big. Too empty.

Except it *isn't* empty. A girl she hardly knows has been spitting toothpaste into their basin, looking in the same mirror that Catherine uses to take off her makeup, washing her hair in their shower cubicle.

She thinks of Lisa asleep in the room next to theirs and realises that she'd never got round to asking any of the things she'd meant to while Gary was out. Such as how her mum had met his dad and whether the two of them ever talked about his son from his previous marriage. Little things, but ones she'd love to know the answer to seeing as Gary refused to talk about that time. The hurt still as raw now as it had been the night his father had left him and his mother.

Outside the window, it's raining hard and even with the umbrella, Gary will be soaked by the time he gets home. She thinks about getting the car keys and driving to collect him but quickly dismisses the idea, knowing he wouldn't want her to. Instead, she gets up and goes over to the window to close the curtains, seeing nothing but her reflection and the flashing images on the television screen reflected in the glass.

The ring on the doorbell, when it comes, is so loud, so unexpected, she jumps back. It's only nine forty-five. Too early for Gary to be home, and anyway, he has a door key. Unless he forgot to take it.

Drawing the curtains closed, Catherine goes into the hall and opens the front door. She's expecting to see her husband standing on the doorstep, his dark hair plastered to his face, but the porch is empty. There's no one there.

'Gaz?'

Behind her, the wind rustles the leaves of the weeping fig on the hall table and she shivers.

'Is that you?'

She peers out into the night. Sees no one. The front garden is just dark shadows, the only sound the rain on the porch roof and the wind that's blowing the front gate on its hinges. Catherine steps out onto the cold tiles. It wouldn't take a moment to put on her shoes and go down the front path to check the street, but something is stopping her.

The thought of leaving the safety of her brightly lit hallway.

'Very funny,' she calls into the dark night. 'Very mature.'

She'd expected to hear teenage footsteps running away, muffled sniggers or foul-mouthed jibes, but there's nothing. Just the pattering of the rain above her head. The wind in the trees that line the street.

Catherine shivers and steps back into the light, but, as she does, her socked foot slides on something. She lifts her foot and looks down to see what she'd stepped on. It's a slim, yellow cigarette lighter, the case cracked where she's just stood on it. She picks it up, her eyes roving over the front garden again, every nerve in her body on high alert as it used to be in the days before Aled died. Gary used to smoke, but he hasn't in years. Surely it isn't his?

The wind has stiffened and a sudden squall sends the rain in a new direction. Needles of it prickling her face. She turns and, thinking she sees a movement at the upstairs window, squints up at it. But the light is off. No one's there.

The lighter is still in her hand and there's no way she's bringing it into the house. With all her strength, she throws it into the wet laurel bush that separates their garden from the road, then steps back inside and shuts the door.

Catherine stands with her back against the glass, eyes closed. Taking long breaths in through her nose, out through her mouth. It was just a knock on the door – kids mucking about most likely. Nothing to worry about. And the lighter? Well, it could be anybody's. It means nothing.

But, if it's just kids, why does she suddenly feel cold? Suddenly afraid?

Stop it. Stop it.

Catherine presses her hands to her head to stop the thoughts that are threatening to get out of control. No good will come from thinking this way. Pulling herself together, she gets her mug from the coffee table and takes it into the kitchen to make herself another drink. But as she switches on the light, she jumps, her hand to her heart.

'Jesus, Lisa. You gave me the fright of my life. Why are you down here in the dark? I thought you'd gone to bed?'

Lisa points to the back door. 'I thought I heard something outside. Went to take a look.'

'It's nothing.' Going to the back door, Catherine twists the key in the lock. 'Just kids mucking about. Go back to bed.'

'I can stay down here if you like. If you're worried.'

She's just trying to be kind, but the suggestion irritates Catherine. That Lisa might think her weak. Scared of her own shadow. A different person to the one she sees at school every day.

'No,' she says firmly. 'You go back to bed. I'll be going up myself soon.'

She switches on the kettle and as she opens the fridge door to get out the milk, she sees the half-full bottle of white wine that Lisa had bought. Feels the pull of it, the flat of her hand hovering over the metal bottle top before continuing to the plastic bottle next to it.

Quickly, she takes it out, slamming the door shut again before the temptation can grow stronger. Her forehead beaded with perspiration. Coffee made, she goes back into the living room. The plan had been to take it upstairs, watch some more TV in bed, but even with Lisa in the house, the idea of going up to bed alone is no longer as appealing as it was. There's a sharp pain in the centre of Catherine's chest and she presses her hand to it. Feels the race of her heart.

She takes her mobile out of her pocket, desperate for Gary to come home, her fingers searching for his number. But what would she say if he answered? *I need you to come back. Someone knocked on our door, then disappeared. Oh, and I found a lighter on our doorstep.* How pathetic she'd sound. How weak. She can just picture her husband's expression as he walked in the door, breath smelling of the beer he'd had to throw down his throat before putting on his coat. His head still in the pub with his mates. Fighting not to show his annoyance at having been dragged away from them.

Of course she won't ring him and, anyway, the pain is subsiding. And it's not as if she doesn't recognise it for it's a pain she's felt many times in the past. A herald of the panic attack that has lain dormant for years now but that she knows is still there inside her. Squatting in some dark corner of her being, waiting for her defences to come down. For her to lose control. And she knows the worst thing she can do is give in to it.

Picking up the mug of coffee she can no longer stomach, she goes into the kitchen and empties it into the sink. Then she climbs the stairs to bed. But, as she reaches up to close the curtains, she can't help looking down at the front garden.

Whoever put that lighter on her front porch could be the one responsible for the fire in her car. Is it kids from the school? Are they trying to spook her?

Catherine drags the curtain closed, shutting out the night. Feels a lick of dread.

Because a lighter is exactly how the first fire started.

ELEVEN

The room is filled with the sound of scraping chairs as the Year 11 children settle into their seats.

As the last pupils come in, Catherine reaches to her bag, takes out her phone and re-reads the message Gary had sent her earlier. *Sorry I was late back last night. Love you and see you later.* A message that had both surprised and delighted her as he wasn't usually one for digital displays of affection... or apology.

Catherine puts her phone back, deciding she won't make a big thing of it when she gets home. She, Lisa and Gary are, after all, still finding their way. Learning how to live with each other.

'Spit that gum out, Toby. Don't think I don't know you're chewing it behind your hand.' Reaching for the bin, Catherine takes it over to him and waits as he spits it out. 'And move that bag before someone trips over it.'

'Heard your car got torched, miss. Know who done it?'

Catherine's fingers tighten around the bin's metal edge.

'The classroom is no place to discuss it.' She puts on her sternest voice. 'But if you've heard anything or have any information at all that will help the enquiry, you need to go straight to Miss Swanson with it.'

Not that it's likely to happen; it's well known that the students are loyal to each other, but if she could just have some proof it was a pupil, or ex-pupil, of the school, she'd feel happier. Know her secret's still safe.

She stands. Starts giving out the books. Last night, she'd dreamt of Aled – couldn't get his accusing eyes out of her head. She'd wanted to wake Gary, have him take her in his arms and tell her everything would be all right, but he was sound asleep. One arm bent across his forehead. His soft snores making her envious of his ability to sleep through anything.

If only she knew the truth about her car. Nothing was worse than the not knowing.

She'd had a call from the police earlier. Without any CCTV in the car park area, they'd had little to go on. There were no fingerprints on what was left of the car and they'd found no one who'd seen what had happened. Neighbours or pupils. The only thing they could tell her was the fire had been started using petrol-soaked rags placed under the car.

'Right, everyone.' She puts the bin back under her desk. Needing things to get back to normal as quickly as possible. 'I know your form tutor will have already mentioned it, but before we start the lesson, I want to give you a quick reminder that whole school assembly is scheduled for tomorrow. Make sure you're all wearing full school uniform.' She points to a girl in the back row who's wearing a royal-blue hoodie over her white school blouse. 'Yes, that applies to you too, Leanne. Now, quieten down and let's make a start. Please open your texts to page thirty-seven.'

The class quietens and Catherine slips into the routine she knows like the back of her hand. Enjoying the moderated level of the young people's voices as they discuss the answers to the questions she'd written earlier on the board.

When she's halfway through the names, she sees Ross pass

her door. He waves and she waves back. Knowing he'll have noticed how well the class are behaving.

The time goes quickly and, before she knows it, the bell is ringing. Catherine raises her hand and waits for the class to quieten – a technique she learnt from Gary, back in the days when they were both teachers. She'd been surprised at how well it had worked and her husband had been right – maintaining order was as much about tricks and confidence as anything else.

She waits for the class to file out, then follows them, shutting the door behind her before bending to pick up a sweatshirt that's fallen from someone's waist. Calling the owner back to collect it.

'You'd lose your head if it wasn't screwed on.'

By the time she gets into the playground, Karen, the other teacher on duty, is already out there.

'Sorry, Karen.' Catherine leans her back against the brickwork and folds her arms. 'Time got away with me.'

'No problem.' Karen points to the mug of coffee by her feet. 'Thought you wouldn't have had time, so I made you one.'

Catherine bends and picks it up. Takes a sip. 'You're a lifesaver.'

'It's all going on with you then.' Karen looks at her over the top of her steaming mug. 'First the car and now I hear you have a new lodger.'

'Yeah.' Catherine gives a deep sigh. 'News travels fast. How did you know about Lisa?'

'Oh, Ross told me. What's the story? I didn't know she was looking for somewhere to stay.'

'Neither did I.'

Catherine pushes aside her irritation that Ross has been spreading gossip. Gary won't be happy about that if he finds out. She wonders what exactly Gary has told him about Lisa. Is it more than he's told *her*? Something that would explain why he's being so odd with the girl?

She looks at Karen, hoping to find out. 'I didn't even know Gary had a half-sister.'

'What? *Your* Gary?' Clearly, it's something Ross had failed to mention... or maybe Gary hadn't told him. Catherine winces, wishing she hadn't said anything.

'Yeah. Not that he knew she was working here. He hasn't seen her since she was a child.'

'That's weird.'

'Isn't it. Anyway, Lisa had been having some problems with her parents and needed somewhere else to live. Asked if she could stay with us. You know, being family.'

She's not going to mention the sleeping bag in the cupboard. Some things are better left unsaid.

Karen blows at her tea. 'Is she still having problems at school? I heard you're now her mentor.'

'Ross again?'

She grins. ''Fraid so.'

'Between you and me, Lisa's a bit, well a lot, out of her depth.' It feels unprofessional to be discussing her mentee, but she needs to tell someone and if *she* doesn't, Ross clearly will. 'The kids don't listen to her and I can't imagine it would have been any different during her teaching practice. To be honest, I'm surprised she passed.'

Karen looks at her. Sighs. 'Sometimes, I think they'll take anyone. I suppose we have to remember that we were all there once... even you, Cath. Though I can't imagine you ever having discipline problems.'

If she's expecting her to comment, Catherine doesn't. In fact, she's hoping Karen will take her silence as an affirmative, because she's never told anyone about her time at her old school. Has let the staff here form their own opinion based on what they see of her now. Allowing the myth to grow that she's always been this way: confident and in control.

It's the best way. The only way.

If only they knew.

A football hits the wall to the right of her head, momentarily distracting her. She points her first and second fingers at her eyes, then turns her hand and points at the boy who'd kicked it. 'I'm watching you, Elliot.'

On the far side of the playground another boy is staring at her. Karen's seen it too. 'What's up with Dean? If looks could kill.'

'I don't think he's forgiven me for the other day.'

'When you sent him to the behavioural unit?'

'Yeah, he wasn't happy about the three days suspension he got. Thinks I'm picking on him.'

Karen smiles. 'And *are* you?'

'Of course not.'

'Just wondered. I reckon we all have a kid at Greenfield who gets up our nose. No one wants to admit it, either that or they hide it well, but I know I'm right. It's no state secret that my nemesis is Amy Cousins.' She points to a girl with pencilled eyebrows who's applying lip gloss to her full lips. 'Precocious little madam. We all have our favourites too.'

'I don't. I treat everyone the same. With clear boundaries, encouragement, and a structure to their day there's hope for them all.'

'So you think a bit of discipline and a shitload of positivity will keep boys like Dean out of the crack house once they leave Greenfield.'

Aled's gaunt face and sunken eyes come into Catherine's head again. His finger pointing at her chest. *They always loved you more than me.* She shakes the memory away.

'I've no idea... but at least I'll have tried.'

She has to. What else can she do?

'All I can say is thank heavens for the likes of you, Cather-

ine. Greenfield Comprehensive needs more teachers made in
your mould.' Karen pushes herself away from the wall. Waves
her mug at a boy who's just shoved another. 'Hey, Lee Chandler. Cut that out.' She turns back to Catherine with a grin.
'See. You're not the only one who can instil fear into the hearts
of the rabble.'

'Clearly not.'

The school building is L-shaped and, as she says it, her eye
is caught by a group of people walking down the corridor of the
maths department on the other side of the playground.

As they move closer, she sees it's Ellen Swanson and one of
the deputy heads, Mark Perry, accompanied by a tall boy with
light brown hair.

She blinks, looks again, her heart beating wildly as the boy
disappears behind a section of wall before reappearing again.
Because, surely, that's Aled who walks beside Ellen.

But, of course, it isn't. It's simply her mind playing tricks
on her.

Karen follows her gaze. 'I reckon that must be the new A
level kid, Jake Lloyd. Didn't Ellen tell you he was coming? It
should have been yesterday but...' She leaves the sentence drifting. They both know what happened yesterday.

'Yes, she told me.' Catherine pulls herself together. 'But
what with my car and everything, I'd completely forgotten. I've
got him next lesson. I just hope he doesn't disrupt the status quo
as my A level group are pretty settled.'

Karen laughs. 'With you as his teacher, he wouldn't dare.
Regardless, they're a bit more human at seventeen, don't you
think?'

'If you say so. Anyway, the bell's about to go and then we'll
find out, won't we?'

Catherine empties the dregs of her coffee into a nearby
bush. 'Would you mind if I went straight in? With Jake arriving,

I really need to sort out some stuff before my A level group get there.'

Karen nods. 'Go on. But you owe me.'

'I do. Thanks, Karen.'

Catherine leaves her and goes inside, heading straight to her classroom. Pulling out her chair, she sits at her desk and wakens her computer. She enters her password, finds the file she's looking for and opens it, bringing the information up on the smart board.

Explore the theme of innocence and experience in The Go-Between. How do the characters grapple with the loss of innocence, and what consequences does it have?

Below the question are bullet points which she'll fill in with the class after a discussion. She's just finished reading through her lesson notes when there's a knock on the door and when she looks up, she sees it's Mark the deputy.

'Ah, Mrs Ashworth. I'm glad you're here... I'd like you to meet our new student, Jake Lloyd. A little late, I know, but he says he had trouble with the buses.' Mark raises an eyebrow at Catherine, indicating his scepticism. 'Anyway, he's here now and I'm sure you'll make him feel at home.'

Catherine stands. 'Of course. Welcome to Greenfield Comprehensive, Jake. I think you'll find we don't bite.'

It's said as a joke, but the youth who stands nonchalantly in the doorway doesn't give so much as a smile. Instead, he looks around the classroom as though assessing whether it's worth his while staying. His dark eyes move to the whiteboard and he reads the questions written there.

'Fuck's sake.'

Catherine bristles. 'Language like that might have been acceptable in your last school, Jake, but we don't tolerate it here. Do we, Mr Perry?'

'We certainly don't, but as it's your first day, we'll let it slide. Any problems, Mrs Ashworth, let me know.'

'I'm sure there won't be.' The deputy leaves and Catherine points to a desk near the front. 'I've put you there next to Aiden. Have you brought a folder of your work from your old school as Miss Swanson asked? It will be good if you have so I can get an idea of what you've already covered and where the gaps are.'

She'd have liked to have known sooner, but Ellen had sprung this new admission to the school on her.

Jake looks at her as though assessing her. He shrugs the rucksack he's carrying off his shoulder and opens it. Takes out a blue folder and tosses it onto her desk before sitting in the place she's indicated. He looks bored. Too old for the school in his jeans and faded black denim jacket.

It's not long before the rest of the class arrive. Unlike the younger year groups, she doesn't expect them to line up, but to come in quietly and sit down at their tables. As they pass him on the way to their seats, his new classmates look at Jake with undisguised interest, but he ignores them.

She waits until everyone has settled, then smiles. 'I want you all to welcome our newest member of the sixth form, Jake Lloyd. It will take him a while to get used to a new class and a new teacher, most likely the texts we're studying will be different too, but it's your job, as well as mine, to help make the transition as smooth as possible.'

Catherine turns away and writes Jake's name on the white-board, taking her time with it. It's not because she doesn't want to start the lesson. No, not that. It's because, after the mistake she'd made when she'd first seen him, she's scared that when she turns around and looks at Jake again, the face that looks back at her will be someone else's.

Her phone pings in her pocket, taking her by surprise, and without thinking, she takes it out and clicks on the message that's popped up.

Her chest tightens.

There are no words on the screen, just a video. It's her car, her beautiful car, barely visible because of the flames that engulf it. Feeling sick, Catherine clicks off it. Stuffs the phone back into her pocket.

If someone's trying to frighten her, they're succeeding.

TWELVE

'Bag off the table please, Jake?'

Catherine clicks her fingers at the rucksack and, with a shrug, the boy lifts it and places it on the floor next to him. He's a strange one, that's for sure. Even though he's only been in the class for one lesson, she's already seen something in his written work that has caught her interest. A spark of intelligence that's missing from the work of the other members of the group. An innate ability to think around the subject and tackle a question from a different direction.

Just as Aled had.

With guidance, he could do well in his exams – has the makings of a grade A student even. Something sorely lacking at Greenfield Comprehensive.

Catherine moves around the classroom giving out texts of *The Taming of the Shrew*. When she reaches Jake's table, she hesitates before putting a book in front of him, hoping that a miracle will happen and he'll participate. Because, so far, he's refused to join in any of the discussions.

Crossing to her desk, she picks up her copy of the text. She leans her back against the hard surface and scans the class, making eye contact with each and every one of her students. Her way of letting them know they are all valued members of the group.

'I want you to open your books to Act 2 Scene 1 where Katherina torments Bianca about her suitors. Janine, I'd like you to read Katherina's part. Carla, you take Bianca.' She selects others from the class to read the rest of the characters. 'And I want you to really think about the meaning of this scene as you read... the reasons behind Katherina's treatment of Bianca. Jake, I'd like you to read the part of Petruchio.'

A boy at the back raises his hand. 'But you said yesterday that I could be Petruchio.'

'Well, I've changed my mind... a teacher's prerogative. As Lord Alfred Tennyson said, Ryan, *Ours is not to reason why; ours is but to do and die*. You can read Baptista instead.'

'Theirs not to make reply.' Jake had been studying his hands, but now he raises his head. Looks at Catherine with barely concealed contempt. '*Theirs* not to reason why.'

Catherine looks at him in confusion. 'I'm sorry?'

'You've misquoted the poem. It's theirs not ours.'

For the first time in a long while, Catherine feels flustered. She's used to backchat from some of the more lairy kids in the lower years, but this boy is questioning her knowledge.

'Okay... well I'm glad you picked me up on it. I can only hope you'll be giving *The Taming of the Shrew* the same amount of attention.' Catherine opens Jake's text and flicks through to the right page. Hands it to him. 'I know you've been studying this play at your last school which will make things a lot easier. Today, we're going to start from where Petruchio arrives at Baptista's house with the music teacher, Licio.'

'I don't want to read.' His head is down on his arms.

'I'm sorry. I didn't catch that.'

'I said' – Jake raises his head and glares at her – 'I don't want to fucking read.'

The class are staring at Catherine, wondering what she's going to do, and she knows it's important she responds correctly.

'I know that being here, the change in routine and new teachers, is hard for you, Jake, but I want you to remember that it was your choice to come to Greenfield Comprehensive, not ours. I will do my very best to help you achieve a good grade in your exams, but I can only do that if you play your part. Be respectful of others in the group and the staff. We want you to succeed here and I think that's what you want too. Am I right?'

She waits, hoping her guess is correct and eventually Jake folds his arms. Nods.

'Yeah. Sorry.'

'Good. I'll accept your apology, and if you don't want to read today, that's fine but—'

'It's okay. I'll read.' He picks up the book and looks around him. 'What are you all staring at?'

Order has been restored and they read the act through with enough time to discuss how well Katherina and Petruchio are suited and, in what seems like only minutes to Catherine, the bell rings to signal the end of the lesson.

She waits with her hand on the door as the class files out. Catches Jake as he's about to leave.

'Look, Jake, I don't know what's going on in that head of yours, but you have potential... a real chance to do well and I don't want to see you blow it. The problem is, there are gaps in your knowledge that need to be filled and time is moving on. If you're to cover what the rest of the class have already learnt, we'll need to find time to work on some of the units outside of lesson time. Are you up for that?'

He looks at her from under his fringe. 'Whatever.'

She presses her lips together, thinking how this will work, then leaves him and goes over to the computer. 'That's a stroke of luck. You have a free period at three and so have I. We can use that time to make a start with it. See where to plug those gaps.'

Jake shrugs. 'If you want.'

'That's a plan then.'

She watches him leave, then turns back to her computer and brings up the lesson plan for her next class. She tries to concentrate, but now she's alone in the classroom again, the video she'd been sent from the unknown number comes back to her. Should she tell the police? Or speak to Gary? Although Catherine knows the answer, she stalls... it could still just be a prank.

A knock on the door makes her look up. It's Ross, a mug in his hand.

'You look pleased with yourself. Thought you might want this.' He comes in, hands her the mug of tea, then perches on the nearest table.

'Thanks.' Catherine smiles. 'Actually, I *am* feeling rather smug. I've had a bit of a breakthrough with the new boy, Jake Lloyd.'

'Really? Already? From what I've heard he's got a bit of an attitude on him.'

'It's more complicated than that.' She thinks of the way he'd sat at the table, his arms folded, his stony expression discouraging anyone from talking to him. 'I get the feeling that what he's showing us is only part of the story. I think there's something else going on that we don't know about and his couldn't-care-less manner is his armour. His defence against the world.'

Ross raises an eyebrow. 'You seem to know a lot about it?'

'It's a hunch, Ross,' she says quickly.

But it's not just a hunch. She's seen it before... in her brother. Only Ross doesn't need to know about Aled. No one does.

'Are you sure that's all it is?'

Catherine folds her arms. 'What do you mean by that?'

'Just an observation. The boy comes from a good background. Clearly has brains.'

'So? What's your point?'

'If one of the current Year 11s were in the A Level group, would you put as much time and effort into helping them achieve good grades?'

'Of course I would!'

'If you say so.'

Catherine eyes him suspiciously. 'Meaning what, Ross?'

'Whatever you want to make of it. I'll leave you with that thought.'

'Are you saying I'm a snob?'

'Your words, not mine.'

Turning his back on her, Ross leaves the classroom, and Catherine watches him, shock and anger fighting for space. But she has to let it go as she needs to heat up her soup in the school microwave before the staffroom turns into Piccadilly Circus.

She leaves her classroom and heads in the direction of the staffroom, passing Lisa's on the way. A glance through the window shows her that the Year 11 class is still in there and Lisa is struggling to get them under control.

Some boys are sitting on their tables, their backs to Lisa, as though she isn't there. The phone they're passing round containing something dubious if the sniggers are anything to go by. And it's not just the boys. A group of girls at the table nearest to her are drawing on each other's wrists with coloured felt pens.

Without thinking about how she's going to deal with this, Catherine throws open the door, making the girls nearest to it jump as it hits the wall.

She points a finger at the ringleader, Dean Gibbs. 'You can cut that out right now.'

It comes out louder than she had intended and the class

goes quiet: the school is full of teachers who shout, but Catherine isn't one of them.

'And I'll have your phone while you're about it, Dean.'

'You can't do that. It ain't your class.'

'I don't care whose class it is. Phones aren't allowed in school unless they're switched off. Now, please.' She holds out her hand.

For one horrible moment, Catherine thinks the boy's going to refuse, but he doesn't. Instead, he kicks the chair away from him and jumps down from the table he's sitting on. He shoves the phone at her, then strides out of the room.

'All right the rest of you. Show's over.'

Knowing all eyes are on her, Catherine walks to the front of the classroom where Lisa is sitting miserably, cheeks flushed. Giving her a reassuring smile, she leans against the whiteboard and stares meaningfully at a group of girls gathered at the window. She clicks her fingers in the direction of the tables and waits for them to sit. Smiles to herself. In less than three minutes order has been restored to Lisa's classroom.

'I'm disappointed in you, Year 11. Bitterly disappointed. At Greenfield, behaviour like that won't be tolerated and I think you know that. Am I right?'

There's a murmur of assent. A nod of heads.

'Then you'll line up and lead out quietly if you don't want to spend the rest of lunchtime in here.'

They do as they're asked and when the last pupil has left, Lisa looks up at her.

'Thanks, Cath. I'm sorry you had to see that.'

'I'm your mentor, Lisa. I'm glad I did. This way, I can see first-hand the things we need to work on. We'll start tonight if you like. After dinner.'

'I'll cook. It's the least I can do.'

'We'll make it together. Now I'm going to have my lunch. This talk of food is making me ravenous.' Catherine's about to leave the room when she stops. Maybe, after the help she's already given her, the girl might be open to offering up some information in return. 'I was just wondering, Lisa, if you had any thoughts about Gary. The real reason why he won't have anything to do with his father.'

Lisa looks away, her cheeks colouring. 'My dad never said. It wasn't something he wanted to talk about.'

'And your mum didn't—'

'No.'

They fall into an uncomfortable silence and Catherine's just wishing she'd never asked when Lisa speaks again.

'Even though I'm not his father, nothing like him, Gary doesn't want me living with you both. Perhaps it's best I leave.'

'No.' The speed with which Catherine says it, surprises her. 'There's no need for that.'

And the reason is, in a house where her needs and ambitions are so often pushed aside, she likes having Lisa there.

THIRTEEN

The door to Catherine's classroom is open and, as the bell goes to signal the end of school, the corridor starts to fill with students. Their voices loud. Their bodies jostling against each other as they make for the double doors that will lead to the stairs down and freedom.

Catherine looks up, then back at Jake who's staring down at his book, his forehead creased in concentration as he thinks about his answer to the question she's just asked.

'There's no hurry, Jake. Take your time.'

Jake picks up his pen. Clicks the nib in and out. 'I think this phrase, the way the poet compared the cloud to a ship sailing without her shows the reader her feelings of abandonment.' He puts the pen down again and taps his forehead. 'It's a metaphor for their suffering, yeah?'

Catherine nods. Although she doesn't want to show it, inside she's bursting with joy. With pride. This boy gets it. Really gets it.

'You're right. When she wrote it, the poet going through a difficult time in her life and longed for some contact with the man she was in love with. She was broken in spirit and felt as though nature itself was against her. What about this next verse? What is it saying to you?'

Jake lowers his head again. His hair is razored short around his ears and the back of his head, the rest falling into a tangled mess on his forehead. There's something untamed and self-reliant about the way he sits: knees bent, feet propped up on the chair next to him as though he's forgotten he's in school and not at home. Or maybe not caring.

A hard lump forms in her throat.

Her brother was like that... a free spirit. Playing life his own way. Brushing off her words of concern like ash dropped from a cigarette. Thinking he was invincible. A cat with nine lives. Until the day he had none left. His sharp tongue and even sharper intelligence, not enough on their own to save him.

'I think it means she's been waiting for the telephone to ring and that's what's caused her to feel like shit. See' – his finger jabs at the line in the book – 'she talks about the mute phone. She's pretty fucked up really.'

Jake doesn't sound like Aled and the picture of him in her head melts away. She smiles. 'We might need to take a look at your turn of phrase, Jake, but your logic is sound. That's exactly what it means.'

She wants him to be pleased with her praise, looks for a sign of it in his face, but his expression is unreadable. As Aled's used to be.

There's a knock on the door and Ellen puts her head around it. 'Just a reminder that it's football practice tonight, Jake. I'll let Mr Mellor know you're on your way, shall I?'

'Oh yeah.' Jake looks at the clock on the wall. Lifts his feet from the chair. 'Shit, I didn't know it had got that late.'

'Time flies when you're having fun.' Ellen looks at Catherine. 'How's it going?'

She smiles. 'Pretty good.'

'Glad to hear it. I don't like to see wasted talent.'

With a nod to them both, Ellen leaves them and Catherine stands, shocked at how time has run away with her. 'You get going, Jake. Tell Mr Mellor I'm sorry for keeping you but well done. You've made a lot of progress today, and I have a good feeling about it. If you put the work in, tidy up your language, I think we have a good chance.' She hands the textbook to him. 'If you're able, read the rest of the poem tonight and I'll see if I can find time tomorrow to go over the rest with you. I just wish you'd contribute more to the discussion in class. The others in the group would benefit from hearing your analysis.'

Jake looks away, his face freezing into a frown. His jaw moving as he chews on the inside of his cheek. 'What's the point? It's not as if the others will be there discussing things with me in the exam. Not when it's a written paper.'

'I hear what you're saying, but the sharing of ideas helps you process information rather than simply receive it. If you voice your thoughts, you're forced to phrase ideas in a way that others will understand. It's a good skill to have.'

Catherine's phone is on the table next to her. It lights up with a message and, distracted by it, she picks it up. Remembering, just in time, the thing she'd been sent earlier. The thing she'd tried not to think about while she'd been teaching. She doesn't want to look in case it's something similar and, with a shock, she sees her hands are trembling.

Jake's studying her.

'There a problem?'

'No, no. It's nothing. You go. You don't want to be late for football.'

'Yeah.'

He pushes back his chair and as he shoves his arms into his black denim jacket, Catherine sees, with sudden clarity, a similar jacket. One that used to hang on the hook on the back of Aled's bedroom door.

She turns away, eyes brimming, and waits for him to go.

When he's out of sight, she clicks on the message and reads it. Smiling with relief when she sees it's from Lisa.

Are you ready to go?

Catherine stares at her phone. Damn. She'd forgotten she'd told Lisa they'd leave early tonight. She looks out of the class-room window at the empty corridor. The poor girl will be wondering what she's been doing.

She's just leaving the classroom when she sees Lisa coming towards her, her bag of books on her arm.

'Sorry, Lisa. I was giving the new boy, Jake Lloyd, some extra tutoring to help him catch up with the others. Hope you had plenty to do.'

'I did. Please don't worry.'

Catherine picks up her box and the two of them make their way through the school and, as they talk, Catherine sneaks glances at the girl who walks beside her. She looks less anxious now and she's glad.

Lisa holds open the entrance door for her and Catherine steps out, her heart sinking when she sees the wet playground. Hears the drum of the rain on the roof of the porch where they're standing.

'Bloody rain. Won't it ever let up? We'd better make a run for it.'

They pull up their hoods and run across the wet tarmac towards the school gates. When they reach the staff car park, Catherine keeps her eyes studiously turned from the blackened space where her car had blazed. Not wanting to see it or think about it. The video of the fire is still on her phone and she knows she should have phoned the number on the card the police officer had given her. But something had stopped her. If she shows them what's on there, more questions will be asked... ones she might not want to answer.

When they reach the hire car, Catherine puts the box in the back, then slides into the driver's side, stretching an arm across the passenger seat to open Lisa's door. But instead of getting in, Lisa leans across the front of the car. Presses her finger to the windscreen as rain drips from her hood.

'Oh, Jesus.' Catherine's breathing shortens. She'd been too busy getting out of the rain to notice the word scrawled across the glass in black marker. A single word distorted by the rivers of water running down the glass. Its brevity only serving to highlight its vileness.

MURDERER

Lisa jumps into the car beside her and slams the door shut, the ends of her hair dripping water onto the handbrake as she twists to secure her seat belt. There's a sharp, quick snap as it locks into place and Catherine wonders if the girl believes the simple action might keep them both safe.

'What does it mean? Who did this?' Lisa's voice is shaking.

'It means nothing.' With a concerted effort, Catherine relaxes the muscles of her forehead, her cheeks. Manages a weak smile. 'Things like this happen all the time at Greenfield. It's just kids messing.'

'But your car. It's the second—'

'Honestly, Lisa, it's nothing to worry about. If we show we're fazed by it, then they'll have won.'

The words are designed to calm, but, inside, Catherine's heart is racing and, too late, she sees Lisa's eyes settle on the fingers of her right hand – fingers that are clutching the steering wheel as though scared to let go.

Catherine fights to regain control of her erratic breathing, knows she has to, because Lisa isn't buying into what she's saying and is it any wonder when Catherine, too, is finding it hard to believe?

Despite having told herself she wouldn't, Catherine's eyes are drawn to the word on the windscreen again. She'd tried to convince herself that the fire had been nothing but a random act of vandalism – something that could just as easily have happened to Ross's car... or Lynne's. But everyone knows lightning doesn't strike twice in the same place. This morning, she'd parked the hire car as far away from the burnt and blackened concrete as she could and that only makes it worse.

Because it means someone is targeting her. And whoever that person is, they know what she did.

Needing to do something, Catherine rubs at the misted window with the sleeve of her coat.

'Why hasn't Ellen got the bloody security light fixed?'

Through the rain, she can just make out the tall fence that surrounds the school but nothing more. She turns the key in the ignition and flicks on the wipers. Leans forward and narrows her eyes in the vain hope she'll catch sight of something that might give her a clue as to who did this.

But there's nothing to see. Nothing but the stark word slashed across her windscreen and the driving rain.

FOURTEEN

Gary is talking too loudly, something he does when he's feeling uncomfortable. The bottle of Prosecco stands empty on the dining table and it hasn't skipped Catherine's notice that the glass he's filled the most this evening is his own.

It's the first evening he's stayed in since Lisa arrived, and she's now beginning to wonder if it would have been better if he'd gone to The Crown as he had the other nights. It's embarrassing the way he's behaving.

'I'm surprised anyone wants to enter the teaching profession anymore.' Gary unscrews the lid from the bottle of red he's just got from the wine rack and offers some to Lisa. When she puts her hand over her glass and shakes her head, he shrugs and fills his own. 'So much bloody paperwork and kids who don't know the meaning of the word discipline.'

Catherine takes a sip of her Diet Coke. 'For God's sake, Gaz, you sound like an old Grinch. In a minute you'll be saying "back in my day". Stop trying to put Lisa off. Just because you didn't enjoy it and decided to jump ship, doesn't mean everyone feels that way. Take no notice, Lisa. It's the drink speaking.'

'It bloody isn't.' Gary pushes aside his dinner plate and

leans his elbows on the table. 'Go on then, Lisa. Tell me why you decided to be a teacher?'

Why is Gary being like this? Why is he trying to make her feel uncomfortable? It almost sounds like a threat.

She puts a hand on Lisa's arm. 'You don't have to answer that.'

But Gary's having none of it. His gaze hasn't left the younger woman's. 'No, tell me. I really want to know.'

Lisa's looking down at her half-empty plate, and it's clear she's lost any appetite she might have had before Gary started his verbal crusade. What's got into him?

'Actually, I don't know why,' she says, at last. 'I suppose I didn't really know what else to do.' She looks meaningfully at Gary. 'Maybe teaching runs in the family.'

Gary looks shocked but quickly recovers. 'At last. Some bloody honesty.' He raises his glass to Lisa. 'My advice is to get out while you can. While you're still young. Believe me, you'll thank me for it.'

Catherine stands. Starts to collect up the plates. 'Ignore him. You've survived your first few weeks, and as you get used to the students, and they get used to you, it will get easier. I promise.'

Lisa pushes her hair back behind her ear. Tonight, she's wearing it down and there's a touch of mascara on her eyelashes. A hint of blusher on the curve of her cheeks.

'Thanks, Catherine. I don't know how I'd manage if it wasn't for you encouraging me. You're so calm. So...' – she thinks for a second – 'on top of things. If that had been *my* car they'd graffitied, I don't know what I'd have done.'

Gary had been refilling his glass, but now he puts the bottle down. He looks at Catherine.

'What's she talking about?'

Catherine stiffens. She hadn't been planning on telling him.

Had presumed that if she didn't mention it, then Lisa would take the hint and not say anything either. She'd been wrong.

'It's nothing. Just some stupid kids. A childish prank. You'd think they'd know better once they were out of primary.'

She hopes that's the end of it, but Gary clearly isn't going to let it go.

'So, what did they write?'

Lisa opens her mouth to speak, but Catherine cuts in. 'Just the usual expletives. Shows a serious lack of imagination so probably one of the Year 11s.'

She stares at Lisa, challenging her to contradict, but she doesn't. It will have to be their secret. Gary must never know the truth.

He takes a gulp of his wine, his lips staining red. 'And when were you planning on telling me this?'

'Oh, for goodness' sake, Gaz. Stop making it into some big thing. You know what kids are like, and I doubt they even knew it was my car. It could have been anyone's. Most likely it was Ellen Swanson they were targeting.'

'Like it was Ellen Swanson's car they were targeting when they lit petrol-soaked rags underneath it.' He gives a dry laugh. 'Do me a favour. Whoever did one, did the other.'

'It was a coincidence,' she says again, weakly. Knowing she's convincing nobody.

Gary folds his arms. 'You might not like the thought of it, but believe me, the kids at the school know what car belongs to who. In fact, Catherine, they know every bloody thing about you. Not just what car you drive, but how many kids you might or might not have, how old you are, where you live...' He stops. 'What's the matter?'

Catherine's eyes are fixed on the kitchen window. She's still not told him about the night he'd gone to the pub... the ring on the doorbell and the lighter she'd found on their porch. If she had, he'd think her hysterical. Believe the anniversary of Aled's death was getting to her.

'Nothing's the matter.' She drags her eyes away. 'Come on. We'll talk about this tomorrow. Let's get this table cleared.'

She stands and Lisa does the same, pushing her chair in as she might in a restaurant. 'If it's all the same with you, once I've cleared the table and helped with the dishes, I think I'll go to my room. I've got some stuff I need to do before tomorrow.'

Catherine gestures at the table. 'Don't worry about this. Gaz and I will do it and as for the dishes, that's what a dishwasher is for. Would you like me to wake you in the morning?'

'No, there's no need. I'll set my phone.'

'Okay. Well, there's muesli in the cupboard and a packet of croissants in the bread bin. We really are happy to have you here, aren't we, Gaz?'

But Gary doesn't answer. He's taken his wine over to the kitchen counter and is stacking the plates in the dishwasher.

Lisa pulls her cardigan around her, looking from one to the other. 'I'll say good night then. And thank you again for everything. You've been so kind, Cath. You too, Gary.'

'Yeah, well...' Gary puts a fistful of cutlery in the plastic basket, doesn't look at the girl, and Catherine knows how that sentence would have finished if he'd voiced it. *I didn't get much choice, did I?*

'Good night then.' The false cheer in Catherine's voice raises its pitch a fraction. 'I hope you sleep well.'

Catherine waits for Lisa to leave them, waits for the door of the spare room to shut, before turning on Gary.

'What the hell is wrong with you tonight? The drinking. The snidey comments. The...' – she shakes her head in frustration – 'the everything. Yes, Lisa did rather spring this on us, and, yes, it's going to take a bit of getting used to, but she's your sister. Pushed out of her house and with nowhere else to go. She'd been sleeping on the classroom floor, for God's sake. Where's your compassion? Where's your pity?'

Gary is crouching in front of her, the knife she'd used to chop the vegetables in his hand. He looks at it, then puts it with the other utensils in the cutlery basket. Wearily, he stands. Goes over to her and places a hand on either side of her shoulders.

'It's not about compassion. It's not about pity.'

'Then what is it?' She searches his face for an answer.

He looks away, his teeth catching at his bottom lip. Tearing at a thin strip of skin. Making it bleed.

'You really want to know?' The way he says it... his tone of voice. It's as if he thinks she should already know the answer.

'I wouldn't ask if I didn't.'

Catherine stares at the bead of red blood on his bottom lip, waiting for him to tell her.

'What's making me like this is nothing to do with Lisa. It's because I'm scared, Cath. There. Happy now?'

'You're scared?' It wasn't what she'd been expecting. 'Scared of what?'

There's a weighted pause. 'God. Can't you see it? Of you, Cath.'

'Me?'

Her face is reflected in the kitchen window. Gary's is too. He moves closer again. Turns her so she's facing him and presses his forehead against hers.

'Yes. You promised, after last time, not to keep things from me and I believed you. You said you wouldn't try to cope with things on your own again. I know I've been a right shit this evening, but I couldn't help it. What's happening, the car and your reaction to it, isn't normal. I see things more clearly than you... how it could end.'

'Meaning?'

'You're under too much stress. Having a house guest is extra work. You don't need this, and I'm sorry for putting pressure on you with Lisa. She's my sister, not yours, and my dad should be the one supporting her. Not us. You can ask her to leave if you want to.' He pauses, waiting for her to reply, then seeing her face, the guilt she's feeling, shrugs in resignation. 'Whatever, I'll apologise to Lisa in the morning. Make some excuse. I'm going to watch the news, then it's bed for me too. I've a meeting in the morning.'

He takes the rest of his wine into the living room, but Catherine stays where she is. Did he really say he was scared of her? But there's something else in what her husband has just said that won't leave her. Something she's only just realised.

She sits at the kitchen table her face in her hands. Why is Gary so desperate for Lisa to leave?

FIFTEEN

'I don't think you should worry too much, Cath. Before you know it, the kids will have forgotten all about the writing on your windscreen.'

It's Thursday morning and Catherine and Lisa are in the car on the way to work.

'You're right. What do they say? Today's news is tomorrow's chip wrapper or something along those lines.' Noting her silence, she qualifies it. 'Newspaper. That's what fish and chips used to be wrapped in.'

Sometimes, she forgets how young Lisa is and that the news she reads is likely to be from an app on her phone. Not from a tabloid.

'Oh, I see.' She laughs. 'Silly me.'

'Anyway, let's talk about nicer things. I hope the advice I've been giving you has been a help.'

Lisa's face brightens into a smile. 'Oh, it has, Cath. It really has. Your way of working is so much more organised than Ross's. His methods are...'

'Chaotic?'

'I wasn't going to say that but... yes. A bit.'

'Still, it seems to work. The kids like him. Ellen likes him.'

'Karen likes him too.' Lisa giggles and Catherine wonders whether she should have told her. Ross had let it slip yesterday that he and Karen were seeing each other. Nothing serious, he'd insisted, but, even so, she'd had to fight to stop herself from ribbing him about it. It had been fun to share Ross's news but now guilt has set in and, with it, the sickly aftertaste of oversharing. Who Ross dates is his business, not theirs.

Yet, even if Gary doesn't share her view, she likes having Lisa around. She feels relaxed in her presence and having someone to talk school with, without having to worry about their reaction, is a novelty. Because Gary's disinterest is obvious whenever she tries to mention it. And it's not just school he doesn't want to talk about... her brother's name on her lips will have him reaching for the TV controller or having a sudden urge to rush off to the toilet.

She glances over at the girl. Yes, Lisa is different, and more than once this morning, she's found herself wanting to open up to her about Aled too. To offload her fears. Her guilt. But there are some secrets she cannot share. Mustn't share.

'I've noticed Gary's been staying late at work a lot. Has he always done that?'

Catherine hears the sympathy in Lisa's voice. Shakes her head. 'Not in the early days but recently, yes. Either that or the pub.'

'It must be lonely in the evenings.'

There's a hollowed-out feeling inside her. 'A little, yes. We used to chat all the time, but now I think he prefers to talk football with the boys.'

With Ross, she thinks.

'I was wondering, has Gary known Ross long?' Lisa asks.

'Since forever.' She thinks of the photograph of the two of them on the shelf in their living room. Arms around each other's necks. Covered in mud from the football pitch. 'They were at school together.'

'And he doesn't mind that you and Ross are friends?'

'What? No, not that he's ever said. Me and Ross... well, our friendship is different. He makes me laugh. I make him irritated.' She smiles to herself. 'But in a good way. What he has with Gary is more blokey. It's based around football and the pub and having a pint. I think we both give Ross something different.'

'I like that.' Lisa shifts in her seat. 'I've never really had any friends. Not good ones anyway.'

'You have me. I never had a sister... I think I would have liked one.'

'Really?'

'Yes. It's why I feel terrible for you that Gary's been so absent. If I had a half-sister turn up out of the blue, I'd be over the moon.' Catherine looks quickly at the girl, her voice suddenly serious. 'You would know this better than me, Lisa. Do you think there's any chance your dad would talk to Gary?'

'My dad?'

'Yes. To explain his side of things. From what I gather, from the minute he left them, Gary and his mum cut your dad out of their lives.'

Lisa looks out of the side window. 'I don't think so. Old wounds like that are hard to heal. No one likes to feel they've been rejected.'

She sounds sad and Catherine wishes she'd never said anything. That sleeping bag in the school cupboard... Gary's not the only one to have been denied their father's love. Yet shouldn't that have bonded the two of them?

'I'm sorry, Lisa, I should never have asked. It was thoughtless of me.'

'It's all right. You're like family to me now and you have a right to know. My father is a hard man, a callous man, and my mum would have been better off had she never met him. No

one deserves to be cast aside. No one.' Catherine feels Lisa's
eyes on her. 'But that question you asked me about Gary and his
past. I hope you don't think I'm speaking out of turn, but if
you're worried, shouldn't it be him you're asking? He is your
husband, after all.'

'He doesn't want to talk about it. There'd be no point.'

'Like *you* didn't want to tell him about the writing on your
windscreen? I know it's none of my business, but there seems to
be a lack of trust between the two of you.'

Catherine's cheeks flush. 'That's nonsense. Look, Lisa,
marriages are complicated. I really don't want to talk about this
now.'

'I'm sorry. I was only trying to help.'

'I know and it was kind of you, but your brother and I are
okay. Please don't worry.' Feeling a pang of guilt, she searches
for a safer topic. 'Anyway, you never told me. How did your
mum and dad meet?'

'They taught at the same school.'

'Oh, so your mum was a teacher too. It must have been difficult for them to have kept the affair quiet. If Greenfield's
anything to go by, it would have been a hotbed of gossip.'

Lisa sighs. 'Oh, they knew all right.'

'So the only one who didn't know was Jan.'

'Who?'

'Gary's mother. They say the spouse is always the last to
know. It must have been a shock. Gary says she never got over it.
Died of a broken heart.'

'Do you believe those things, Cath?'

Catherine tries to imagine what it would feel like to lose
Gary that way. 'Yes, I think I probably do.'

'Well, *I* don't.' The words come out sharply, surprising
Catherine. 'Men like that are not worth crying over. They
should be made to pay.'

'Goodness, Lisa. That's a bit harsh, isn't it? Surely there are two sides to every story.'

'You think my dad was right to want nothing to do with me? To prefer me to sleep in a classroom than to live with him?'

Catherine hears the hurt in the girl's voice. 'No, of course not. It's just that you've never explained why he asked you to leave. You don't have to tell me, but it might help me understand if you do.'

'I told him the truth. That's what. And he didn't want to hear it.'

'You told him the truth?'

'Yes.'

Catherine indicates and drives into the staff car park. She desperately wants to know what that truth is, but she's already asked too much. Maybe in time, Lisa will trust her enough to tell her.

SIXTEEN

Catherine leans her elbows on the table in front of her. Presses her fingertips against her temples. Every so often, she hears the scrape of a chair leg, a cough, the voice of a student asking their neighbour a question about the text they're working on, but her thoughts are not on the class but on the conversation she had with Lisa in the car. In particular, the comment Lisa had made about her and Gary. How, from where she was standing, it looked like there was no trust between the two of them.

And it worries Catherine that she might be right.

She thinks back to the last evening she and her husband had spent alone together. The one before Lisa had entered their home. They'd talked, yes, but it hadn't been about anything important – her worries, her needs. Any time she'd brought up the subject of school, he'd shut her down and when he'd kissed her, it had been less about love than about ownership. An expectation of sex.

When had it started? That's what she asks herself now. When had the rot set in, leaving a huge hole between them, making her afraid to ask Gary the questions she wanted answers to? She thinks of his odd behaviour recently. How he's never properly explained why he doesn't want his sister in their house.

She presses her fingertips harder into her skin. The car fire and the writing on her windscreen had only happened after Lisa had come clean as to who she was. Might Gary have been behind those things? Could he have been trying to frighten Lisa away from their family by pretending Catherine was in danger? The thought seems preposterous and yet...

'I don't think it's right, miss,' a voice calls from the back of the class, bringing her back to the present. 'That bit where Petruchio tries to tame Katherina by not letting her eat or sleep. If I had a husband like that, I'd report him.'

In the seat beside Catherine, Jake shakes his head. 'Jesus, what an idiot. How did she even get to be in the A level group?'

Catherine twists round in her chair and makes eye contact with the girl who had asked the question. 'You have to remember that the play was written in Elizabethan times, Bethany... that's over four hundred years ago and things were very different then. Marriages were often thought of as business arrangements between a father and the husband-to-be. We'll be studying that in more detail next lesson.'

Jake huffs out a breath. 'I don't know how you can stand to do it. Day after day teaching kids this dumb.'

She turns back to him. 'Then why don't you give the other students the benefit of your wisdom, Jake? You sit there, refusing to answer questions, never contributing... it makes the others think you're struggling when, clearly, you're not.'

While the rest of the class had been answering the questions she'd set on the board, Catherine had been working with Jake on the poem they'd started the day before. Now, as he sits beside her, irritation at her comment written across his face, she considers him. The more she talks to the boy, the more she sees how quick he is at picking up the subtle nuances of the verses.

How easy he finds it to extract words the poet has used to give the poem light and shade.

'What does the poet mean by the sun wounding her, Jake?'

A student at a table the other side of the aisle from Jake's puts up his hand to ask Catherine a question, but she pretends not to see him. Once she knows Jake has got a grasp of the poem, she'll be able to concentrate on the other students in the class.

She smiles at him. 'Come on. What is it saying to you?'

'Miss, I need to ask you something.' The boy next to them leans across the gap between the tables, but she ignores him, wills Jake to come up with the answer, because she knows he can if he puts his mind to it.

There's a knock at the door and Ellen Swanson looks in. 'Mrs Ashworth. Do you have a minute?'

'Of course.' She gets up and walks over to her. 'What can I do for you?'

Ellen smiles. 'I'm the bearer of good news. The emails haven't gone out to the other candidates yet, but I wanted to tell you myself that the interviews for Head of English will be next Monday. We'll be interviewing five candidates and you will, of course, be one of them.' She lowers her voice, looks behind her at the empty corridor. 'I wanted you to know that I've been impressed with what I've seen since I took over from the old head. Like how you've been managing Jake and the progress he's made already. Between you, me, and the bedpost, I don't think you have anything to worry about and the position is practically yours for the taking.'

Inside, Catherine's glowing. 'Thank you for taking the time to tell me.'

'You're welcome. There's just one thing, Catherine.'

'Yes?'

Ellen lowers her voice. 'That business with your car, the arson... I know it's not your fault, but it hasn't been good for the school's reputation. Nothing else has happened, has it? Anything we'd need to consider before the interview?'

The image of the fire on her phone flashes into her head.

'No, nothing.'

Ellen's eyes are boring into her. 'It's just that there have been some rumours.'

Catherine forces a laugh. 'Oh, you mean the silly thing written on my hire car? Honestly, that was something and nothing. It's been dealt with.'

'Well, that's good.' She looks unsure. 'In future, I'd appreciate it if you came to me with any incidents like this.'

'I will.'

With a nod, Ellen leaves her and Catherine goes back to Jake's table. Picks up where she left off, though it's hard to concentrate. Not just because she now knows for sure she's been picked for interview, but because she's worried about how Gary will take the news. What can of worms it might open.

Maybe it's better to face up to whatever it is that's going on with him.

Without thinking, she takes her phone out of her pocket. Starts to type a message to her husband. *I need to talk to...*

'What the fuck?'

She looks up. 'Jake, I'm sorry. I didn't—'

'You're no better than the teachers at my old school.' Jake stands. Shoves away his chair. 'I'm done with this.'

Picking up his bag, he swings it onto his shoulder, then, without looking back, slams out of the classroom.

The phone with its unwritten message hangs limply in her hand. She looks at the faces of her A level students, then at the empty corridor. Stands and goes after him.

SEVENTEEN

When she gets back to the classroom, Catherine is surprised to find Ross at her desk. Her Year 13 class packing up for the end of lesson. She glances at her watch and is shocked at the time. She'd only planned to be a few minutes, but she's been gone nearly half an hour. Trying to persuade Jake to return to the class. Making him understand how important it is that he succeeds.

'Mr Walker. I'm really sorry... something important came up that couldn't be left.'

Ross puts his pen down. Looks up, his face inscrutable. 'I heard. Something about Jake Lloyd kicking off.'

'He didn't kick off, he...' She feels suddenly flustered. 'Look, it's complicated.'

'You can tell me later. Anyway, there's no harm done.'

'I really didn't plan to be away so long.' Catherine feels her cheeks warm.

It's only now she sees how unprofessional she's been – leaving her class unattended, dashing off after a student simply because he reminded her of her brother. In the past, it would have been inconceivable to do such a thing but now...

The fire, the scrawled word on her windscreen and the memories the two things had brought back. This is why she'd behaved out of character. Lost her grip.

She'll have to make sure it never happens again.

'I'm sorry, Ross.'

Ross raises his hand. 'It's fine, honestly. I made an excuse for you when Ellen came by. Said you needed to have a word with Head of Pastoral about a kid in one of your classes.'

'Thanks. You're a star.'

'No probs.' He grins. 'And, yes, I am.'

He leaves her to it and the bell rings. A couple of the boys stand, push back their chairs, and Catherine puts on a suitably stern face. Raises her eyebrows at them.

'Hey, you two. The bell is for me not for you.'

'Sorry, miss.'

They sit back down and she waits a moment before allowing the class to leave. When they've gone, she puts her face in her hands and exhales slowly, annoyed with herself for her earlier lack of judgement. Knowing how she would have reacted had it been Lisa who'd neglected her class. What an idiot.

But she can't let one slip-up knock her back. Everyone makes mistakes and, because of Ross, everything's fine. She must put the incident behind her... think about her next lesson and try not to worry about it.

Catherine turns to her computer and slides the mouse on the pad to wake it up. The screen springs to life and at the same time her phone pings. She bends, takes the phone out of her bag and, without thinking, clicks on the message. There are only five words, but it's enough to make her heart miss a beat.

I KNOW WHERE YOU LIVE

She gasps, her hand flying to her mouth, her stomach knotting. She turns to the door as though expecting to see the perpetrator standing there, but of course they're not. No one's outside. The corridor is empty.

Catherine looks back at the screen. Hoping it was just her imagination, her eyes playing tricks on her. But it's a vain hope. The words are still there. It's a simple statement, but the menace behind it is there all the same and it brings back the moment when her doorbell had rung. When she'd stood on the empty porch and looked out onto the equally empty garden.

She looks at the message again. Checks the number to see if it's the same as the one containing the video of the fire. It is.

'Cath? Are you all right? Has something happened?'

Catherine turns. Sees Lisa in the doorway, her fingers worrying at the sleeves of her blouse.

'I'm really sorry about earlier,' she continues. 'Your class were getting loud and Ross was passing by. I asked if he'd look in and find out what was happening. I hope I did the right thing.'

Quickly, Catherine turns her phone over. Thankful that, from where she's standing, Lisa wouldn't have seen the words written on it. But this is news to her... that Lisa was the one to tell Ross. Still, it's what she would have told her to do if it had been anyone else's class.

'Of course you did.'

'So you're not angry?'

Catherine hesitates, wondering how much to tell her. 'Why would I be when it was my fault for leaving the class for so long? I was having a bit of a problem with Jake, but it's all sorted now.' She straightens her back. 'Look, Lisa, I may be a bit late home tonight. I know I said I'd give you a lift, but are you happy to get the bus?'

'Yes, of course. Just because I'm living with you, doesn't mean I expect you to run a taxi service for me. I'll see you when you get home.'

'Thanks, Lisa.'

She leaves and Catherine turns back to the computer. All the time she'd been talking to Lisa, she'd been fine, but now, as she moves her hand to the mouse, she sees how it trembles. On the table next to her is her phone, the words written on it a soundless threat. Putting down the mouse, she turns the mobile over and clicks delete – as though the simple act of removing the words is all it will take to allow her to breathe again. But it doesn't work, any more than it had when she'd cleaned the windscreen of marker pen. For the words are still etched onto her brain. The memory of them too strong to eradicate.

Ellen had said that after the arson, she should report anything else that happened to her straight away. But she can't show her the message she's just received... or the video she'd been sent of her blazing car. Because, if she did, then the rest would come out.

Her involvement in the fire at her old school.

The guilt that had caused her breakdown.

And she's not prepared for that to happen. Not now she's reinvented herself. Not now she's on the verge of promotion.

It must stay her secret. Always.

EIGHTEEN

Catherine looks at her watch, shocked that it's gone six thirty. The cleaners already left. The sun dipping below the houses opposite the school.

She's spent the last few hours looking up websites and sifting through revision guides that Jake might find useful. Sticking Post-it notes into the relevant pages. Scribbling thoughts in the margins. Now she stands, thumbs massaging the small of her back, before filling her plastic box with the work she hasn't yet marked and making her way downstairs.

As Catherine pushes the door open, she feels the breath of evening on her face. It has a chill edge to it and she pulls her coat around her and hurries across the playground making for the car park. All the while, trying to ignore the churning in her stomach at the thought of what she might find when she gets to her hire car. She'd parked it next to Ross's knowing he's often leaving late, but when she reaches it, the spaces either side are empty.

Steeling herself to look at the windscreen, she breathes a sigh of relief: the glass is clean of any writing. But, even so, she can't help scanning the car park as she gets in, as now everyone has left, the area of parking bays feels too quiet – the lights on their tall poles, in the absence of cars, casting long shadows across the spaces outlined in white.

As she prepares to drive away, the illuminated clock on the dashboard catches her eye and she frowns. It will be gone seven by the time she gets home and she's not sure how she'll explain her lateness to Gary. For while she'd been sitting at her desk, the A Level texts open in front of her, she'd given neither him, nor Lisa, more than a moment's thought. Her mind too occupied with how best to help Jake and the ways in which she could steer him down a different route to Aled's. A path that might lead him to a brighter future.

Twisting in her seat, she retrieves her purse from her bag, opens it and slides a photograph from the clear pocket. It's been cut from a block of four identical ones which she keeps in the drawer in the kitchen, amongst the tape measures and packs of cards – miscellaneous things with no other home. Aled's eyes stare back at her from under the fringe that's been combed across his forehead in an unnatural way by the school photographer. He was seven or eight years old when the photo was taken and she'd chosen it for its size. And for the memory. Because, once upon a time, he'd been okay, the shadow of what he'd become not yet descended. The spark in his eyes not yet snuffed out.

She touches a finger to his cheek. 'I'm sorry, Aled.'

Catherine returns the photograph to her purse and replaces it in her bag. Reaches up a hand to reposition the rear-view mirror.

The roads are empty and it doesn't take Catherine long to get home. Once, she would have been excited about getting home. Spending time with Gary. Now, though, she feels nothing but trepidation at the thought. There would be no kiss at the door, just an atmosphere.

As she drives, her thoughts are on what she'll find when she gets there. Gary and Lisa haven't been on their own together since Lisa moved in, and she hopes it hasn't been too awkward.

As she reverses into the drive, she sees in the rear-view mirror that the downstairs lights are on. She turns off the engine, gets out and collects her bag and the plastic box from the back seat. But as she crosses in front of the kitchen window, raised voices stop her in her tracks. She looks through the glass. Sees Gary pacing, his red face turned away from her. Lisa is by the cooker and, as she watches, he stops in front of her.

She hears Lisa's voice now, the words distorted by the glass. Whatever she's said, Gary doesn't like it. He takes a step towards her and Lisa presses herself back against the worktop, an arm shielding her face.

Shocked at what she's just seen, Catherine runs the last few steps to the front door, puts the box down and shoves her key in the lock. Her bag slipping from her shoulder.

'Gary!' she yells from the hallway. 'What the hell is going on?'

Not bothering to take off her coat, she runs into the kitchen, terrified of what she's going to find. Gary has never been a violent man. Still...

'Oh, hi, Cath. You're home.' Lisa's voice stops her. 'Would you like some tea? I was just going to make one for me and Gary.'

Catherine stands stock-still in the doorway, her eyes moving from the kettle in Lisa's hand to her face.

'Are you all right, Lisa? Did Gary? Did he—?'

'Actually, I'll have a coffee, Lisa.' Linking his fingers, Gary stretches his arms above his head and widens his mouth in a yawn. He's no longer standing but sitting at the kitchen island. 'I had the most nauseatingly boring meeting this afternoon with HR to discuss employment benefits and could do with something to keep me awake.'

Catherine points to the window. 'I saw you both. You were arguing. Gary, you—'

Gary raises his eyebrows at her. 'Rubbish. Look, the window's all steamed up. You imagined it. Were we arguing, Lisa?'

Lisa tucks a strand of hair behind her ear. 'No. Why would we do that?'

Catherine frowns. 'I don't know. You tell *me*.'

She looks at the window. It is indeed steamed up from the pan that's bubbling on the stove. Maybe she hadn't seen what she thought she had. She takes off her coat, drags a barstool from under the island and sits next to her husband. Is it possible she'd made a mistake?

The mug of tea Lisa hands her is hot, burning her fingers. But as she puts it down, a thought comes to her.

The glass of the kitchen window may well have been steamed up, but she knows what she heard. Gary's voice telling Lisa she'd never get away with it.

The girl replying that she would.

NINETEEN

The plates are in the dishwasher and the kitchen still holds the aroma of tomatoes, garlic and herbs. Their supper had been delicious, but it had been eaten in silence unless you counted the polite comments Lisa had made about the food or the tap of Gary's fingers on his phone after their plates had been cleared. All through the meal, Catherine had been watching Gary and Lisa carefully. Searching for evidence that she wasn't losing her mind. That she'd seen what she'd seen. Finding nothing.

Hating the strained atmosphere, she'd tried to make conversation, asked Gary whether he'd known about Ross and Karen. Surprised when he'd folded his arms and said, *what about them?* Giving her no alternative but to tell him. Although he denied it, she'd seen from the narrowing of his eyes he hadn't known. Knew that the lie was because he was upset she'd been the first of the two of them to hear. It was only when she'd told him it was Karen she'd heard it from that his mood had lifted a little.

Gary's upstairs now, in the bathroom. He'll be cleaning his teeth, sorting out a shirt for tomorrow, as though nothing is wrong. As though this had been just an ordinary day.

She closes the kitchen door. Takes the tea towel out of Lisa's hand.

'Sit down, Lisa.'

'I don't mind doing it. I want to help.'

'Sit down.'

Lisa sits, the tea towel limp across her knees. She looks warily at Catherine as though knowing something unpleasant is coming.

Catherine stands in front of her, her arms folded. 'I know you both lied to me. I know what I saw.'

Lisa looks as though she's going to argue, but instead, releases an audible breath. 'I'm sorry, Cath. It wasn't as bad as it looked.'

'So you're not denying it?'

Lisa bites her top lip. Looks away. 'I don't want to say too much. Drop him in it. He *is* your husband, after all.'

'I don't care if he's the bloody ace of spades, Lisa. If there's something going on that I should know, then please do me the courtesy of telling me. Gary was shouting at you. I heard him through the window. He looked...' She closes her eyes a second. 'He looked as though he wanted to hit you.' She frowns at the recollection. That expression he'd worn – it was one she'd never seen on him before. Reaching out, Catherine puts a hand on Lisa's shoulder. 'No one should feel frightened by a man that way or be scared in the place where they live.'

And yet *she* had, the night the doorbell had rung and no one had been there. It makes her think of the message on her phone, the capitals driving home their message. *I KNOW WHERE YOU LIVE.*

Upstairs, she can hear the pipes as the toilet flushes. Hopes Gary won't come down. She needs Lisa to open up to her. To help her understand what's going on.

'Maybe I deserved it.' Lisa bites at some loose skin on her thumb. 'I probably shouldn't have said anything.'

'What did you say? Gary might be my husband, but I need to know.'

'All right, but it wasn't anything contentious. I was just defending you.'

'Me?' She feels a weird sense of displacement. Why would Lisa need to defend her?

'Yes. We were talking about school.' She lowers her eyes. 'He went weird when I was telling him about Jake.'

Something inside Catherine grows cold. Why would Lisa need to mention him? 'What did you say?'

'Nothing much. Just that you've been helping him with his coursework. Spending a lot of time planning his revision which was probably why you were late this evening. I'd only said it to make conversation. You know as well as I do how Gary doesn't like talking to me, can barely look me, and I thought, with you not here, it would be a chance to engage. Only, the minute I mentioned Jake, he went off on one. It was after I'd told him you believed you had it in you to save him.'

Catherine feels a red flush creep up from her collarbones. Had she really said those words? On Lisa's lips they sound odd. Evangelical even. No wonder Gary flipped. What was it he'd said to her the other night? Not that he was scared *for* her but *of* her.

She hadn't imagined that look in Gary's eyes as he'd stepped towards Lisa. He'd no right to take it out on her. The poor girl was only the messenger.

'Tell me exactly what he said to you.'

'I don't remember the exact words, but it was something about hating you working at the school. That he wished you'd give it up.'

Catherine leans her elbows on the island. Rests her forehead in her hands. 'But why? It was Gary who got Ross to see if there were any jobs going at Greenfield. Encouraged it.'

But he'd also agreed to Lisa staying with them even though

he hated the idea. The more she thinks about it, the more contradictory Gary's behaviour seems to be. Now *and* in the past.

She feels Lisa's hand on her arm. 'I think he sees the school as a threat. That's all.'

She turns confused eyes to her. 'A threat? Who to?'

Lisa shrugs. 'I'm not sure, but I think he meant to your relationship. Maybe he thinks it's taking you away from him. That you spend more time thinking about school than you do him.'

'He *said* that?'

'Not in so many words, but I've experienced jealousy before in my life. Know how hard it can hit you in here.' She presses a fist to her chest.

'Jesus.' Catherine pushes herself up onto the barstool, lets her leg swing. 'I had no idea. It explains why he never likes me talking to him about school. But the way he reacted was ridiculous. I'm sorry he took it out on you, and I'll definitely be having a word with him when I go up.'

'No!' Lisa grabs her arm, her fingers cold on her skin. 'Please don't do that. He doesn't want me here as it is, and if you say anything, if he knows we've been talking like this, he'll make me leave. I can't go back to sleeping in that classroom, Cath. I can't.'

'Of course you can't, and you won't, but I can't just leave it like this. You must see that, Lisa. Gary feeling this way is...' – she searches for the word – 'is unhealthy. I take my job seriously, but I spend no more time at the school than the other teachers.'

'I know that.' Lisa drops her hand back into her lap. 'And that's what makes you brilliant. But sometimes when you love someone, you don't see what others see. Don't let Gary stop you from doing what you love.'

Catherine frowns. 'He wouldn't do that. Whatever you might think, Gary respects me. Wants me to be happy.'

'If you say so.' Lisa slips down from the stool. 'In the morning, it will all be forgotten, I'm sure, and you two will be like this again.' She crosses her second finger over her first. 'The perfect couple.'

'There's one other thing, Lisa.' Catherine stops her as she walks by. 'What I overheard was Gary saying you'd never get away with it. What did he mean by that?'

Lisa blinks. Shifts her feet.

'I threatened to tell you if he carried on talking as he had.' Crossing her arms, she grips an elbow in each hand. Digs nails into her skin. 'And, like I say, he didn't like it.'

'I'm sure he didn't. But I don't want you to worry. I won't say anything about our conversation tonight. I like having you here and I don't want to make things worse for you.' She looks at Lisa and sighs. 'Families really are the strangest things.'

Lisa laughs. 'Tell me about it. And thank you, Cath. You really are the best. My brother doesn't deserve you.'

She leaves the room and Catherine remains where she is, staring at the place where Lisa had been sitting. Unsure if she really knows her husband at all...

TWENTY

Catherine and Ross are standing in the playground, watching a group of girls practise a dance routine they've copied from some YouTube video or other, their white shirts untucked and tied at the front to reveal their stomachs. Bare legs turned pink by the chill air.

'I have a question, Ross. It might sound odd, but have you ever suspected Gary of being jealous of me working here at Greenfield?'

'You're right, it is a strange question. What? Because you're working with me?'

'Get over yourself!' She raises her eyebrows at him. 'No, I mean everything. Wanting to—'

'Please do not say, make a difference.'

'I wasn't going to. I was going to say wanting to give everyone the best chance in life.'

Ross folds his arms. 'Like, Jake, you mean?'

'I didn't say that.'

'You didn't need to.' He frowns. 'Anyway, do I detect things aren't as rosy as they usually are chez Ashworth? Is it that cuckoo in the nest?'

'What, Lisa?'

'Yeah. From what Gaz has told me, she's proper got her feet under the table. Can't believe he never let on he had a sister.'

'Half-sister.'

'Whatever.'

'God, Ross. Put you in a Greenfield uniform and you could almost be mistaken for one of the Year 11s.'

'That's what happens when you've been teaching here as long as I have.'

'Well, whatever Gary thinks, I like having Lisa there. She's company.'

'You mean Gaza isn't?'

'I wouldn't know.' Despite herself, her shoulders stiffen a little beneath her coat. 'He's always out with you. Anyway, how's it going with Karen?'

'Oh, you know.'

'Very coy.' She nudges him with her elbow, in the hope he'll expand, but he doesn't answer. In fact, he looks a little irritated by her question.

In front of them, a boy jumps into the girls' line-up. Mimicking their dance moves. One arm wrapped across his chest, the other wagging a finger at an imaginary audience.

'Piss off, Jayden.' The chief choreographer, a girl with long hair and gold hooped earrings, gives the boy a shove. 'Go play with yourself and leave us alone.'

Catherine watches as the boy slopes away to rejoin his friends, middle finger raised. She pulls the zip up higher on her coat and adjusts her scarf so it covers her mouth. 'Don't these kids ever feel the cold? Look at their legs. They're as marbled as my kitchen island. Would it harm them to wear some tights? Maybe I should have a word.'

This at least elicits a smile from Ross. 'Methinks you're showing your age, Mrs Ashworth? Have a word if you like but don't try to tell me you never flouted the uniform rules when you were at school. When I was a teenager, we were convinced a tie made us look like John Major, so it was tie on for the lesson, tie off for the playground – unless we had them wrapped around our heads that is. Jesus, we must have looked a right load of prats.'

A commotion over by the wheelie bins lined up outside the door of the school kitchen halts their conversation. Two teenage boys are scuffling near them, their feet kicking aside the boxes and the empty cans that have spilt out onto the playground. A small ring of onlookers surrounds them chanting *fight, fight*.

Ross steps forward. 'Hey, you two. Stop that now!' He turns back to her. Delivers a heavy sigh. 'You want to sort it, or shall I?'

Catherine frowns. One of the boys is lying on his back amongst the rubbish. The other stands over him, his fist raised. To her horror, she sees it's Dean, the boy whose phone she'd taken, who lies prostrate, his shirt bunched tight in the fist of Jake Lloyd.

Catherine feels a flash of impatience. Why is Jake even out here? As a sixth former, he has his own area inside the building with a kettle and comfy chairs. He must have gone out with the sole purpose of finding Dean.

Ross is looking at her strangely. 'Looks like it's me then. I just thought you had a bit more of a rapport with our new boy than I have. To be honest, he gets on my wick with his bloody arrogance.'

Catherine shakes her head. 'No, you're right. I'll go. He'll listen to me. You tackle the crowd.'

The circle of teenagers has grown and she runs across the playground, hoping against hope that by the time she gets to them, Jake won't have hit the boy.

'Everyone line up at the door. Now!' Behind her, Ross is pushing through the sea of Greenfield sweatshirts jostling for the best position to see the fight. 'Show's over.'

Heads turn his way. There's a moment's hesitation, then the crowd reluctantly starts to disperse. Some walking backwards, others craning over their shoulders so as not to miss anything. Disappointed that the fight has ended as quickly as it had begun.

Catherine pushes through the stragglers. Grabs Jake by the arm.

'Let him go, Jake. He's not worth it.'

As she speaks, she steals a look at Dean's face. He doesn't look as if he's hurt, unless his pride is factored in. She's got there just in time and she's relieved. If Jake had landed a blow, it would have meant an automatic exclusion.

The boy's fist is still raised. Ignoring Catherine, he pulls Dean's face close to his. Fingers tightening on his collar. 'Do something like that again and I'll fucking kill you.'

'Stop it. Jake. That's enough.' Catherine pushes herself between them. Forces Jake to look at her – to focus on what she's saying and not on what he wants to do to Dean. 'I mean it. Think about what you're doing.'

Jake's eyes meet hers and he blinks. It's as if the boy's been in a trance.

'Come on. Let him go.'

'Why should I?'

'Because I'm asking you to. Not just for his sake but for yours.'

Reluctantly, his fingers release their grip on Dean's shirt. He pushes the youth away from him. 'Someone had to teach the scumbag some manners.'

'Maybe so... but that person is not you. Once you've passed through those gates, it's the school's job to deal with these things. Now go inside and wait in my classroom. Whatever Dean's done, it will be sorted out, I promise you, but brawling in the playground is not the way to do it.' She turns to the other boy. 'You, Dean. Get yourself cleaned up and I'll talk to you later.'

Jake's eyes are dark with anger. 'He's scum and you know it.'

'Mrs Ashworth, are you done here?' Ross has cleared the crowd and they're lining up by the door.

'Yes, thank you, Mr Walker. It's all under control.' Trying not to let him see how flustered she feels, she throws Ross a smile. 'There'll be no more trouble.'

'Let's hope you're right.' He jerks his thumb at the door. 'You two boys go inside. You should know better, especially *you*.'

The comment is directed at Jake, and Catherine wills the boy not to retaliate. Is relieved when he doesn't. His only act of defiance a withering look at Ross before picking up his bag and striding, head down, towards the entrance door. When he gets there, he runs up the steps, pushes through the waiting teenagers and disappears inside.

She turns back to Dean. He's still on the ground, but now he gets up, his fingers investigating a sore-looking graze on his arm.

'Okay if I go now, miss?'

'Yes, you can go.'

Catherine walks back across the tarmac, her head in turmoil. What crazy idea had made Jake act like that? She thinks of him, of his raised fist, and her anxiety rises. What had Dean said that had made him retaliate in that way? Aled had always fought himself out of a problem and she can't let Jake do the same.

She goes back inside, knowing she has to talk to him. What he did was stupid, but she needs to reassure him that what happened in the playground hasn't stopped her from wanting to help him. And she has to succeed... she owes it not just to Jake but to Aled's memory.

Yet, even as she thinks this, she knows how wrong it is. The boy is not her brother and the amount of time she's putting into teaching him, is over and above what is expected of her. But the need to help him is obsessing her and there's nothing she can do to stop.

If only she could talk to Gary about it, get his opinion, but he's the last person she can talk to about Jake. The time she's spent helping the boy has taken her away from her home, and she can't help wondering if, instead of it worrying him, Gary would be happy if she spiralled out of control again. Because then she'd be dependent on him again.

Recently, she'd had the horrible feeling that the car fire and the writing on her windscreen might have been Gary's sick attempt to scare his sister off, but now she's not so sure. She puts her hand to her chest. Feels the fluttering of her heart. What if *she* is the real target? What if he wants to make her feel so vulnerable that she'll quit her job?

She can't believe she's thinking it, but the truth is, as the days go by, Gary's becoming more and more of a stranger to her. And it scares her.

TWENTY-ONE

The crash makes Catherine jolt awake. She lies in the darkness listening. What had she heard? It sounded like it had come from the garden or the road outside.

Beside her, Gary snores softly. She wants to wake him, but he'd gone to bed late and it seems mean, especially as she knows he has a meeting tomorrow. Outside the window, she can hear the rain. Needles of it being driven onto the glass by the wind. What she should do is go back to sleep, but she can't. So, instead, she lies with eyes wide open, her head turned to the window. Staring at the faint light beyond the curtains. Waiting for the sound to come again.

When it does, louder this time, she gives in. Reaches and shakes Gary's arm.

'Gaz, wake up.'

He groans. Turns over so he's facing her. His face just visible in the dark room. 'What the hell, Cath?'

'I heard something. In the garden, I think. It was loud. How could you not have heard it?'

'Because I was asleep and so should you be.' He's annoyed,

she can tell. Hates his sleep being broken. 'I've got meetings all day tomorrow. Or maybe you've forgotten?'

She turns her face to him, wondering if he's doing it deliberately or whether it's *him* who's forgotten. Because, tomorrow, at ten o'clock, she'll be sitting in front of the interview panel. Putting her career in their hands.

She lies back, but sleep is impossible. Something had caused the noise and she needs to know what it is. Her hire car is parked in the drive, and in the darkened bedroom, pictures play out behind her eyelids. The glass of the windscreen scratched, her tyres slashed, a petrol-soaked rag bursting into flames beneath the chassis or, worse still, pushed through their letter box.

'I'm going to check.'

'Suit yourself.' Gary turns over, pulls the pillow over his face, the rest of his words muffled. 'And for God's sake, Cath. Turn the bloody light off.'

She does what he asks, lifts her dressing gown from the end of the bed and feels her way to the door. Out on the landing, she notes that someone has forgotten to turn off the light.

Wrapping her robe around her, Catherine walks quietly past Lisa's room, so as not to wake her, and makes her way downstairs. At the bend in the stairs, she stops and looks down into the hall, worried when she sees the front door ajar. She hurries down the rest of the steps and, when she gets to the door, searches for her raincoat under the others on the coat stand. But it's not there. The old gardening shoes she wears to take out the rubbish are missing too.

Catherine pushes the door wider and steps out, the red tiles cold beneath her bare feet. The front garden is mostly in darkness, only the bushes either side of where she's standing lit by the small porch light. A gust of wind blows and something white flies past her. It snags on the bush to her left, and when she pulls it out, she sees it's a bag from their local bakery. And now, as her eyes adjust, she sees other things too. Pale shapes on the grass. Some in the borders. She peers out through the veils of rain, trying to see better... but it's impossible.

She shivers, feeling conspicuous under the porch light with just her dressing gown hiding her nakedness. And when something moves, over to the side of the house, she takes a quick step back. There's a person moving in their garden.

'Hello?' she calls into the darkness, her heart pounding. 'Is someone there?'

The wind is blowing the rain in the direction of the porch. It flaps the bottom of her dressing gown against her legs and her bare feet are cold and wet. There's a scrape and another bang and then the shadow moves closer.

She rubs at the small, raised hairs on her forearms. 'Whoever you are...' Her voice comes out as a whisper. 'Please show yourself.'

'It's just me, Catherine.' Lisa steps into the light. Her face half hidden by the hood of Catherine's raincoat. The gardening shoes she's wearing, too big for her narrow feet. 'I didn't mean to scare you.'

She steps onto the porch, rain dripping from her hood. Catherine's hood. 'I heard something and went out to see what it was.' She points to the side of the house. 'The rubbish bins had been blown over and stuff was all around the lawn. I've managed to pick as much up as I can, and have righted the bins, but it was hard to see what I was doing.'

'The bins blew over? What both of them?' When Catherine had put things in the recycling bin the previous evening, it had been full. The garden waste one too. Both would have been heavy. 'I can't believe that even in this wind they'd blow over?'

'Well, they did, and it was hard to lift them back up.' Lisa flexes her fingers. She's shivering, her teeth chattering, and Catherine's not surprised. Her legs are bare under the raincoat.

'Come inside, Lisa. Let's get you warm.' With a last look

into the rain-drenched garden, Catherine ushers the girl in and shuts the door behind them. She takes the raincoat from her and hangs it on the coat stand where it drips onto the hall floor. 'I'll make you a hot drink.'

'You don't have to.' Lisa bends and prises off one wet shoe then the other.

'It's true but then I'd be responsible for you catching your death. Go into the kitchen and I'll find you a throw.'

When she comes back, the throw under her arm, Lisa is perched on the barstool at the island. 'That's kind of you, Cath, but I don't need it. I found this.'

Catherine stares, aghast. Lisa is wearing one of her sweat-shirts. She's larger than Lisa and the item swamps her slight frame. The bottom reaching to midthigh.

Seeing her face, Lisa looks down, her brows pulling together as realisation dawns that she's done the wrong thing. 'You don't mind, do you, Cath? It was on the banister at the bottom of the stairs.' Lisa lifts the edges of the top. 'God, I'm such an idiot. Of course you mind. I'll take it off.'

'No, don't be silly. You can leave it here when you go up. I'm sorry you were woken. Next time it's windy, I'll make sure I secure the bins. I just wish you'd knocked on our bedroom door when you heard the crash, then either me or Gary could have seen to it.'

Lisa pulls the cuffs of her sweatshirt over her hands. 'I didn't want to disturb you. I was hoping I could get it sorted and you'd not be any the wiser. I know it's your interview tomorrow.'

'It's nice of you to remember, but to be honest, I'm not unduly worried.' Catherine flicks the switch on the kettle. 'I've prepped well and Ellen's as good as told me the job's mine for the taking. The interview will be just a formality.'

She spoons chocolate powder into two mugs and pours in

hot water, praying that she's right. That the external candidates will be wasting their time.

'You'll be great, Catherine. Everyone knows what a good teacher you are. How well you manage your classroom.' Lisa takes a sip from the mug Catherine has just handed her. 'It's just...'

'Yes?' Catherine places her own mug on the island opposite Lisa and waits for her to finish. When she doesn't, she frowns. 'Is something the matter, Lisa? If there is, I'd rather you said. Is it Gary?'

'No, of course not.'

'Then what is it?'

Lisa puts the mug to her lips again and they fall into silence. What had she been going to say?

She tries again. 'Whatever it is, I won't mind. I'm tougher than I look.'

Lisa blows at her hot chocolate, sending ripples across its surface. 'Okay,' she says at last, her reluctance obvious. 'All I was going to say was I'm sorry the interview came at such a bad time for you.'

She's not looking at Catherine as she says it but at the calendar on the wall. Catherine's eyes follow and her heart sinks knowing her eyes are on the date that's circled in red pen. The anniversary of the night her classroom had been engulfed in flames. The night her brother had died.

But there's nothing written there. No name or other indication to show why she's marked it. How does she know?

'It was the same day your car was set alight, wasn't it, Cath? That must have been so awful... I wish you'd told me.' She stops. 'Oh, God, I'm sorry. Gary said I shouldn't say anything. I've let my mouth run away with me again.'

The colour has drained from Catherine's face. 'Gary told you?'

'It came out when we were having the argument about you

spending so much time at school helping Jake. He didn't mean to. He was just so angry, he blurted it out. Said the anniversary of your brother's death was sending you crazy.'

In that moment, Catherine hates her husband. How dare he say such a thing about her to Lisa. But then another thought comes to her. Gary is the only person who knows the truth. That Aled had been sleeping in her classroom when the fire broke out. That the cold floor had been his final resting place. Surely, he wouldn't have told her *that*.

'What else did he...' – she draws in a breath through her nose – 'blurt out?'

'Just that your brother died in a fire. He didn't give details.'

'And that's all he said?'

'Yes.' She looks embarrassed. Lifts the neck of Catherine's sweatshirt over her chin as a child might. 'But maybe it's better I know about Aled. Seeing as I'm living here now.'

Catherine presses her fingertips into the sockets of her eyes. Waiting for the stars. Her brother's name on Lisa's lips sounds wrong to her ears. She hadn't known him, hadn't met him, any more than Gary had. Slipping down from the stool, she takes her half-drunk mug of hot chocolate to the sink and pours it down the plughole. Hoping Lisa will take the hint and go up to bed.

But Lisa is beside her now. A tentative hand on her arm. 'What was your brother like? When he was a boy, I mean? You don't have to tell me, but I'd love to know.'

Catherine stiffens, her breath catching at the back of her throat. The mug she's rinsing hanging limply from her fingers. She doesn't want to answer, but Lisa's face is so earnest she knows she should be glad that she asked. It's more than Gary ever does.

She puts the mug on the draining board. 'Aled had a big heart and a quick mind, but he was troubled. Misunderstood.

The kids made fun of him because he was different. Said he was a loser when the truth was he was cleverer than the lot of them.'

'Do you have a photograph of him?'

Catherine doesn't turn. She doesn't want Lisa to see the pain on her face. 'In the drawer of the island. It was taken when he was seven... maybe eight. He was a good-looking kid.'

She hears a rattle as the drawer is opened and Lisa searches for it. When she hears the drawer close again, she waits, feeling, in some way, that it's important Lisa agrees.

'Yes, he looks nice. Kids can be cruel. When he was an adult, did he—'

It's only now Catherine turns. 'If you don't mind, Lisa, I'd rather not talk about this now. Aled couldn't cope with being an adult. Needed professional help but wouldn't accept it. Remembering that time brings back too many memories... bad ones. You understand, don't you?'

'Of course and I'm sorry, Cath. I've asked too many questions. I'll go back to bed now.' Crossing her arms around her waist, she lifts off the sweatshirt and puts it on the island. At the stairs, she turns. The hall light picking out the white of her nightdress. 'Oh, and good luck for tomorrow. You'll do brilliantly despite what my brother thinks.'

She climbs the stairs and Catherine walks to the window. Watches the rain crying down the glass for a moment before going to the front door to lock it. Seeing the key isn't in the lock, she searches the hall table, then the windowsills either side of the door. Finds nothing.

What has Lisa done with it?

There's a puddle on the floor where water has dripped from her raincoat. Dipping her hand into one of the pockets, her fingers find only bits of torn sweet wrapper and an old plaster. She finds the key in the other pocket, but there's something else in there too and, when she pulls it out, her heart jolts. It's the yellow lighter she'd thrown into the bushes the other evening. The plastic body of it cracked from where she'd stood on it.

Catherine stares at it. Presses her hand to her mouth to stop herself from crying out. Why is the awful thing in her pocket?

The clock on the wall shows her there are only a few more hours until daybreak. She has to sleep. Has to be fresh for tomorrow. But she knows she won't sleep until she's spoken to Lisa.

She goes upstairs and knocks softly on her door, hoping she's not already asleep. Is glad when it opens.

'Yes?' Lisa looks surprised to see her.

'I found a lighter in the pocket of my raincoat... the one you were wearing. Is it yours?'

'Oh, that. No, I found it on the grass where the bin had blown over. There was still some lighter fuel in it and I thought it should be taken to the recycling centre. I must have left it in the pocket. Is there a problem?'

'No. There's no problem.'

She closes the door, goes to her own room and climbs into bed, being careful not to wake Gary. She's still angry with him for having blurted out to Lisa about Aled, but her interview's tomorrow and this is not the time for an argument.

The staccato rhythm of rain on glass should be soothing, but try as she might, sleep evades Catherine. As she lies there, she's filled with a creeping unease, because, whatever Lisa had told her, she's certain of one thing. The two bins, as full as they were, had been sheltered by the wall of their house. They'd never have fallen over by themselves. Not even in this wind.

But why would Lisa lie?

TWENTY-TWO

'Thank you for your time and for sharing your insights with us today, Catherine. We saw from your teaching observation how you inspire your students to achieve their potential in English.'

Ellen stands and Catherine does too, relieved that it's over. 'I'm glad you thought so.'

'The presentation, too, on how you'd improve the English department.' It's the deputy head, Mark Perry, who's speaking now, rifling through the papers in front of him. 'It was very sound. From what I've heard, the other teachers in the department like and respect you. You really are an asset to the school.'

Inside, Catherine is filled with a warm glow. She's proud of herself – of how she coped with the data task they'd set and the ease with which she'd answered their questions. She doesn't want to jinx it by being too optimistic, but the signs had been good. *Very* good. And that's with everything that had happened last night on her mind. On the way in, she'd managed to calm herself down: remember that Lisa hadn't done anything wrong and that the bins had simply blown over in the wind. The strange events of the past week had spooked her, that's all.

'Thank you.' She reaches out and shakes Ellen's offered

hand, then Mark's. 'It's been a pleasure to show you how much teaching at Greenfield Comprehensive means to me.' She smiles, not the polite smile you might give at the end of an interview but a genuine one. 'This is what I was born to do, and if you think I'm the right candidate to take the English department forward, then I'm grateful.'

Ellen returns her smile. 'Obviously, we still have candidates to interview before we can make a decision, but rest assured, your application has been, and will continue to be, given our thorough consideration. Thank you again for your application and we'll be in touch just as soon as we've made our choice.'

Catherine leaves the room, shutting the door behind her, and closes her eyes. It's over and she can do no more. She gets out her phone and types out a message to Gary. *It's done. Dare I say I think it went well?*

His lukewarm reply comes back quickly. *I suppose I should say well done… though you know what they say about not counting your chickens. I'll try to get off early. Pick you up from school and we can do something nice. Maybe try that new restaurant in town. I'll be waiting outside. About sixish. Message if there's a problem.*

Disappointed by his response, she puts her phone back into her pocket. Looks at her watch. Lisa has been standing in for her while she's been away and there are only fifteen more minutes until the bell rings. It isn't worth disrupting her lesson by taking over for such a short amount of time, so she might as well go to the staffroom and make herself a coffee.

With the bell yet to ring, she'd been expecting the room to be empty, but it isn't. Ross is sitting at the long coffee table, a folder open in front of him. He looks tired. It's the first time Catherine's seen him since she came in that morning.

He looks up. 'How did it go? Bet you aced it.'

She smiles. 'The presentation went well, though my mind went blank when I was trying to remember some of the stats.

Thankfully, they came back just when I was starting to panic and I don't think either of them noticed.' She doesn't mention how, without warning, an image of the upturned bins had entered her head, the yellow cigarette lighter too, and how it had been a struggle to regain her thoughts. 'The kids were good too. Probably shell-shocked at having both the head and deputy in the room at the same time. Doesn't happen very often.'

She laughs, but Ross doesn't join in.

'Are you okay, Ross?'

He blinks. Presses the soft space between his eyes with his thumb and first finger.

'Yeah. Sorry. Had a bit of an argument with Karen last night. Something and nothing. Ignore me. I'm glad it went well. You deserve it.'

'I wish Gary felt the same.'

'Been difficult, has he?'

'Let's just say he's made his feelings on the subject pretty clear.' She sits down next to him. 'I really don't know why he's so against me going for the position. Lisa reckons he feels threatened by it.'

'Seriously?' He glances at the staffroom door. 'Look, Cath. I know she's living with you and all that, but I wouldn't believe everything that girl says. She's an odd one. If you had a half-brother you'd barely met, would you turn up on their doorstep and expect to be taken in?'

'She didn't exactly—'

'You know what I mean and you have to admit, it *is* pretty weird. I'm not sure I'd want her creeping around my house. Poking her nose into my things.'

'She doesn't creep around...' And yet hadn't she found her in the garden last night?

'Ross?'

'All ears.'

'When was the last time you saw Gary smoke?'

Ross looks at her then away. 'Why?'

'I just wondered. If he's taken it up again, I'd rather know. I don't want him to feel he has to keep it a secret from me.'

'Look, he has the occasional one at The Crown after a couple of pints. That's all. It's no big deal, Cath.'

Not to him, maybe, Gary knows only too well what the smell of a match, the click of a lighter, might do to her.

'You know, I've been thinking I might go and see his dad. Do a bit of delving.'

Ross looks surprised. 'What for?'

'I'm not sure really. It's just that there's something that's not adding up. His dad left him and his mum, I get that, but refusing to speak to him, not answering the phone if he sees it's his number, it's a bit OTT. Lisa said I shouldn't go, said her dad was a hard man, *callous* was the word she used, but I've never met him, not even heard his voice on the phone, and I think it's time I did.'

Catherine wants to tell him that the real reason she needs to go is to find out if she can trust her husband. Whether he's dangerous and how far he might go to make sure she's not promoted... or not work at all. But she can't, because although Ross is her friend, he's Gary's too, and she can't trust him not to tell her husband her fears over a pint at The Crown.

'So, what do you think?'

Ross raises his hands to her. 'Oh no. Don't go dragging me into this.'

'I'm sorry to interrupt.'

They both turn. See Lisa in the doorway.

'Oh hi, Lisa.' While she and Ross had been talking, the bell had rung. 'Any problems?'

She feels her neck redden. It's Lisa's dad they've been talking about, and there's no way of knowing how long she's been standing there or what she's heard.

'No, none at all. I just wanted to say that I'll take the kids' books home and mark them.'

'You don't have to do that.'

'I know, but I'd like to. I'll see you later.'

Lisa disappears down the corridor and Ross sticks two fingers down his throat.

'Stop it, Ross.' But she knows what he means. Sometimes, Lisa can be too much.

'Anyway.' He picks up his bag. 'I'll have to love you and leave you. Playground duty awaits. Hopefully, we won't have a repeat of Friday's performance.'

'You mean Jake and Dean?' With this morning's interview and what had happened last night, she'd barely given it a thought.

'Yeah.'

'I'm sure there won't be. Jake's not a violent lad.'

'And you know that how?'

'I just do.'

Ross raises his eyebrows in answer, then leaves the staffroom, the door swinging closed behind him.

TWENTY-THREE

'Oh, Cath, just the person.' Sonia Jackson, Head of Pastoral, is hurrying down the corridor in her direction. 'I wanted to have a word.'

'Really?'

'Yes.' She stops next to her. 'It's about Jake. I'm worried about him. Several of the teachers say he won't participate in class and then there was that incident in the playground on Friday with Dean.'

Catherine frowns. 'What happened out there... it wasn't his fault. It was Dean's. The boy had been provoking him and he was reacting to something he'd said.'

'With his fists? A bit extreme, don't you think?'

Catherine thinks of the fights Aled used to have. Coming home with a bloodied nose. Skinned knuckles. Their mother turning away, lips pinched together, leaving Catherine to deal with his wounds. To listen to his explanation.

'Can you blame him? Dean would have said something to him. Wound him up.'

'I'm afraid that's no excuse. It's not the way we expect A level students to behave and I'm surprised you're defending him.' She taps at the folder in her hand. 'I wanted to tell you that I've filled out a behaviour contract for him which I'd like you to look through. I'll be getting Head of Year, you as Head of English, and the heads of the other departments to take a look too.'

'But I'm not Head of English.'

'Not yet.' Sonia smiles. 'It's Greenfield's worst kept secret. You'll be bossing all of them around before the week is out. I'll take a bet on it.'

'Well, thank you for your support. It's appreciated and, I have to say, I'm pretty confident, but this...' She takes the copy of the contract Sonia is holding out. 'Jake is seventeen and I'm not sure how he's going to respond to it. Do you really think it's necessary? I saw what happened. It really wasn't Jake's fault.'

It wasn't Aled's fault. She's eighteen again, standing in her brother's form room, her mother having refused to go to the school. *He's sensitive. He doesn't know how to react to the other boys when they tease him.*

'Please, Sonia. Give me a few days, a week even, to work with him and if it doesn't work, we can go down your route. I think a behavioural contract will be detrimental. We could be doing more harm than good.'

Sonia thinks, her eyes straying to the window where children are now gathering on the playground. Finally, she smiles. 'All right... a week. Let's hope for his sake it works.' She holds the tips of her thumb and first finger an inch apart. 'Between you and me, he was *this* close to an exclusion on Friday. I had to talk Ellen out of it.'

'Thank you.' Catherine returns her smile. Gestures with the behavioural contract. 'Hopefully, we won't be needing this.'

'Let's hope so.'

But how does she know? How is it she has so much faith in him? The answer isn't difficult. It's because she understands what the boy needs – the same thing Aled had needed but hadn't received.

Someone to believe in him. Someone to have faith.

She leaves Sonia and is about to go back to her classroom when she stops. This business with Jake needs sorting out and now. Turning back, she walks past the staffroom to Karen's classroom door. The door is closed and she knocks on it. Puts her head round the door.

'I'm sorry to bother you, Miss Langley, but could I have a quick word with Jake?'

Karen turns from the whiteboard and puts the lid on her black marker. 'Can it wait? We're in the middle of a lesson.'

Catherine's surprised at her sharp tone. 'I know, and I really am sorry. It won't take a minute.' She scans the class. Sees Jake at the back, his rucksack on the chair beside him. He's staring out of the window, clearly disengaged.

'Jake?' She jerks her thumb at the door. 'Can I speak to you?'

Catherine raises a finger to Karen. *One minute*, she mouths. Karen nods but doesn't look best pleased and it makes her wonder. Recently, she's had the feeling she's been avoiding her, seeking out Lisa instead for her staffroom chats. There's no time to ruminate on it, though, as for now, her priority is Jake.

The boy lifts his head. Pushes his book away from him and, with hands deep in his pockets, follows Catherine out of the classroom. He leans against the noticeboard.

'Yeah?'

'Look, Jake. I really could do with having another look at your A level coursework before we submit it. With the move from your old school, there's no denying you've fallen behind and I need to give some thought to how we can get you back on track. If you can give me fifteen minutes or so of your time after school, I'd be grateful.'

Jake folds his arms. 'I don't have the work on me. Anyway, it's not finished.'

'That's not a problem and a digital copy will do just fine. I can print it off here, then take it home and look at it. Make some notes highlighting areas for improvement.'

He gives a slow smile. 'You mean do it for me?'

'Not at all. The help will be no more than I've given the other A level students. What I eventually submit will be your own work and that's why I need to show you examples of high-quality coursework so you know what standard I'll expect. You've got it in you, Jake. I know you have.' Through the window, she can see Karen. Her face says it all. 'Look, you'd better get back or Miss Langley won't be best pleased with me. Three forty then?'

Jake shrugs. 'Whatever.'

He goes back in, the door shutting behind him and, with a smile of satisfaction, Catherine hurries back down the corridor. Seeing Lisa through her classroom window, she pushes open the door.

'I never said thank you for looking after my class. You're a star.'

Lisa turns from the computer. 'I didn't mind, honestly and it's the least I can do. You've done so much for *me* recently. So, so much.'

Since she's been living with them, she's changed: the way she holds herself, the way she walks. It lacks the tension that had been there. Her face too – the anxiety in her large eyes all but gone. It makes Catherine happy.

'How did the interview go?' Lisa asks. 'Good, I hope.'

Catherine smiles. 'Pretty good. In fact, I'm not sure it could have gone any better.'

'I'm very happy for you. Really I am. All this... your job... your beautiful home... your marriage. You deserve it all, Cath.'

'Well, I don't know about that.'

Seeing her sceptical look, Lisa places a hand against her heart. 'No really, you do. Good things come to good people, but I didn't mean to embarrass you.'

Catherine shakes her head. 'There's no need to apologise, Lisa. It was very sweet what you said... and very unnecessary. Everything I've achieved in life is through hard work.' She laughs. 'And, although luck played a large part in meeting Gary, marriages need working at too. You'll find that out when you're older.

Anyway, I'll make sure I take one of your classes next week when I'm timetabled for some non-contact. And remember, you won't be an ECT forever.'

'I know.'

Catherine goes back to her classroom. Prises the lid off a marker pen and starts to write on the whiteboard: *Writing to Argue.* She hopes she hadn't come over as patronising, but Lisa had made it sound as though everything she has, everything she loves, had simply fallen into her lap.

If only she knew the truth. How hard she'd had to work at keeping it all together. How she'd nearly lost everything and how close she feels to losing it all even now.

She puts the pen down, stares out of the window. If only she could figure out what is happening with Gary. Get to the bottom of it.

TWENTY-FOUR

Catherine stands at the window watching the children as they leave the school, heading for the metal gate and freedom. A teenage boy takes his rucksack off his shoulder and swings it round, catching his friend on the back and sending him to the ground.

Usually, she'd open the window and call down. Let them know she's seen. This afternoon, though, she has other things on her mind. Jake will be here soon and helping him makes her feel powerful, in control.

Because, recently, she's felt on the edge of losing everything.

Gary's words come back to her, *I make enough money to support us both.* He's never hidden from her that he'd be happy with a stay-at-home wife and Lisa's seen it too. Had told her as much – that she thought Gary saw the school as a threat. That he was jealous of it.

She'd like to ask Lisa for her father's address so she can find out more, but the girl's made it clear she doesn't want Catherine going there. She'll have to find another way of getting it.

'You wanted to see me.'

Jake's early. He swings his bag to the floor, pushes himself up onto one of the tables, his legs swinging. One pale knee visible through the rip in his jeans.

Catherine points at it. 'Didn't the head speak to you about appropriate uniform? I know she was going to.'

'Maybe.' He worries at a thread, making the rip bigger. His eyebrows pushing together.

'I know it seems trivial to you, Jake, but, as a teacher, it's my duty to remind you. Just as I remind all the students.' Catherine points to one of the school laptops. 'If you could send your coursework to me now on the school email, I can have a quick check on how you've set it out and then tomorrow, once I've had a better look, we can go through my feedback.' She's standing with her back to her desk. Leans into it, the hard edge pressing into her back. It's not the only reason she's asked him to stay behind and she needs to deliver this well. 'Before you do, though, there's something I need to talk to you about. I've been speaking to Mrs Jackson.'

He frowns. 'Who?'

'Mrs Jackson. Head of Pastoral. She's the one who looks after the students' welfare.'

His frown deepens. 'Why? What did you say?'

'Mrs Jackson wanted to talk to me about what happened in the playground the other day... between you and Dean. It's school protocol.'

He gives her a sharp look. 'Why? What's she got to do with anything?'

Catherine draws in a deep breath. 'A lot, as it happens. After an incident like that, the usual course of action would be that we offer you a behavioural contract. One that you and your mother would need to sign. It would outline your behavioural obligations while you're in school as well as the teachers' obligations once you've met those requirements.'

'You're kidding, right?'

'I'm afraid I'm not.' She continues quickly, scared he'll bolt.

'Anyway, I'm sure you'll be glad to hear that, in this case, Jake, I managed to persuade her that we should hold off… for a week or so at least. As, in my opinion, a behavioural contract isn't necessary. I believe this is something we can sort out ourselves.'

He puts his head on one side. Runs blunt-nailed fingers through his fringe. 'Yeah? Why?'

'Because, unlike Dean, you have maturity on your side. In a matter of months you'll be eighteen. An adult. Threatening Dean was wrong, however much you dislike him, and Miss Swanson won't tolerate fighting in her school. So let's agree that nothing like that will happen again. That it will be the end of it.' She hopes with all her heart he'll agree. 'Email the work you've done through to me, then you can go. And please, Jake, try and make a bit more effort to engage in your classes. You'll find it a lot easier with the teachers on your side.'

He considers what she's said. 'And why would I care about that?'

'You might not care, but I do. Like it or not, by persuading Mrs Jackson not to issue that behavioural contract, I helped you dodge a bullet.' She folds her arms. 'And you also owe me for not bringing it up with the head when I probably should have. Use that brain of yours because I know you can… you've shown me that and now I need you to show the rest of the world. You know, Jake, there's not long to go before the exams and the time will vanish like this.' She clicks her fingers to emphasise her point. 'With the extra help I'm giving you, you have a great chance of getting good grades, so please don't give it all up because you're trying to prove something. By making out you're hard.'

She thinks of Aled. Acting as though he didn't care. Pushing them all away and only crawling back when he had no other choice. Broken. Needing money for the drugs that he couldn't live without. When it was much, much too late.

The sound of the door opening makes them both turn. Lisa

is pushing into the classroom, a pile of books in her arms. When she sees the two of them, she stops, her cheeks reddening.

'Oh, I'm sorry. I thought the room was empty. I marked the work you set when I was covering your class this morning and thought I'd drop it back. The rest I'll do at home. Are you coming now?'

'No. I need to stay here for a while. Jake's sending me his coursework and I want to look at how best we can get him up to speed. I need to print off what he's emailed me before I leave, so I'll see you later. You've got your key, haven't you?'

'Yes, I have. I'll leave you to it then.' Lisa puts the books on the table and goes out, the door closing again.

Catherine watches her through the window and, when she's out of sight, pulls her eyes back to Jake. Annoyed at the interruption. 'I mean it, Jake. You're different to the other students in your year, but that's not a bad thing.'

He's not listening. His eyes are on the door.

'She's living with you, isn't she?' It's a statement rather than a question.

'It's none of your business, but, yes, at the moment she is.' She folds her arms. 'And it's Miss Prescott to you, Jake.'

'I don't like her.'

'What a ridiculous thing to say. You don't know her. She doesn't even teach the A level class.'

'You don't need to *know* someone like that. You can see it in their eyes. The neediness.'

Catherine folds her arms. 'Well, I never took you to be judgemental. Maybe you should take the time to get to know Miss Prescott better, then you'll see how hardworking she is. How much she wants to succeed... as *you* should. I really did think better of you.'

Jake jumps down from the table. He points a finger at her. 'Don't pretend you know anything about me. You know nothing.' He marches to the door. Turns when he reaches it. 'You say

I'm the one trying to prove something, acting hard, well, just take a look at yourself. Pretending to care about my education when you don't. I recognise a fake when I see one.'

'That's not true. I care very much.'

If she told him about her brother, it would prove it, but she can't. It wouldn't be appropriate. Yet, if she did, it might help him understand better. Show him how important it is to work hard. Stay out of trouble. Pass his exams.

'I had a brother,' she blurts out. 'His name was Aled.'

Jake stops, his hand on the door. 'Yeah? So?'

'He was like you, Jake. Gifted... so much to offer the world.'

He looks unsure. 'And? What's your point?'

'My point is, I don't want you to make the same mistakes he did.' She stands, goes over to him and puts her hand on his arm. 'He needed someone to save him... I should have been that person.'

Jake looks down at her hand, his brow creasing. Steps away. 'I've got to go.'

He leaves the room, closing the door behind him and, as Catherine watches him hurry down the corridor, she feels a terrible shame. She should never have said what she did.

She goes back to her desk and opens her school emails. While she'd been talking to Lisa, Jake had sent his coursework through like she'd asked. That's something. As she clicks on it, she thinks about how she's handled things. Worried that the talk they've just had might actually have the opposite effect to the one she'd intended.

She rests her forehead on the pads of her hands, pushing her fingers into her hair. She should stop now, go home, but the thought of the atmosphere there isn't something she can face at this moment. Not while she's still wondering what made Jake say those things. He'd called her a fake and her fear is that it might be true. That by helping the boy achieve something with his life, she's simply assuaging her guilt.

But, if it is, so be it.

Jake's coursework is open on her screen. Catherine reads the first paragraph, then the next, her mouse hovering over the words. The work is good. More than good. Rough around the edges, yes, but something that could, with help, be great.

She prints it out and starts to jot down notes and pointers. Things that will steer him in the right direction. References he could look at. How to use proper citation. And as she scrolls through more, all other thoughts leave her head. The unnerving things that have happened to her recently: the burnt-out car, the lighter on her doorstep, the message on her phone that proves the person who did it knows where she lives.

If Catherine had left her desk and gone to the wide expanse of glass and looked out, she'd have seen the person who's standing outside the school gates, eyes trained to her classroom window. Caught the cold blankness of their expression.

But she *doesn't* see. She's too engrossed in what she's reading. So caught up in it that she also fails to hear, deep in the bowels of her bag, her phone ring. The ping of the message that's left when she fails to answer.

TWENTY-FIVE

Catherine picks up her bag, switches off the light and makes her way out of the building, noticing how low the sun is in the sky. How long the shadows are.

She's just putting her box and bags into the car when she has an urgent need to pee.

'Why didn't I go before I left?' she mutters as she slams the back door. 'I'm as bad as the kids.'

Not wanting to be bothered to go back into the school building, Catherine locks her car door and runs to the road where, on the other side, is a public convenience. It wouldn't be her first choice, but with all the cups of tea she's drunk today, beggars can't be choosers. She waits for the traffic to clear, then crosses the road and takes the narrow path around the side of the red-brick toilet block with its high narrow windows criss-crossed with wire. Pushes at the graffiti-covered door, hoping it will still be open. Offering up thanks when it is.

She steps into the dim interior. The lights aren't working, and the ivy-crusted windows let in little natural light. There are three cubicles to her left and she heads for the nearest, her feet crunching on the glass from the broken tampon machine. She locks the door and sit down on the toilet, groaning in relief as her bladder empties.

Her hand is on the old-fashioned chain pull, ready to flush, when she hears the outside door slam. Then footsteps. Not wanting to be caught in the toilets by one of her pupils, she stays where she is. Thinking that she'll leave when whoever it is enters a cubicle. But they don't.

There's the scuff of feet on the cement floor then silence. Catherine waits, thinking they might have come in to use the mirror, but no one would see anything in the gloom. She knows she should flush the toilet and come out, but she's waited too long, so, instead, she stands with her shoulder to the door, hoping they'll go out again.

Another sound. Not the run of water, or the gush of air from the hand drier, but something that makes her stomach clench.

The sharp click of a cigarette lighter.

It has to be a kid from her school – one of the younger ones, most likely. A teenager who still cares what their parents think and wants to avoid being seen while they have a quick smoke on their way home from their after-school club.

Catherine holds her breath and waits for the whiff of a cigarette or a joint to permeate through the space under her door. But, instead, there's a stronger smell of burning – one that grows more pungent by the minute. Like the clothes on a Guy on bonfire night.

The outside door slams and Catherine grapples with the lock with terrified fingers because the smoke is seeping under the door now. Suddenly, the lock gives and the door bangs open. Lifting her jumper to her face, she runs to the smoking basin in front of her and turns both taps on full force. Jumping back as the gush of water extinguishes the flames. She turns the taps off again and stares at the soggy rag in the bottom of the cracked ceramic bowl.

'What the hell?'

Her heart is still jittery. Her eyes still fixed on the blackened fabric.

She leans heavily on the cold edge of the sink. Raises her eyes to the speckled glass. It's getting darker, what's left of the daylight blocked by the overgrown press of ivy against the window, but even so, she sees how black her pupils are in her pale face. How pinched her lips.

Her fear's still there. Had someone seen her go into the toilets?

Bending to the basin, she puts her nose to the wet cloth and breathes in. There's a lingering smell of damp smoke, but underneath it, she can detect something else – the faint underlying whiff of petrol.

She straightens. Her heart beating into the silence. Memories of her smouldering classroom tugging at her. Making her remember the terrifying moment when she'd realised Aled would have been in there. The nightmare she'd been forced to enter when she'd realised he must be dead.

The pain of her loss is a crushing weight in her chest. Whoever did this knows what happened back then. Had seen her go into the toilets and followed her in to frighten her.

Or... her heart skips a beat as she thinks of Greenfield Comprehensive across the road, behind its security fence... maybe they'd been heading somewhere else with their lighter and rag. Had watched with disappointment as they'd seen her leave through the school gates.

Her hands drop to her sides. Water from her fingertips dripping onto the floor. Darkening the concrete. The basin is cold against her hip bones. She should tell someone. Call Gary, at least.

With fingers numb with shock, she feels in her bag for her phone. Takes it out. There are three missed calls from him.

Messages too. *Where the hell are you? Ring me back, Cath. This isn't funny.*

But, instead of ringing him, she puts her phone away.

Not because he wouldn't understand, but because after what Lisa had said, what Ross had confirmed, she's no longer sure about him. The man she's been married to for ten years is the only one who knows about Aled and that makes her mistrust him.

Catherine leaves the building. Looks one way then the other along the street as though expecting to see him before crossing to her car. If this really is what her husband is thinking, then he's made a mistake. Because although Gary thinks he knows everything about what happened with Aled, he has no idea what *she* is capable of.

TWENTY-SIX

When Catherine gets home, she doesn't park in the drive but leaves her car a little way down the road. She unlatches the gate, as quietly as she can, and, staying close to the bushes, walks to the side of the kitchen window. On the drive home she'd been thinking about what she'd seen through the window the last time Lisa and Gary had been home alone together and she wants to watch her husband. See if she can find some answers to her unvoiced questions.

The room is brightly lit. Lisa is sitting on a stool at the kitchen island, a large paper carrier bag with handles on the worktop beside her. As Catherine moves closer to the glass, she sees the four empty takeaway cartons she and Gary have been eating from, their discarded lids slick with yellow sauce and grains of white rice.

At first, she thinks Lisa is alone in the kitchen but then Gary comes into view. Ignoring Lisa, he picks up the cartons and pushes them into the bag along with the remains of some naan bread. Then he crosses the room and shoves it into the bin.

It looks a domestic scene, something from a TV sitcom, but when Gary turns, the vision of domestic bliss is shattered.

Because, freed from their load, his fingers are bunched tight. And, with a gasp of shock, Catherine sees him slam his fist into the nearest wall.

Her hand rises to her mouth. Is Lisa safe in there? But when her husband turns, it isn't anger that's written on his face but despair. He brings his knuckles to his lips, winces, but Lisa hasn't moved. She's sitting at the island, watching him dispassionately. Her lips move. She's saying something to Gary, but unlike the other evening when their voices had been raised, the glass mutes her words.

In the dark garden, Catherine presses her ear to the glass. Trying to hear... to make sense of it. Desperate to understand. A drip of water from the earlier rain they had, drops from the gutter onto her cheek, but she daren't wipe it away for fear of being seen.

Inside the house, Gary's face has darkened. His hand moves to his back pocket and, to Catherine's surprise, he drags out an envelope. Its contents thick and weighty. He throws it at Lisa, but it's done with such force that it misses the island and disappears out of sight onto the kitchen floor.

Catherine gasps. What the hell is going on? Gary is usually so difficult to rile. So composed.

A gust of wind blows, whipping the ends of her hair around her, and she shivers. Is it because of what she's just witnessed inside her house? Or is it a delayed reaction to what happened in the public toilets? Whatever it is, Catherine's sick of being a silent observer. All she wants now is to go inside. To confront him.

She slips her key into the lock and lets herself in, the smell of Indian food hitting her empty stomach. Making her nauseous.

'I'm home.' Unsure of what she'll find now she's here, she makes her tone as neutral as possible. 'Sorry I'm late.'

'So you're back then.' It's Gary who comes out of the

kitchen, a small teardrop-shaped stain of yellow sauce on his work shirt. He folds his arms. 'Why didn't you message me? Phone me back?'

'Message you?' She can't take her eyes off the stain. Struggles with his question. Through the open kitchen door, she can see an open bottle of wine. Craves it. His question throws her, removed as it is from what she's just witnessed. 'What about?'

'Are you for real?' He turns abruptly and stomps back into the kitchen.

Catherine follows him in, her eyes lowering to the floor. To the place where the stuffed envelope would have landed. Sees nothing.

Lisa smiles. 'Hello, Cath.'

It's said with such warmth, such sweetness, that Catherine is floored – a feeling, like the one she'd had the other evening, coming over her. That she's stepped into the wrong house. That everyone knows what's going on, except her. As though she's Alice emerging from the rabbit hole into Wonderland.

Though there's nothing wonderous about *this*.

What she needs is to talk to Gary on his own, but it doesn't look as if Lisa is going anywhere. If it was *her*, she'd make an excuse to leave the room – say she's left something in the bedroom or needs to charge her phone. Anything. But Lisa doesn't. Instead, she remains where she is, her glass of wine pressed to her lips. Curtains of dark hair falling across her pretty face.

Trying to ignore her, Catherine concentrates, instead, on her husband. 'Tell me, Gary. What did I need to message you about? And what could possibly be so important that you couldn't be bothered to wait until I got home before stuffing your face with tikka masala?'

Gary doesn't answer her question but asks one of his own.

'So what was it? Were you too busy celebrating with your work chums down the pub to remember me? If Karen hadn't

seen me parked outside in the road and told me you'd left the
building, I'd have been sitting in my car like a bloody lemon for
the next half hour.' He shakes his head bitterly. 'I thought I was
being nice, Cath. Supportive of your career as you're always
telling me I should be. Next time, I won't sodding bother.'

Catherine stares at him blankly. Shocked at his words.
Confused how, after what she'd witnessed through the window,
the spotlight has now fallen squarely upon *her*. Then, like a bolt
of lightning, it comes back to her – the messages they'd
exchanged that morning after her interview. Her husband had
been going to meet her after work. Take her for a celebratory
meal. It had completely slipped her mind.

How was that possible?

Catherine feels sick with guilt. Just as she'd been wondering
if she should trust him, he'd been waiting to treat her. Confusion takes over. She doesn't know what to think anymore.

'So, what were you doing?' The chill in Gary's voice is
unmissable. 'You haven't told me.'

Catherine opens her mouth to speak, but before she can,
Lisa has answered for her.

'She was helping Jake.'

Gary's frown deepens. 'Jake?'

'Yes. That new boy I told you about.' She looks up at
Catherine. 'You don't mind me saying, do you? I didn't want
him to think anything else.'

Catherine notes how she's been demoted to a collection of
pronouns – as though she's unable to tell her own story and
needs Lisa to do it for her.

'And that's why you didn't meet me?' Gary folds his arms.
'Because I've come in second place to your bloody school again.
To some kid who you think is more deserving of your time than
me. Is that it, Cath?'

The shaking has stopped, but tears are coming now. 'Of

course not.' She swipes at the tears with the back of her hand. Embarrassed by them. 'It's not like that.'

'Then what *is* it like?' His voice is hard and thin.

'You knew where I was, Gary. You could have phoned me. I'd have come straight home.' But even as she says it, she's remembering how her mobile had been turned onto silent. The messages he'd left only read when it was too late. 'Okay, I forgot we'd arranged to meet, but when I didn't come out of school, you could have come in to find me.'

'Which is exactly what I did. There was no sign of you when I got there. Lynne on reception confirmed what Karen had already told me, that you'd gone, but I thought I'd check anyway. Your classroom was empty, the lights off. I'd no idea where you were. If Lisa hadn't told me later that she'd spoken to you before she went home, I'd have imagined something terrible had happened. And with the fire at school... Go on tell me. Did something else steal your precious time?'

It did... but she can't tell him what.

Catherine smells again the smoke that had drifted under the toilet door, bringing with it the memories. The fear. How long had she stood in those toilets? Too scared to confront what might be waiting for her outside? Smoke must be in her hair, on her clothes, and she wonders if they can smell it too. How dearly she wants to tell Gary about it, but she can't.

Because he'll use it against her.

TWENTY-SEVEN

'There's nothing to tell,' Catherine says wearily. 'I simply forgot the time.'

Gary pulls out a chair and sits. Sinks his head into his hands. And with that, the moment has passed.

Lisa is staring at her and Catherine knows it's because she's never seen her like this before. 'Please don't be upset, Cath. You've been so good to me. If there's anything I can do to help, just ask.'

Catherine almost laughs. The girl's barely more than a child herself. Has no idea what she's had to deal with over the years. The fine line she has to tread each day in order to stay in control: pitching her voice just right, phrasing her words just so – not so strict that the children despise her. Not so informal they think she's trying to be their friend. The art honed over the years. Out of necessity.

It's a technique she uses with Gary too... except, recently, she's found that mask slipping.

Lisa's cheeks are pale, her large blue eyes magnified by her glasses, and Catherine finds herself doubting the sincerity of her words. It's suddenly all too much and she holds out her hand to stop Lisa saying any more. She'd thought she liked having her here, but now her presence makes her feel like she's a stranger in her own home.

'Lisa, could you give us a minute? I want to talk to my husband alone.'

Lisa doesn't say anything and, wanting something to do to break the awful tension in the room, Catherine picks up the takeaway menu and slides it into the drawer under the island. She's just shutting it again when something stops her.

'Have either of you seen the photos that were in here... the ones of Aled?'

Gary looks at her distracted. His head still in their argument. 'What? No, why would I have?'

'What about you, Lisa? You were looking at them the other day. Are you sure you put them back?'

There's a second or two's pause before she answers. 'Yes, I definitely did. Would you like me to help you look for them?'

Catherine doesn't reply but stares at the place where they had been. The loss of those photographs is visceral. A deep pain within her. She has the one in her purse, but if she were to lose that too, she'd have nothing. No other reminder of her brother.

'You're shaking.' Lisa slides off her stool. Comes over to her and puts an arm around Catherine's shoulders. 'Are you unwell?'

'I'm fine.' Catherine shrugs off her arm. She looks across at Gary, hoping he'll say something – that his concern for her will outweigh his annoyance at having been stood up – but he's staring into space, his expression unreadable.

'I'll ask you again, Lisa. Please can you leave us? I'm sure you must have some marking to be getting on with.'

'Yes, of course.' Lisa picks up her bag from the back of the chair. Lowers her voice so that only Catherine can hear. 'I hope you two can sort things out.'

She leaves the room and Catherine waits until she can hear

her upstairs and then she takes the seat Lisa had been sitting on. Puts her hand on Gary's arm.

'What's going on with you, Gary?'

He looks at her with haunted eyes. 'Nothing's going on.'

'I wish I could believe you. Lisa thinks—'

'Jesus. What does it matter what she thinks?' He lowers his voice again. 'She needs to go, Cath. Can't you see she's poison?'

'Go where? Back to her parents where she's not wanted?'

Catherine thinks of the sleeping bag stuffed into the supply cupboard in Lisa's classroom, wondering where she would be now if they hadn't taken her in. Would she still have been sleeping on the floor with an arsonist on the loose?

'She orchestrated the whole thing. Can't you see? She put that sleeping bag in the cupboard to make you feel sorry for her. Knowing you'd never allow her to continue sleeping on the classroom floor. She planned it all. The girl knew about your brother and how he died. Knew you'd never let that happen again.'

He waits for her reaction, his eyes pleading, but Catherine's having none of it. Lisa hadn't known about Aled before she moved into their house. *He'd* been the one to tell her.

'It wasn't me you were angry with, was it, Gary? It was Lisa. What was that envelope you gave her?'

Gary's face pales. 'It wasn't anything.'

'Stop playing games with me. I saw it with my own eyes. What was in there? Oh God. Don't tell me it was money.'

When he doesn't answer, she knows she's hit the nail on the head.

'What was it for?' She shakes his arm. 'Gary, I'm talking to you.'

His expression is closed. Defensive. 'Okay, Okay. I thought if I offered her money, she might leave, all right? Happy now?'

'And she took it?'

His eyes slide away from her. 'No, of course she didn't.'

'But why would you try and bribe her?' Catherine's mouth tightens. 'What has Lisa ever done to you?'

'Nothing, but I don't trust her. What's that smell?' Lifting a lock of Catherine's hair, he sniffs it. 'Is it smoke?'

She could deny it, but why should she? She no longer cares if he knows.

When she's finished telling him about the dark toilets, the blackened rag in the basin, Gary's face is grey, slack, as though the stuffing's been pulled out of him.

'What the hell?' He reaches out a hand to the island to steady himself. 'Is this some kind of sick joke? Because if it is, Cath, it's not funny.'

Catherine stares miserably back at him, wishing she'd never told him. 'It's not a joke.'

Gary sits up straighter in his seat. On edge. 'Did you see who it was?'

'No, the lights weren't working and, anyway, they were gone before I came out of the cubicle.'

'Did anyone see you leave the school? Think, Cath. It's important.'

'I don't know. I don't remember.'

Gary's questioning is making her uncomfortable, reminding her of the days at her old school after Aled had died. He'd pressed her then too, begged her to open up, until finally she'd broken down in front of him. Told him everything. Not just how the problem kids, having picked up on her distress, and unaware of what had caused it, had made her their target, but how the drink she kept hidden in her classroom was the only way she could get through the school day without crumbling.

At the time she'd been glad she'd told Gary everything. He'd helped her through it. Had persuaded her to leave her school and asked Ross to look out for any job vacancy that might come up at Greenfield. And, by the time they'd married and settled into their new lives, all that had happened before – the fire, her brother's death, her breakdown – had become a distant, unpleasant memory.

Recently, though, she's felt the weight of Gary's scrutiny. As though he's searching for signs that it's happening again. And she doesn't like it.

Gary lifts dark eyes to her. 'It was *her,* wasn't it? My *sister.*' He points to the ceiling. Spits out the word as though it's a curse. 'Your car being set alight... the thing that happened to you tonight. Don't you see? All this crazy stuff only started after she'd joined the school. Before that, everything was fine. *We* were fine.'

'That's madness. How can you even think it's Lisa? She's just a kid.'

'She was there,' he hisses. 'At the school. She followed you out. Isn't it obvious?'

Catherine's eyes don't leave his. 'And so were you, Gary. You were there too.'

Maybe Lisa had been right. That he was jealous of her and what Greenfield Comprehensive meant to her. What if his obsession with her leaving her job had taken a darker, more sinister turn?

Shocked at what she's thinking, she stands. This is Gary, for God's sake. Her husband. The man she's been in love with since he scooped her up and put her back together again. He'd never do anything to hurt her. It's impossible.

'Look, Gary. I'm dead on my feet and nothing's making any sense. I'm going to bed.'

Catherine opens the kitchen door and goes out into the hall. At the bottom of the stairs, she listens. Hears nothing. Gary hasn't followed her. She climbs the stairs and, with a heavy heart, crosses the landing, but as she passes Lisa's room, something makes her stop. The door is half-open, the light on. Normally, she'd avert her eyes, let the girl have her privacy, but tonight, there's a voice in Catherine's head telling her it's *her* house. That she can look in any room, enter it even, if she wants.

She moves closer, struck by how the room, even the small bit she can see, looks different. There are new pictures on the wall above Lisa's bed. Ones that have been hung from nails the girl must have hammered in before she got home. The dressing table has been moved to the other end of the room and beside the bed is a colourful rag rug that she's never seen before.

'Is everything all right, Cath?' Lisa's voice comes from behind her and she shoots round. She must have been in the bathroom.

'Yes, of course.' She pulls her eyes away from the books that are lined up on the shelf next to the girl's bed. 'Why wouldn't it be?'

'That's good. I'll say good night then.'

Lisa goes into her room and shuts the door, leaving Catherine standing on the landing. She waits a moment, looking at the closed door, listening to Lisa moving around behind it, before making her way to her own room.

When she gets there, she sits on the edge of the bed and thinks. What could Lisa possibly gain by trying to scare her? All of this started happening as soon as Gary was faced with his sister in his home. All Catherine knows is that she needs to make that visit to his father. Needs to know her husband's secrets. Before it's too late.

TWENTY-EIGHT

When Catherine arrives at school the next morning, she's met by a cluster of students at the gates. She'd slept fitfully the previous night, only falling into a deeper sleep just before her alarm was due to go off – Gary's shake of her shoulder the only thing to wake her. And now she's tired and grouchy.

After parking the car, she makes her way to the gate where, in front of the school building, she can just make out the flashing blue lights of a police car. On the drive to school, she and Lisa had hardly exchanged a word and she's relieved to have the distraction.

Hating that she's late, she pushes through the group of students, needing to find out what's going on. Knowing she'll feel better if she goes in armed with the relevant information.

'What's happened? Anyone know?' She puts a hand on the nearest girl's shoulder. 'Becky, I'm talking to you.'

The girl, whose face had been pressed to the railings, turns to her, a ridge down her forehead. 'Someone's been beat up. Literally. Blood everywhere... that's what Craig Johnson says anyway.'

Catherine's heart thuds against her ribs. 'Do you know who?'

An image of Aled comes into her head. Lying on the school playground, his face bruised, his lip split. Brighter than the rest of his peer group, unable to fit in, he'd been an easy target for the tougher boys.

Her grip on the girl's shoulder tightens. 'I said who, Becky? Answer me.'

The girl pulls away. Rubs at her shoulder. 'I don't know, miss. Honest. I don't think anyone does.'

'But it's someone from the school?' She moves closer to Becky, fighting the urge to shake her. 'Come on, Becky. What do you know?'

Other students have gathered at the gate. Heads are turning their way. Lisa's staring too. Remembering herself, Catherine steps back again, shocked at the way she's behaving.

'I'm sorry. I didn't mean to frighten you. It's just that this is very important.'

Across the playground, she can see Karen and Lynne. They've just come out of the main doors and are standing at the top of the steps, their heads together. Faces serious.

Catherine turns to the students. Holds up her hand for silence. 'I'm sorry, everyone. I can't let you in until I know what's going on. I need to have a word with Miss Langley.'

Catherine touches her card to the keypad. Waits for the gates to open, then goes through to find out for herself.

'What's happened?' she says, when she reaches them. 'The kids say someone's been hurt.'

Karen looks at her meaningfully as though waiting to see what her reaction will be. 'It's Jake Lloyd.'

'Jake?' The shock hits her like a punch to the gut. Knocking the wind out of her. He was the last person she'd been expecting. 'How?'

'No one knows. He was found this morning by a delivery

driver... round the back of the school by the bins. He thought it was a rough sleeper at first and it scared the life out of him when he found it was just a boy.'

Just a boy. Catherine shivers. It's what she'd said about Aled. When she was apologising for him. Excusing his behaviour.

As she stands there, the blue lights of the police car flashing their warning, the fear of what might have happened gathers and grows. Who would do something like this to him?

The touch of a hand on her arm brings her back to the present.

'Cath, what's the matter?' It's Lynne, her voice laced with concern. 'You're as white as a sheet.'

'Is Jake okay?'

'I can't say at the moment. He's been taken to hospital, but he's unconscious.'

Catherine closes her eyes and breathes in deeply.

'I'm sorry, Lynne. It's a shock, that's all. How long will they keep him in?'

'I'm not sure. Apart from the concussion, they suspect he has some broken ribs. Whoever was waiting for him gave him quite a kicking. Ellen will tell you more when you go inside.'

Lisa has joined them. She points to the straggle of teenagers waiting outside the gates. 'Did she say we were to let the kids in?'

'Not yet.' Lynne follows her gaze. 'You go in. Karen said she'd talk to them.'

'Are you all right with that?' Catherine turns to Karen who's standing to one side checking her phone. When she'd last looked at the playground roster, she'd noticed it had been changed so they are no longer on duty together.

'Yeah.' Her eyes don't meet Catherine's when she speaks. 'I'll sort things out here, Lisa can help me.'

Lynne nods. 'Thanks, Karen. I've a feeling we're going to be getting a lot of calls this morning. Not just from antsy parents but from the press too. Ellen's not going to like it. Speaking of which, she says the police would like a word with you, Cath. You'd better go straight in.'

'With me?'

Finally, Karen is looking at her. 'That's what she said.'

She turns her back on them and walks away. Catherine's eyes on her.

'What's up with Karen?'

Lynne shrugs. 'Search me. She was moody all last week.'

They go inside to find Ellen Swanson in reception. With her are the two police officers who'd come to the school after the arson attack on Catherine's car.

'Ah, Cath. Perfect timing. PC Dawson and PC Olds would like to have a word with you about Jake. I'm sure Lynne has filled you in on what's happened.'

'Yes, of course. But I'm not sure I'll be of much help.' Catherine's stomach is churning. What do they think she knows? What have they heard?

'You never know.' Ellen gestures to the door. 'You can use my office again if you like. I'll stay here and help Lynne fend off the calls from parents. This was a serious assault.'

Catherine tries not to react. Squashes the image of the boy on the ground. Arms crossed over his head to deflect the blows. Aled's face not Jake's.

PC Olds is looking at her questioningly. 'Whenever you're ready, Mrs Ashworth.'

'Yes, sorry. I'm still coming to terms with what happened. Please come this way.'

The officer nods. 'Thank you. It shouldn't take long.'

Catherine takes them upstairs. Shows them into Ellen's office. The radiator is on in the small room, making it oppressive, and, as she sits and waits, she can feel the back of her skirt sticking to her legs.

PC Olds gets out her notebook, her eyes skimming Ellen's walls, alighting on the framed certificate of her honours degree and a photograph of her standing outside the school next to the Greenfield Comprehensive sign.

'A bit like Groundhog Day, isn't it?' A smile hovers on her lips. 'Us sitting in here like this, I mean. But it shouldn't take long.' She flicks open her notebook. Taps her pen against her chin. 'Firstly, can you tell me how long you've known Jake Lloyd?'

Catherine thinks. 'Not long. He only joined the school recently.'

PC Olds makes a note. 'And am I right in saying you've been giving him extra lessons?'

'Yes. He's fallen behind with his A level work. I've been helping him catch up.'

'I see.' She looks up. 'And you've had no problems with him?'

Catherine holds her gaze. 'No. Should I have?'

It's PC Dawson's turn to speak now. 'Not really. It's just that the head says that some of the other teachers have found him a bit difficult. As far as you know, did he have any enemies? Anyone he disliked more than others?'

Catherine folds her arms. 'As I said, he was new to the school. I wouldn't know.'

PC Dawson shows something he's written in his notebook to his colleague who nods. 'I believe there's a boy in the school. A...' – he consults his notebook again – 'Dean Gibbs. Am I correct in saying you were in the playground when they had a fight?'

Where is this going? Surely, they can't think it was Dean who did this to him? He's half the size of him.

'I was, but the boy's younger than him. Smaller than him. I can't quite imagine it.'

'I've no reason to doubt it, but I'm not sure of the relevance. You saw the fight he had with Dean. You were there.'

'Well, yes, but I wouldn't call it a fight. More an argument.' For some reason she thinks it important to play it down. 'Ross Walker will tell you the same. He was on crowd control while I talked to the boys. It was just a schoolyard scrap. Nothing we haven't seen a hundred times.'

PC Dawson folds his arms. 'And this argument... Any idea what it was about?'

'I'm sorry... no. Neither boy would say.'

He makes a note of Catherine's answer. 'And, while we're here, there's nothing else you'd like to tell us about? Nothing that's caused you concern since we last spoke to you about your car?'

It feels like a test. One for which she hasn't read the questions. What is she supposed to say? That she suspects her husband of being behind it all? They'd think her crazy.

'Mrs Ashworth?'

'Sorry. No, there's nothing.' Like before, Ellen's room is too hot. She draws the back of her hand across her forehead. 'But surely Jake must have seen who attacked him?'

'That's something we won't know until he regains consciousness.' PC Dawson stands. The interview at an end. 'Thank you for your time. We'll leave you to get on with preparing for your classes. Let us know if you think of anything else.'

'Of course.'

Catherine sees them to the door and is about to walk down the corridor to her classroom when Ellen arrives. Shuts the door behind her. This is the moment she's been waiting for since the head teacher shook her hand when the interview had ended. The moment of truth. She'll have either got the job or will have to welcome someone else into it. Try and pretend it doesn't matter to her that she's been cast aside. Been found wanting.

She makes herself smile. 'Ellen.'

This must be how her A levels students feel when they get their exam results.

Ellen's face is hard to read. 'This shouldn't take too long.'

Catherine waits, her fingers twisted together. Head of English is what she's been working towards since she joined the school. Final proof that she's changed. That she's overcome the obstacles of her past.

When she can stand it no more, she forces herself to look at the woman who sits in front of her. Sees Ellen is sitting straight-backed. Her own slim fingers, with their shiny red nails, spread wide on the table in front of her as if she's waiting for the polish to dry.

'Don't make me wait any longer, Ellen. Just tell me straight. Did I get the position? Was my interview successful?'

Now it's Ellen's turn to look away. She looks stressed, tense – as though she hasn't slept well. The middle fingers of each polished hand tap a rhythm on the shiny wooden surface. It's this business with Jake. She knows how she feels.

As if surprised that she's the one making the irritating, tapping sound, Ellen lifts her hands from the table and steeples her fingers instead. Presses them to her lips.

'This isn't about the interview, Cath.'

Catherine's eyebrows raise in surprise. 'It's not?'

'No, it's more serious than that.'

A million thoughts are pushing into her head. Twisting and colliding.

'If it's about what happened to Jake—'

'It is about Jake, yes.' Ellen lowers her hands. Closes her eyes a second. 'But it's nothing to do with him being in hospital. Look, Catherine, I won't beat about the bush. This morning, after I'd spoken to the police, I took a look at Jake's coursework that you'd uploaded onto the school's shared drive.'

'Yes.' She's not sure where this is going. 'I've been working on it. Making suggestions on how it could be improved – all within the guidelines, of course.'

Ellen looks at her nails, smoothing one shiny tip with her index finger.

'There's no easy way of saying this.' Ellen presses her lips together and looks back up at her before speaking again. 'I checked the coursework following some information I'd been given.'

Alarm bells are ringing. 'What sort of information?'

'That you'd been doctoring his work.'

A laugh bursts from Catherine. 'This is a joke, right? I work on the texts of all my students. All the English teachers do. It's not doctoring... it's legitimate feedback. Constructive criticism showing areas for improvement.'

Ellen shakes her head. 'I'm sorry, Catherine, but what I saw was more than that. Jake's coursework has been tampered with. Whole pages affected, the edits incorporating sophisticated language Jake would never have used... ideas he'd be unlikely to have on his own. Also, there's been some concern by another member of the teaching staff which ties in with this. I have to follow it up. It's my duty.'

Catherine can hardly believe what she's hearing. 'Concern? From who?'

'I'm afraid I'm not at liberty to say.'

Catherine pushes herself from her chair. 'This is nonsense. You know that, don't you? Have you spoken to Jake? Have you asked him?'

And then she remembers. Of course they won't have asked him. He's lying in a hospital bed unconscious.

Blood is ringing in her ears. 'But I didn't do it, Ellen. It's a set-up. Show me what it is I'm supposed to have done.'

She thinks of how she'd saved the work onto the school server from home the previous evening when she'd been struggling to sleep. What could have gone wrong?

'I'm sorry that's not possible at the moment. You'll get a chance to view it, and have the opportunity to respond, once all the evidence has been collected. In situations like this, a formal investigation has to be initiated with an external investigator to ensure impartiality.'

Catherine goes cold. 'Is that really necessary?'

'I'm afraid it is. Do you also have a hard copy somewhere of Jake's work?'

Catherine brightens. Once they see it, see how the changes suggested don't match with the altered digital copy, they'll know she's telling the truth. 'Yes, it's in the drawer of my desk. I used the hard copy to jot notes on before I marked up the digital ready to give back to Jake. It's what I do with all the students' work.'

Ellen nods. 'That's good then. If you'll give me a minute, I'll go and find it.'

She leaves the office and Catherine waits, her breathing tight in her chest. Everyone knows how serious coursework tampering is... but she didn't do anything wrong. The notes she'd scribbled onto the hard copy would show that.

Minutes tick by and by the time Ellen reappears again, a sheaf of paper in her hand, Catherine's lips are dry. In contrast, the back of her blouse, where it's pressed against the back of the plastic chair, is damp.

'Is this it?' Ellen's face is grave, frown lines etched between her brows. She holds the pages out to Catherine. 'Is this your writing?'

Catherine glances over it, noting the fine red pen she always uses, the brevity with which she jots her notes. The overlarge letter g and the sweeping tail of a y.

'Yes... yes, I think so. But I'd need to—'

Ellen takes it from her hand. 'I had a look on your computer, just the first pages, and the notes you made in the margins here correspond exactly to the changes you've made to Jake's work.'

'But that's impossible!' Catherine's composure is slipping. Her forehead prickling with perspiration. 'Surely—'

'Please. Enough. There will be plenty of time to state your case when the investigation begins. But there's something more... something just as serious.' There's a hint of steel in Ellen's tone and Catherine wonders what on earth could be more serious than what she's already heard.

'What is it?' Her voice is small, tired.

'I found this in your drawer.'

Catherine had been too busy looking at the pages of Jake's coursework to see that Ellen had been carrying something else. But now she holds it out to her – a plastic bag. One she recognises because it contains the bottle of vodka she keeps in her drawer. How could she have forgotten it was there? Allowed Ellen to look?

'I can explain.' She turns desperate eyes to Ellen. 'This isn't what it looks like.'

She'd been willing to tell her everything, how she'd once had a drink problem but hadn't touched a drop in fifteen years – the sealed bottle kept in her drawer to reassure herself, every day, that she was strong enough to resist. But as Ellen takes the bottle out of the bag, she knows she can't.

Because the seal on the bottle has been broken. Half the contents gone.

TWENTY-NINE

Catherine closes her eyes, the fight drained out of her. Wanting to wake from the nightmare. Finding she can't.

'So, what happens now?' She could explain about the bottle, but what's the point? Ellen would never believe that someone had opened it, poured away half the contents to make it look like she'd drunk it – any more than she'd believed someone else had tampered with Jake's work.

Ellen's face is grim. 'Although it pains me to say it, I'm going to have to suspend you with immediate effect.' She slides open a drawer, takes out an envelope and hands it to Catherine. A letter written before this talk – more proof that Ellen has already made up her mind about her guilt. 'The terms of the suspension are explained in this letter. You'll remain on full pay and are required to leave the premises immediately.'

'But I have classes to teach. The exam syllabus...'

'We'll cover it. After the investigation has been initiated, all relevant parties will be interviewed. Then, once the witness statements have been logged and evidence, such as the two versions of Jake's coursework and the digital logs showing file access and modifications, have been collected, you'll have an opportunity to respond.'

'Then you'll sack me.' The inevitability sickens her.

Ellen laces her fingers. 'I didn't say that. Based on the findings, we'll decide on the appropriate course of action, but in the meantime, I do have to let you go. It might take time, but these things have to be done by the book... You understand that, don't you, Cath? I have no choice.'

Catherine doesn't answer. The only thing she understands is that her carefully built life is falling apart and she's unable to stop it. And that this all seems like exactly what Gary would want...

The walk down the corridor to her classroom to collect her things is a living nightmare. As she passes the windows, faces turn her way, making her feel like a prisoner to the gallows, even though there's no way the students can possibly know what's been said behind Ellen's closed door.

She's done nothing wrong, but, inside, she's dying of shame. Soon all the staff will know. The teacher they all aspire to knocked down from her pedestal. And it's not just the teachers. Soon the pupils will know too... and their parents.

Lynne looks up as she enters the reception and Catherine's heart sinks further. She can see from her expression that she's already heard. Of course she has. The reception desk is the hub around which the school revolves.

'Cath, I—'

'You don't have to say anything, Lynne. It's just a big misunderstanding and I'll be back before you know it. No harm done.'

But she doesn't believe it herself. The harm has already been done. Those sayings: *No smoke without fire. Every rumour has a kernel of truth...* she's heard them all. Mentioned them, in some of her classes, when they've been discussing clichés. Even if the rumours are proven to be untrue, she'll be tarred by them. Stained. A cheat and a drunk.

She pushes open the door with her shoulder, the box she's carrying heavy, but before she can leave, Lynne is on her feet. Arm extended to her, palm flat. 'Your lanyard, Cath. I have to take it. I'm sorry. And I'm afraid you'll no longer be able to use your login details to access the school's network.'

'You don't believe I did it, do you, Lynne?' Suddenly, it's important to know. 'We've worked together for fifteen years. You know me.'

Lynne has the decency to look embarrassed. 'I'm only doing what I'm told. I don't know any more than anyone else. Look, Cath, my advice would be to talk to the union. Get some help. Maybe you should even think about getting a solicitor.'

'A solicitor?' Panic rises. 'But I haven't done anything.'

'That's not the point and even if it's true, you might still need help to fight it.'

Catherine notes the words *even* and *if*... is saddened by them. Whatever happened to innocent until proven guilty? 'I'll think about it.'

'Take care, Cath. Look after yourself.' Lynne sits herself back down on her swivel chair. 'I'll open the gates for you from here.'

'Thank you.' She walks across reception to the doors, then turns. 'And, Lynne, will you do one thing for me?'

'Of course, what is it?'

'If you hear anything about Jake, if he regains consciousness, will you let me know?'

'I will.'

'Thank you.'

Catherine lets herself out, crosses the playground, then waits, her arms aching from the weight of the box she's carrying, until the gates open. She passes through, hears the clang as they close behind her, and only then does she let the tears fall.

When she reaches her car, she slides the box into the back, then gets into the driver's seat. She's just securing her seat belt when there's a sudden rap at the window. Looking up, she sees it's Ross. Quickly, she wipes her tears away with the back of her hand, relieved that it's not some parent who's heard the news on the school's jungle grapevine and has come to make a complaint.

She winds down the window. 'You heard then?'

'Yeah, I heard.' He sounds out of breath, as though he's been running, and a quick glance at the car's clock shows her it's already lunchtime. He must have sprinted out of school to catch her.

He goes round to the passenger side and opens the door. Gives a rueful smile. 'Fancy a drink? I'll stand you a Coke.'

'I don't know, Ross. What if someone from the school comes in? I couldn't bear having to explain.'

'Unlikely. It's not as if it's Friday. Come on, you look as though you could do with someone to talk to. A friendly ear to bend. Let's get away from here.'

Getting a tissue out of her pocket, Catherine blows her nose. 'You're right. Everything's such a bloody awful mess.'

There's a lot going on that she doesn't understand and she hasn't had the chance to properly think about it. Not with the image of Jake's battered face constantly in her head.

'Cath? I asked you if Gary knows.'

'Sorry.' She hadn't been listening. 'No, I haven't had the chance to speak to him. It's all been so sudden and I'm still trying to come to terms with what happened to the poor kid.'

'I'm not talking about Jake. I'm talking about what happened to *you*, Cath. Have you told Gary you've been suspended?'

'Not yet. I was escorted off the premises like a bloody criminal, if you remember.'

Ross rubs at his sideburn with his index finger. 'I think it's a good thing you haven't told him, if I'm honest. You need to calm down first. Get yourself together before talking to him. Gary needs to see that this isn't entirely your fault. Everyone makes mistakes.'

Catherine turns sharp eyes on him. 'Am I hearing you right, Ross? Are you saying you believe this crap?'

Ross holds his hands up in submission. 'No, of course not, that's not what I'm saying. It's just that Gary's going to see things differently to most people. After what happened at your old school—'

'So he told you!' She feels the pain of her husband's disloyalty like a stab to the back. Gary had promised he'd never tell a soul. She should have known. 'When?'

'I dunno... years ago. Me and Gary are mates, Cath, you know that. We go way back. Look, he was worried about you, that's all. Worried it might happen again.' He looks away, awkward now.

'Go on. Say it. You mean the drinking.'

He sucks in his top lip. Nods. 'Yes. That.'

'I don't know what he told you, but there were reasons for what happened back then. Good reasons. I was young, barely older than the students I was teaching, and didn't know what I was doing. The kids saw it... used it against me. Just like they do with Lisa. The thought of a drink once I got home was the only way I could get through another day of it – another term. Kids can be cruel and when they found out Aled was my brother, it was only more ammunition. They thought it funny that I was the sister of a junkie. Related to the weird guy who used to hang around the school.'

Her voice breaks and Ross reaches over, puts his arm around her. 'I'm sorry. I didn't mean to upset you. Bring it all back. Thank God for Gary.'

'Yes, he saved me... but I guess you know that. If he'd chosen another school to do supply in, I'd never have met him. I know it sounds corny, Ross, but when I bumped into him at the photo-copier, it was like someone had sent me a guardian angel. He taught me how to stand up to the more difficult kids. How to close the chinks in my armour and see alcohol wasn't the answer. I owe him a lot, you know. My career. My sanity. My sobriety. I haven't touched a drop since. I promised him I wouldn't and I haven't. But I don't deserve this.'

Ross doesn't say anything. Just stares at his reflection in the car window. He's never been one to be stuck for words and she's unsettled by it.

'What is it? What aren't you saying?'

He looks at her with sad eyes. 'We both know that isn't true.'

She's shocked. 'It *is* true. I haven't touched a drop in years.'

'That bottle in the drawer of your desk. I saw it when I was looking after your class.' He stares at her, exasperated. 'You didn't even try to hide it. What if the kids had seen?'

She's filled with indignation. 'You were snooping in my drawer?'

'Not snooping. Looking for a board marker. For fuck's sake, Catherine. What did you think you were doing?'

'It wasn't there for me to drink, I swear. I brought it in to test myself. To prove that, however hard things got, I'd never need it. Not like back then. You have to believe me.'

Ross puts a hand on her shoulder. 'If you say that's the case then, of course, I believe you. I know you wouldn't lie to me.'

Relief washes over her. 'Thanks, Ross.'

'Ellen, though, is another story. Do you want me to have a word with her?'

Catherine shakes her head. 'No. And, please, Ross, don't say anything to Gary.'

She hasn't had the time to visit his father yet, but she needs to do it soon – just as soon as she finds out his address.

Ross gives her shoulder a squeeze. 'You have my word. Now

let's get that drink or the bell will ring before I've ordered anything.' He stops. Frowns. 'Unless you'd rather the café.'

'No. You're good. If I was going to give in to temptation, I'd have done so by now.'

He gives a half-hearted smile. 'You'll get through this, Cath. I know you will. Everything will be okay.'

'I hope so.'

But the words are empty. He's wrong. Things will never be the same again.

She starts the engine and reverses out of the parking space. As she enters the road and drives past the school, she turns her head. Across the playground, in one of the first-floor classrooms, she can see Lisa. Her arm raised as she writes something on the board. And Catherine knows she will do whatever she needs to in order to get her job back.

THIRTY

'You've been suspended?' Gary paces the living room. Fingers laced behind his head. Elbows wide. He's only recently got back from The Crown, a quick meetup with the lads after work and his hair is plastered to his head. The material of his thin rain jacket darkened in the places where the waterproofing has worn off. 'Please, tell me you're joking.'

Catherine shifts her weight forward on the settee. Hugs the cushion she's holding to her chest. The idea had been to catch him out. Watch his face carefully when she told him, but his reaction to her news seems so genuine it's making her start to doubt his involvement.

Either that or her husband's a good actor.

'Why would I joke about such a thing? And, to be honest, I'm surprised you didn't hear all this from Ross at the pub.'

Outside the window, the rain that had battered her windscreen as she'd sat at the side of the road summoning up the courage to go home, has got harder. A rumble of distant thunder promising more rain to come.

'He didn't say anything. Wasn't himself, if I'm honest.

Looked as though he had a lot on his mind. Trouble with Karen I think.' Gary stops in front of her, his face pained, and she wonders if he's hurt that his best friend kept something from him. 'So you've been accused of what? Of altering a student's coursework in the hope of getting them a better grade?'

'That's just it. It's an accusation, that's all. I didn't do it, Gary. I'd never take that risk. Oh God, I can't believe this is happening.'

Gary drops onto the settee beside her. 'Okay, let's get this straight. You've changed a bit of his work. Added a word or two to make it sound better. It's not a hanging offence. We've all done it.'

She stares at him.

'That's just it,' she says carefully, her eyes meeting his. 'It was more than just the odd word. It was whole paragraphs – replaced with ideas Jake would never have come up with himself. Language he'd never have used. He's bright, has flair, but his work is rough around the edges. From what Ellen said, the changes stood out a mile.'

Gary draws in a breath, his nostrils flaring slightly. 'The whole thing is ridiculous. Ellen must know you wouldn't do anything as stupid as that. Put your whole career at risk.' He stares at the floor a moment, then back up at her. 'You wouldn't, would you?'

Catherine's horrified. Surely, he doesn't think that?

But of course he doesn't. It's what he wants her to believe he thinks – all part of the act. And if he can go along with this charade, then so can she. Sooner or later, he'll trip himself up. Say something incriminating.

'Jake Lloyd is the brightest boy we have in Year 13. With his change of school he's dropped behind and I did what any good teacher would do – gave him my time, helped him in any way I could. But I'd never resort to cheating. I just wanted to give him a chance and now he's lying in a hospital bed.'

Her voice catches as she thinks of it. And not knowing how he is, makes it a hundred times worse.

'I know it's a terrible thing to have happened.' The tone of Gary's voice has altered. Taken on a new, bitter edge. 'But everything recently has been about this Jake... no thought for me or the reputation of our family. What the fuck were you thinking playing fairy godmother to that boy?'

'Is it so hard for you to understand?' Her words are fuelled by resentment at his inability to read her and by the callousness of his comment. For all they know, Jake might never regain consciousness. 'I couldn't risk making the same mistake again.'

'If you're talking about what happened—'

'Yes, Gary. I'm talking about Aled. Is that so terrible?'

He shakes his head. 'Jesus... not this again. I knew it had something to do with him. Can't you get over it? It was years ago.'

'I'll never get over it. Never. If it wasn't for me, if I'd tried harder, he could have been anything – a doctor, a mathematician, a road sweeper, for all I care. He could have been whatever he wanted, but I took that away from him.'

Gary's face softens slightly. 'You didn't. It wasn't your fault.'

But Gary doesn't know it all. Only what she's wanted him to hear.

'It's that girl.' He points to the ceiling where her room is. 'She's behind it.'

'Don't be ridiculous.' The speed with which Gary has condemned her for the second time is shocking. It's like he wants her to believe it was Lisa, is desperate for it, and it makes her question why.

'You can't go accusing people without evidence. Of course it wasn't her. But that's not all, Gary.' She has to tell him. It will come out soon enough.

'You mean there's more?'

'While Ellen was looking for a printout of Jake's work in my desk drawer, she found a half-empty bottle of vodka.'

She waits for his reaction. Knows this will trigger him more.

His face freezes into a frown. 'Now you really *are* joking.'

'I'm not. The bottle was in there, I don't deny it, but it wasn't me who drank it, I swear.'

Gary presses his palms against the top of his head. Groans. 'People are going to talk. True or not, they'll make their own judgements.'

'So this display of concern has nothing to do with your worry for me, it's about *you*.'

Without warning, he reaches over. Grabs her wrist. His fingers biting deep.

'Do you not understand? This could affect my job at the council. My reputation.'

Catherine stares at his fingers. Feels the dull ache in her wrist. He's never hurt her before. 'Get your hand off me, Gary.'

'Is everything all right?'

They both turn. Lisa has come home and neither had heard her.

Behind her glasses, the girl's eyes are worried. 'I don't mean to pry, but you both sounded so upset.'

Gary's face is tense. 'What do you want, Lisa? We're having a private conversation here.'

'I'm sorry. Would you prefer it if I went upstairs? I've got some marking to do.'

Gary folds his arms. 'Yes, that would be a good thing.'

But Catherine's not having it. How dare Gary dictate what Lisa should or shouldn't do? It's not just his house but hers too and he needs to be reminded of it.

'No. Stay, Lisa. I suppose you've heard what's happened.' She hates how far she's fallen. Wonders what Lisa thinks of her mentor now.

'What happened? No, I was supervising the homework

club, then came straight home. Is it something to do with the attack on Jake?'

'No, but it is related to him. Someone altered his course-work and, not surprisingly, Ellen presumes it was me who did it.'

Lisa's hand flies to her mouth. 'Oh my God, Cath. You'd never do such a thing.'

'Oh, don't play the innocent.' Gary's looking at Lisa with disgust. 'You know only too well. Because it was *you* who changed Jake's coursework, then made your phoney little complaints about my wife to Ellen. And after everything she's done for you. Letting you stay with us when it was obvious you weren't wanted.'

'That's enough.' Catherine turns on him. 'Lisa asked if she could stay because she's your flesh and blood.' She presses the palm of her hand to her forehead. 'You know, I don't think I can do this anymore, Gary.'

He stares at her in surprise. 'Do what?'

'Live in this house with you, when all you can think about is yourself.'

She walks past the two of them. Heads for the stairs.

'Where are you going?'

'I'm going to pack some things. I need space.'

Gary runs to her. Grabs her arm as she reaches the bottom of the stairs. 'You can't do that? What about the girl?'

'What about her? Your sister can stay until she finds some-where to live, but I can't be under the same roof as you any longer. Not when you keep so much from me. I might as well be another ornament on the mantelpiece for all the notice you take of me. For all the care you have for my well-being. It's all about *you*, Gary. It always has been.'

And she no longer trusts him. Is surer than ever that he's behind everything that's happened.

Lisa has joined them. 'This is all my fault. You two were

happy before I came to live with you. I should be the one leaving.'

'Yes, maybe you should.' Gary's looking at the girl as though he hates her. 'It's what we'd all like.'

'Then I will. But first, I'd like to have a word with Cath.'

Gary tenses. 'Can't you see this is crazy? It can be sorted out. We need to all calm down a bit. This business with Jake, Cath... it's got to you. Taken its toll on your mental health. Stay and talk and I wouldn't be surprised if after a good night's sleep, you didn't agree with me that your suspension might actually be for the best?'

Catherine feels the dark swell of anger. 'Are you for real? Get out of my way.'

Pushing past him, she runs up the stairs. When she gets to her bedroom, she slides open the wardrobe doors and drags a holdall from the shelf above the hanging rail.

Gary's shout comes up the stairs. 'Don't be stupid, Cath. Come down.'

She ignores him. Throws tops and jeans into the bag, then moves to her dressing table and shoves underwear and makeup on top. And, as she does it, she tries not to think about what she's doing. Because the decision to leave was made in anger and she has no plan. No place to go.

She's also not sure how safe it is for Lisa to stay... but she can't be worrying about that now.

Gary's in the doorway now. 'You can't leave.'

'Watch me.' She pushes her brush into the outside pocket of the bag. 'What happened to *for better or for worse*? It doesn't get much worse than this.'

He looks on helplessly. 'But this is stupid. Where will you go?'

'Anywhere.' Catherine heaves the bag onto her shoulder. 'As long as it's away from *you*.'

With tears blinding her eyes, Catherine runs down the stairs and slams out of the front door. She gets into her car and reverses it out of the drive, narrowly missing the gatepost.

She has no idea where she's going, but she doesn't care.

THIRTY-ONE

Catherine sits on the edge of the bed, the polished floorboards cold under her bare feet. The holdall she'd thrown things into on the floor beside her. She's seen this room before, has stayed in it on occasion when she and Gary have been to the pub down the road and neither of them have wanted to drive home. But, here on her own, the street light shining through the gap in the curtains, the carriage clock on the bedside table ticking down the minutes since she'd left her home, she feels lost, untethered.

There's a knock on the door and Ross comes in, a mug of tea in one hand, a glass of whiskey in the other. He hands the tea to Catherine.

'Drink it while it's hot.' He perches on the bed next to her. 'My mum used to swear by a cup of tea. Used to say that whatever the situation, nothing would seem so bad after you'd drunk it. Probably why they're always doing that in films. Giving out tea when someone's witnessed a death or an accident.'

Catherine points to the mug. 'It's for the shock.'

'Eh?'

Catherine takes a sip, burning her lips. 'It's the sugar they put in. Helps with the shock, or so they say.' She puts the mug down on the bedside table. 'Thank you for letting me stay, Ross. I didn't know who else to call.'

Ross shifts on the bed. Takes a large gulp of his whiskey. 'I could hardly let you roam the streets. But I need to ask you a favour.'

'Anything. I owe you.' It's true. If it hadn't been for him, she'd be in some soulless B&B, counting the stains on the ceiling, rather than in Ross's smart spare room.

'Please don't tell Gary where you're staying. He's my friend too and I don't want things to be awkward between us.'

It's not something she'd thought of and the fact that she hadn't makes her cheeks burn. Of course this will be awkward. By letting her stay here, Ross will, in effect, have chosen her over Gary. His newer friend over his old.

'It only needs to be for tonight. I can find somewhere else in the morning. Karen might be up for having a lodger for a bit.' It's said half-heartedly. The way Karen's been with her recently, it's hardly likely.

At the mention of her name, Ross tightens his lips. 'No, there's no need. You can stay here as long as you want. Just... well, keep it to yourself. Karen's not known for her tact.'

'Did you two have a falling-out?'

'Something like that.'

Catherine nods. Blows on her tea. 'Thought so. She's been snappy for days. What happened?'

'She got a bit needy, that's all. It was never meant to be more than a bit of fun, but maybe I didn't make that clear enough at the start.'

'Poor Karen.'

Ross laughs. 'Poor me.'

'Yeah, that too... and I'm sorry, Ross.'

'No need to be. All water under the bridge. Anyway, your

troubles are bigger than mine at the moment.' He tips his head back and empties his glass. 'What are you going to do about it, Cath? Are you going to fight it?'

'I don't know.' She looks at him. Desperate for him to understand. 'You know I didn't do it, Ross. It would be madness to. More than my career is worth.'

'Of course I know, I told you that. But if you didn't change Jake's A level coursework, who did?'

Catherine stares miserably at the bag by her feet. 'I don't know.'

What she wants to say is that the obvious candidate is Gary, but she can't. She has no evidence, and Ross will think she's crazy if she tells him her theory. And even if she did voice her suspicions, how could she be sure he wouldn't change his allegiance back to his old friend once he'd heard her out.

'But how would they have done it?'

'I'm not sure. Jake sent his coursework through to me on the school email and I uploaded it to the school server that evening.'

'But how would anyone have been able to get into your email? It's password protected.'

'That's what I'm wondering. They'd also added notes to the printout in my drawer for good measure. In case anyone questioned it.'

'Jesus.' Ross shakes his head. 'That's devious. But why on earth would anyone want to go to all the trouble of doing that? What would be their motive?'

'I don't know. Maybe they want to discredit me. Gary thinks it's Lisa.'

She hadn't meant to tell him, but it's too late to take it back.

Ross barks out a laugh. 'You're kidding me, right? He accused his sister? Lisa might not be a good teacher, but that girl hasn't got a nasty bone in her body.'

'Well, whoever it was has done a good job of wrecking my

life. They've succeeded in wrecking my career and my marriage.' She swallows down the painful lump in her throat. Feels one small step away from breaking down. But it's something she can't do in front of Ross. 'I'm lucky to have you; otherwise, it might have been me sleeping in a sleeping bag on the classroom floor rather than Lisa.'

Ross leans forward, the tips of his fingers against his nose. 'What? You mean Lisa was sleeping in the school? Jesus, I had no idea. So, where does Gary stand on all this?'

She gives a small shake of her head. 'You don't want to know.'

'Tell me anyway.'

'Let's just say, the straw that broke the camel's back was when he had the audacity to tell me I might be better off with the suspension. Can you believe it?' She's hardly able to believe it herself. 'And the way he's treated Lisa since she moved in is frankly embarrassing.'

She looks down. Sees she's cupped her hand over her wrist. Is massaging, with her thumb, the soft place where Gary's fingers had gripped. Quickly, she stops, but it's too late. Ross has seen.

He lifts her fingers. Sees the four small round bruises that are starting to fade.

'Did Gary do this?'

She's going to lie, but what's the point? 'He's been stressed having Lisa around.'

'*He's* been stressed!' He puts her hand down gently. 'What about you? Look, I don't know what's going on with him recently, but my advice is to give him time, Cath. You've been together a long while. I'm sure you'll work things out.'

'I wish I could believe it.' She feels a bilious wave of panic. 'All those years... did they mean nothing to him?'

'Of course they did.' She feels the bedsprings move as he

stands. Feels the kiss he presses to the top of her head. 'Finish your tea and get some sleep. Things will seem better in the morning, I promise.'

'And if they don't?'

'Then I'm a liar. Seriously though, Cath. We'll sort this. Whatever's going on, we'll rumble it. My guess is that by next month, you'll be back in your job and back in your home.'

Catherine looks up at him. 'You think so?'

'I know so. I'll say good night now and see you in the morning.'

Ross leaves the room and Catherine switches off the main light. She pulls a vest top and pyjama bottoms from her bag and, checking the door is closed, changes into them.

She turns back the duvet, gets into bed and switches off the bedside light. Wondering what Ross is doing. Whether he's watching TV or having an early night. Fighting against thinking the same about Gary and whether he's missing her.

A message pings on her phone. It's from Lisa. *I just wanted to make sure you're OK.*

She messages back. *I'm fine, thanks. Just need time to think.*

A car drives by, its headlights sweeping an arc across the ceiling. Try as she might, sleep won't come. She's too wound up. Too heartbroken. Rolling onto her side, she feels for her phone. Wakes it up in the hope of finding a message from Gary, but there's nothing.

Catherine pulls the duvet around her as she did as a child, finding no comfort in it. She closes her eyes and thinks of Jake in his hospital bed. Attached to monitors. Oblivious to everything going on around him in the ward. Thinks of Aled with no plaque to mark his final resting place. Thinks of Lisa and Gary.

Only a week or so ago, she had a job, a home, a husband. Now she has nothing.

The silence in the room is black and heavy and now her ears are playing tricks on her. Filling the void with the roar and crackle of the flames that started all this. Making her smell again the smoke and the fumes of the petrol-soaked rag.

Catherine stares into the darkness, forcing her mind away from the thing she fears most. She's a fighter. She won't lose everything.

Tomorrow, she's going to find out the truth.

THIRTY-TWO

Catherine wakes suddenly and opens her eyes, heart racing. Unsure where she is. She doesn't recognise the room at first. The slice of light coming through the door from the landing picking out the edge of a chest of drawers that isn't hers. A strip of alien polished floor.

She'd thought she'd felt a hand on her shoulder. Had been terrified by it.

'Gary, is that you?' She feels again the deep press of Gary's fingers on her wrist. The intent on his face. 'Please don't hurt me.'

Her eyes strain to see and panic overtakes her as she realises her instinct had been right. She's not alone. There's someone hovering over her. She sits up and as she does, her recollection returns, the weight of it dragging her down to a darker place. This isn't her home. This is Ross's flat.

'It's all right, Cath. It's only me.'

A light snaps on, blinding her, and it takes a moment or two for her to realise it's not the intruder she'd imagined but Ross who's standing beside her bed.

'Jesus, Ross. What the hell?' Catherine presses the palms of her hands to her face. The shock of what she'd imagined still with her. The terrible guilt at imagining Gary could hurt her.

'I'm sorry I frightened you.' Ross sits on the edge of her bed. He's wearing a pair of blue tracksuit bottoms. 'You cried out. Scared the living daylights out of me.' He rubs at his bare chest with the flat of his hand. 'You were having a bad dream.'

'I was?'

Concern for her is etched into the lines between his brows. 'And some! You were shouting out... something about a fire. I wasn't sure whether waking you was the right thing, but I didn't know what else to do. When I shook your shoulder, I wasn't expecting you to jump out of your skin.'

'I'm sorry.' She releases her grip on the duvet. 'I do that sometimes... have nightmares. Well, I used to.'

Ross pinches the soft space between his eyes and yawns. 'It's the stress. It's not surprising considering what you've gone through. I'm really sorry, Cath. You must think the universe has dumped a load of shit on your doorstep.'

'Something like that.' She reaches across to the bedside table, picks up her glass and takes a sip of the lukewarm water. 'I have to ask you something, Ross. Do you think the person who set fire to my car was the same one who attacked Jake?'

Ross shrugs, the movement flexing the smooth muscles of his shoulders. 'Maybe. But I can't think how the two would be connected.'

'The connection is me.' Without realising it, her eyes have strayed to the tanned skin of his stomach. Embarrassed, she slides them away to something safer. The mobile on her bedside table. She reaches for it. Wakens it.

'I want to show you something.'

'What?'

Catherine scrolls to her videos and finds what she's looking for. She holds it out for Ross to see. 'Whoever did it, sent me this.'

She watches Ross's face darken as he watches the flames. Sees himself come into view, the extinguisher in his hands.

'The bastard's laughing at us.' A muscle twitches in his cheek. 'Look at the angle it's taken from. Whoever took this was standing in the road watching. Gloating over what they'd done.'

Ross watches to the end and Catherine knows he's remembering. Blaming himself for not having got there in time to save her car.

He hands the phone back to her. 'The resolution is low. Probably a cheap pay-as-you-go. These things are hard to trace. Why didn't you show it to the police?'

She hangs her head. 'Because of what happened before... at the other school. I couldn't face the questions. The suspicion that the two things were linked. It was safer to have them think it was just a stupid prank. A kid from the school with a grudge.'

'Safer?'

'Yes... for my mental health. If I didn't show them, then I could pretend it was nothing too.'

'Someone's trying to frighten you, Cath.' He points at the phone, then folds his arms across his chest, the overhead light catching the golden hairs on his forearms. 'This isn't a prank. It's targeted.'

'Do you think I'm in danger?'

'I don't know, but I'm glad you're here.' He looks at her, his face serious. 'I meant what I said yesterday. You mustn't tell Gary where you are.'

He says no more, and Catherine can't help wondering if there's something he's not telling her. If he suspects her husband too.

'Thank you for not telling Gary about my suspension. It was better I told him myself.'

'I agree, but I didn't get the chance to anyway. Gaz never turned up at the pub yesterday evening.'

'What do you mean? He said he did.'

Ross shakes his head. 'I don't know why he'd do that. It was just me and a couple of the lads. Gary was a no-show. It's happened a few times recently.'

'Really?'

'Yeah. And even on the nights he has been there, he's not been himself. The other guys have noticed it too.' He looks hard at her. 'I'm serious, Cath. It's best he doesn't know. I've no idea what's going on, but the fewer people you tell where you're living the better.'

'I won't say anything.' She puts the phone back on the bedside table. Lies back on the pillow. 'You don't really think I'm in danger, do you, Ross?'

The bed moves as Ross lies next to her. 'Not now you're here.'

He puts his arm around her, his hand cupping her shoulder and Catherine takes comfort from it. She captures his fingers in hers and kisses the knuckles. Thankful for his friendship. Grateful that he hasn't taken Gary's side against hers.

But why hasn't he?

She turns onto her side, her eyes fixed on the gap between the curtains. Remembers Lisa's words when she'd been talking about Gary, *I think he sees the school as a threat*. If anyone had a motive for scaring her, Gary did and she wonders if Ross thinks that too. And, if he does, why is he protecting him?

She needs to find out if her husband was the one behind the arson on her car and if it was him who had caused her to lose her job. She also needs to know why he hates Lisa so much.

Because, despite what Ross says, until she has the answer to these things, she can't know, for certain, if she's safe now.

THIRTY-THREE

When Catherine wakes the next morning, sunshine is filtering through the curtains. She tries to turn over, but something heavy is weighing her down and it takes her a moment to realise its Ross's arm.

She lies there, not daring to move. Trying to remember the night before. She'd had a bad dream, had cried out. Ross had comforted her. His arm is numbing her hip and, trying not to wake him, she lifts it and places it by his side. Slides out of the bed and slips her arms into her dressing gown. She looks at Ross's sleeping form. He's lying on top of the covers and she gives a small sigh of relief when she sees he's still in his blue tracksuit bottoms. Because it means nothing happened.

Not that she'd have let it, because, despite everything, she still loves Gary. And for another reason too – that in all the years she's known him, she's never seen Ross as anything more than a friend. Someone to rib when he's shown them his latest Tinder match or to shake her head at when he's dumped that one for the next.

She tiptoes over to the bedside table, picks up her phone

and looks at it, seeing there are three missed calls and several messages. All from her husband. She heads out onto the landing, turns in the direction of the kitchen with the intention of making herself some tea, and clicks on the first one. Reads it.

Answer your phone, Cath. I need to tell you something. Something important.

The next message is more urgent. *For fuck's sake, pick up. I have to speak to you. It's about Lisa.*

Catherine stares at the screen, anger surging through her. She doesn't want to hear any more of Gary's accusations against the girl. He needs to change the record. She places her phone on the worktop and is just filling the kettle when it rings. The kettle jumps in her hand, water spilling onto the shiny surface.

'Damn.'

Putting the kettle down, she jabs at the phone.

'Leave me alone, Gary.'

His voice is urgent. 'Thank God you picked up. I really need to speak to you, Cath.'

'You should have thought of that before you lost your temper. Before you suggested my suspension was a good thing. What's wrong with you, Gary? Leaving you was something I should have done years ago. I'm worth more than this.'

Gary's voice comes to her through the phone that's pressed to her ear. Tense. Urgent. As though someone might overhear. 'I know you are and that's why you have to hear me out. I can't lose you like this. You need to know the truth.'

Catherine had been pacing the room, but now she stops. Ross is in the doorway, hands tucked under his armpits. The blue jogging bottoms loose on his hips. He points to the half-made tea on the worktop, a wide grin on his face.

'You needn't have done that, Cath. I'd have made it.'

Catherine lowers the phone. Presses it to her chest as she mouths the word *Gary* at him.

Ross's face falls. He turns his back on her and fishes a tea bag out of one of the mugs with a teaspoon. Swearing as it slips back, hot tea splashing onto his bare stomach. He rubs at it and Cath has to force her eyes away from the dark line of hair that trails from his navel to the cord of his joggers.

In her ear, Gary's voice has turned hard. 'Who's that with you?'

'It's nobody you know,' she says quickly, hating that she's lying to him.

'Fuck's sake. I'm not an idiot. It's Ross, isn't it?'

'Don't be stupid. I'm at Lynne's. Her husband Pete's just off to work. Not that it's any of your business.'

'Right.' He sounds unsure. 'Okay, but I have to see you. To talk to you. Something's happened and I need you to hear it from me, not from—'

Something in his tone calls out to Catherine, but then her resolve hardens. 'As if I can trust you... Get out of my life, Gary. Don't call me again.'

'Wait, Cath. It's import—'

But Catherine's already ended the call. Has turned the phone over so she won't see the pleading messages that she knows will follow.

'You did the right thing.' Ross is leaning against the work-top, his mug of tea to his lips. 'I wasn't sure before but now...' He points to the bruises on her arm. 'Now I am. I can't believe he did that.' He sucks in his lips. 'Not to you.'

Catherine pulls out a chair and sits. 'I'm not sure I trust him anymore, Ross. I used to think he was my knight in shining armour, but I now wonder if he was only happy when he was controlling my life. The stronger I get, the more confident, the less he likes it. You should have seen him when I told him I was going for the promotion... when I told him I was working with Jake to help him get better grades in his A levels. He really wasn't happy.' She remembers the look on his face. 'Wasn't happy at all.'

'And now the kid's in hospital.'

It's said lightly, but something in the comment resonates. She looks at her phone. Thinks of the conversation they've just had. Gary wanted to tell her something important. Did he have something to confess? But the idea is so ridiculous, she pushes it away. Gary's not a violent man. Her fingers stray to her wrist. Not usually, anyway.

Catherine picks up the phone and wakens it.

Ross frowns. 'What are you doing?'

'Getting him out of my life, as I should have done years ago.'

Tapping through to her settings, she finds Gary's name and, with a certain satisfaction, blocks it. It might be childish, a knee-jerk reaction, but it makes her feel better. She's got nothing to say to her husband and nothing she wants to hear.

Ross gives a reassuring smile. 'I would have done the same in your shoes. Anyway, I'm going to grab a shower. Some of us still have to go to work and it looks like I'll be winning "first into school" today.'

'That's not funny, Ross.'

'It wasn't. I'm sorry.' He looks suitably embarrassed at his gaff. 'You'll be okay here on your own?'

''Course I will. Garden leave will give me a proper rest.'

But seeing Ross get ready for work brings it painfully home to her. While he's teaching his classes, she'll be sitting in his apartment twiddling her thumbs.

Anger and indignation had carried her through the first day of her suspension, but now the weight of disappointment, of loss, hits her hard. She'd loved teaching at Greenfield. Would never have done anything to jeopardise it.

Catherine listens to the gurgle in the pipes as Ross runs his shower. If only they'd let her see the altered pages of Jake's work, the notes she supposedly made on the printout, but they won't. And with no access to the school server now, there's no way to find out what's been added. What's been changed.

But there *is* something she can do. She can find out about Gary. Pay his father and stepmother a visit. She thinks of the message on her phone from Lisa. The easiest way to find out where they live is to ask her, but she can't. Lisa had made it clear she didn't think a visit from Catherine would be a good idea and it's unlikely she'd tell her their address.

Taking out her phone, she clicks onto Facebook. Adds Gary's surname to the search bar. She scrolls through the names that come up. There are several Ashworths, but they are mostly too young. If only she could remember Gary's father's first name. As she scrolls down, a couple of the profile pictures show men who are older, but when she clicks on them, one is living in California and the other has pictures of himself and his five grandchildren. This isn't going to work.

She puts her phone on her lap. Thinks. If Gary's father isn't on social media, the chances are he'll still have and use a landline. It's worth a try.

Ross has come through again, the collar of his shirt up, his hand tucking the long end of his tie into the loop of material he's created. Pulling it through and working the knot up to his throat.

'Bloody ties. Wish they'd never been invented.'

'You sound like one of the kids.'

He puts on his jacket, comes over to her and places his hands on her shoulders. 'Because that's what I am at heart... a big kid. Seriously, though. You'll be all right, won't you?'

'Of course I will.'

'Use whatever's in the fridge for lunch. While you're here, what's mine is yours, Cath.'

'I know and thanks.'

Catherine smiles up at him, meaning it. She's grateful for his support. Grateful he hasn't sided with Gary.

'I know it's an odd question, but do you by any chance have a telephone book, Ross?'

He thinks. 'I'm not sure. If I have, it will be with the other things I never use in the cupboard over there. It won't be up to date, though. I haven't used it in years.'

'That doesn't matter.' With any luck, Gary's parents won't have moved house any time recently.

'Why do you want it?'

She hesitates, wondering whether to tell him. Deciding not to. 'I wanted to look up an old friend, that's all.'

'Hope you find her.' Ross takes his hands from her shoulders. 'I'll see you later then?'

'You certainly will. Now get out of here and teach those damn kids.'

'Yes, ma'am.' He gives a mock salute, picks up his plastic box of files and walks to the door. 'I mean it, Cath. Make yourself at home.'

She hears the click of the front door. Parts the net curtain at the window to watch him get into his car. As he drives away, she turns her wedding ring round on her finger, seeing the indentation it's left on the skin beneath: evidence of the years she's worn it and never taken it off.

There's something about Ross that's very attractive, but is she really ready to give up on Gary? Walking out of the house yesterday had felt like a strength, but now it feels the opposite. To give up her marriage so easily would be weak and it comes to her now, with clarity, that she should be fighting to understand what went wrong.

Catherine gets up and takes her mug to the sink. Then she goes to the cupboard and rummages through it until she finds the telephone directory. Despite being four years old, she finds the address she's looking for immediately. Jots it down on some paper and puts it in her bag.

She's not going to sit here doing nothing, she's going to find out what's going on. And although neither Lisa nor Gary will like it, the only way to do that is by paying their father a visit.

THIRTY-FOUR

The house is nothing to look at. An ordinary semi in an ordinary street of buildings. Red-brick. Small with neat front gardens.

Catherine rings the doorbell. Waits. At first, she thinks no one's in, then she sees a shadow through the glass panels of the front door. When it opens, it's a middle-aged woman who stands in front of her. A questioning smile on her lips.

'Can I help you?'

As she speaks, she pats at her neat, fair hair as though worried about how she might look to a stranger. She's shorter than Catherine and the jeans she's wearing are tight around her ample thighs. There's no makeup on her face save for the fuchsia pink lipstick that clashes with her red jumper.

Catherine holds out her hand. 'I'm sorry to bother you. I'm Catherine. Catherine Ashworth.' She pauses, wondering how the woman will take it. 'Gary's wife.'

'Oh, good grief!' She presses a hand to her chest. Turns and calls out to someone in the house. 'Neil. You'll never believe who's here, love.'

'Who is it?' A man appears in the narrow hallway. He's

older than the woman, his hair receding at the temples, and Catherine sees at once his resemblance to Gary. He joins Lisa's mother at the door. 'Did I hear you say something about Gary?'

'It's his wife, Catherine. Would you credit it?'

The man's face lights up. 'Really? I never would have thought... How marvellous.' He steps back. Gestures to the hall. 'Come in. Don't get cold standing on the doorstep. If I remember rightly, you're a teacher. Like Gary used to be. You didn't take the day off specially to see us, did you? Gary's all right, is he? Nothing's happened to him?'

'Gary's fine. I didn't mean to worry you. And I'm on sick leave at the moment.' She presses a smile to her lips. 'Nothing contagious.'

'I'm sorry to hear that. But where are our manners? Can I get you anything? Tea? Coffee?'

'No, thank you.' Catherine follows the two of them inside. 'I don't want to take up any more of your time than I have to.'

'I know we've never met, but you're family, love.' The woman smiles at her. 'Take all the time you like.'

She's shown into a living room at the front of the house. Takes a seat on one of the red velveteen settees and waits for the other two to join her. Wondering where she should begin.

But the decision is taken from her as it's Neil who speaks first.

'How is Gary?'

'Gary's all right.' How can she tell him the truth? That she no longer knows who her husband is.

'We haven't seen him since...' He turns to his wife. 'Oh, it must have been my mother's funeral.'

'Yes.' Catherine nods. 'He mentioned that. I'm sorry if Gary was rude to you both, Mr Ashworth.'

Gary's father crosses his legs. 'Please, call me Neil. And he wasn't rude to us. In fact, he never uttered a word to us the whole time he was there. To be honest, I'm not even sure why he came as he wasn't particularly close to his grandmother. Thought he ought to show his face, I expect. What do you think, Jackie?'

'There's no need to be like that, Neil.' Gary's stepmother frowns at her husband. 'The girl has come all this way to see us, and I'm sure the last thing she wants is to hear any of your bitterness.'

'It's okay.' Catherine puts a hand on Jackie's arm. 'I know it must have been difficult for you. For Gary too. It's so sad knowing you're estranged from each other, but at least you have your daughter.'

Had their daughter. Do they know Lisa is now living in her house? Do they feel any guilt at all for having thrown her out?

At the mention of their daughter, Jackie's face breaks into a smile. 'She's such a wonderful girl. I don't know what we would have done without her. You know she tried to heal the rift between Gary and Neil?' She looks surprised when Catherine shakes her head. 'No? Well, she did. She really is a lovely girl and, under different circumstances, I'm sure Gary would have grown very fond of her, but the damage had already been done.' Jackie pulls a tissue from her sleeve and dabs her eyes with it. 'And I don't mind admitting I'm ashamed of the part I played in it. It must have been very hurtful to Gary's mother to find out about us, but we were in love.' She smiles at Neil. 'And I'm afraid it was bigger than the both of us.'

If it had been anyone else, Catherine would have found it moving – a love so great it was impossible to fight – but she knows how much damage Neil's affair had done to his family. The heartache it had caused.

'You're probably not going to believe this, but your daughter works at the same school as me... has done for a few months.' Catherine composes her face. 'In fact, I'm her mentor. The truth is, neither Gary nor I knew who she was. It's such a coincidence.'

Jackie puts her cup down. 'Really? How odd. What is it our daughter does there? The accounts?'

'The accounts? No, she's a new teacher in our school. She teaches English.'

Neil leans forward, his elbows on his knees. 'I don't think so, dear. There must be some mistake. Our Anne's an accountant.'

'Anne?' Gary hadn't said anything about another half-sister. Possibly she's a daughter from Jackie's previous marriage. It would explain why she'd never heard her name mentioned. 'Oh, sorry. No, I didn't mean Anne, I meant Lisa. Your other daughter.'

Only the ticking of the clock on the mantelpiece breaks the silence in the room. Jackie and Neil are looking at each other as though they're wondering whether they've done the right thing in inviting Catherine inside. As though it's a stranger who's walked in, instead of their son's wife.

Next to the clock is a photograph. Jackie gets up and holds it out to Catherine. 'This is my daughter, Anne. Neil and I only had one child. We tried again, but we weren't lucky enough to have another.'

Catherine takes the photograph from her. Looks closely at the three of them. The picture's been taken on a holiday – several years ago by the look of it. The three of them are tanned and smiling. They're standing on a beach with a camel behind them and the girl between Jackie and Neil is the spitting image of her mother. Pretty. Her fair hair blowing around her face. No other child is in the picture.

'But I don't understand. She's been living in our house. She's talked about you.'

But what has she said? Not a lot. Only that her parents threw her out.

'Do you have a picture of this girl? This Lisa?'

'No, I don't. Oh, wait a minute, it would be on the school website.'

Catherine gets out her phone and puts the name of the school into the search engine. When it comes up, she clicks on the tab marked *Staff* and scrolls down to the English Department.

Her own picture comes up near the top, underneath the head of department, and it hits her again how close she'd been to reaching that pinnacle. Becoming Head of English with the validation of her worth that would have come with it.

Ross's picture is next, followed by a few others, then at the bottom, is Lisa. Her dark hair loose around her shoulders. Her eyes serious behind her glasses.

'This is Lisa.'

She holds her phone out for them to see. Sure they'll recognise her.

Neil takes the phone from her. Adjusts his glasses on his nose so as to see it better.

'I'm sorry, Catherine. I've never seen this young woman before. Have *you*, Jackie?' He hands the phone to his wife.

'No, I'm afraid not. You say she's been living with you and the question I'm asking myself is why she'd pretend to be someone she's not. But I've another question too. If you believed this girl's lies, that she's Gary's half-sister, then that must mean Gary believed it too.'

'He said he did.'

'And do you have reason to doubt him?'

'Should I?'

Neil exchanges a glance with his wife. Stands. 'You know my son better than me, Catherine, and my advice is to go home and talk to that husband of yours. See if you can get some answers. Though if he's anything like he was when he was a boy, it might be difficult. He always kept things close to his chest. Liked to be in control of a situation even if it meant deviating from the truth.'

'I see.' Not knowing what else to do, what else to say,

Catherine gets up too. 'Thank you for your time. I'm glad I finally got to meet you both.'

Neil smiles kindly at her. 'Us too. We always wondered what our daughter-in-law was like. But, of course, the downside of meeting you today, is knowing what we've been missing all these years...'

Catherine says her goodbyes and gets into her car, but instead of going straight home, something makes her turn right at the traffic lights. Take the road that leads to the school.

Not wanting to be seen, she parks a street away.

It's not breaktime yet, so the playground is empty, but through the windows of the classrooms she can see the heads of the students she used to teach. An arm raised here and there in answer to a question.

She stands, her hands clutching at the cold metal bars of the security fence, overcome with a sudden loneliness. This was how Aled must have felt when the world had turned its back on him. When *she'd* turned her back on him. And she understands how it feels. Really feels. Not just the loneliness but the fear.

But she won't let it beat her; she's stronger than that now.

Turning her back on the school, Catherine walks away. Only by fighting for what is rightfully hers, for what she wants, will she prove her strength. She won't be walked over by a slip of a girl. Won't give her the satisfaction. And she won't let Gary tell her any more lies.

With a last look over her shoulder at the classroom window, she walks back to the car. In her bag are her house keys and, legally, the place is still hers as well as Gary's. She'll park in a nearby road, let herself into the house, then sit and wait it out. Because she plans to be there when Lisa gets back from school. Have it out with the girl, before Gary comes home, and find out what the hell she's doing in their house. While she's waiting, she'll see if she can find any evidence to explain why Lisa's been lying about who she is, because now she's wondering if Gary was right all along. If it was Lisa who'd tampered with Jake's work. Had set light to her car.

Feeling better for having made a plan, Catherine gets her phone out of her bag and leaves Ross a message on his voicemail.

Hi, Ross. I'm not going to be back until later. I've been to Gary's dad's house and, you know what? He and his wife have never heard of Lisa. She's a liar. Not Gary's half-sister at all. Do you think Gary knew? It's time to sort this mess out and, with any luck, I won't be needing to stay another night at your house. Thank you for being a good friend.

She clicks send, then starts the engine. Enough is enough.

THIRTY-FIVE

Catherine slides open Lisa's wardrobe door and stands looking at the few things that hang there. Unsure of what exactly she's looking for. Hoping that her search will turn up something that will show the girl for who she really is. Her anger rages. She'd thought the girl so nice, had liked her, and all the time she'd been a fake.

She looks around her. In the short time Lisa has been here, she's made the room so homely and now it seems incredible to think she imagined she'd get away with her lie.

Had the plan been to live here forever?

Who is this girl?

On the right-hand side of the wardrobe, below the hanging rail, is a set of drawers just asking to be opened. Catherine's the only one in the house but even so, she gives a quick glance behind her before pulling the top one open. Disappointment filling her when she finds nothing except some underwear and a few pairs of socks. The next drawer down is completely empty. The one below it too.

On the wardrobe floor, next to the chest of drawers, is Lisa's holdall. It's unzipped and, even though she knows she shouldn't, she slides her hand into its depths. Feels around for she knows not what. There's not much there, just an old notepad with what looks like preparation notes for the interview she'd had for her job, a Biro and an unopened packet of tissues. Nothing interesting. But there's an outside pocket she hasn't looked in yet. She unzips it and gasps. The envelope full of money she saw Gary throw at Lisa has been stuffed inside. Why had he wanted her to have it? So she could leave?

As Catherine's fingers continue to search, they touch something smooth and shiny at the bottom of the bag. She grabs at it, her breath shortening as she pulls it out, knowing even before she sees it that it's Aled's photographs she holds in her hand. Why has Lisa got them? Why did she lie to her when she told her she hadn't moved them?

The front door slams and Catherine freezes. She should leave the bedroom, but it's too late and already she can hear Lisa's footsteps on the stairs. And, as they get louder, a strange feeling comes over her, that despite what she's just found in Lisa's drawer, it's *she* who's trespassing. *She* who's the wrong-doer. Not Lisa.

Knowing there's no time to leave, she sits on Lisa's bed. Readying herself. And as she waits, heart galloping, adrenaline coursing through her, her eyes fix on some of the titles of the books that line the shelf next to Lisa's bed. New books she's never seen before: *Where is Baby's Birthday Cake?*, *In Grandma's Arms*, *Creep from the Deep*. Picture books designed to be read on a parent's lap. Certainly a strange choice of reading material for a young woman Lisa's age.

'What are you doing?' The bag Lisa's holding drops to the floor and it takes a moment for her to recover from the shock of seeing Catherine. 'You have no right to just let yourself into the house like this. No right to be in my room.'

The ridiculousness of the girl's statement makes Catherine laugh. 'You mean let myself into my own house?' She lifts the photographs of Aled from her lap. Stands and waves them in Lisa's face. 'And talking about rights. What right have *you* to steal my photographs?' When Lisa doesn't answer, Catherine carries on. 'The question I'm asking myself is why you would have my brother's photographs in your holdall when you didn't even know him? Don't you see how weird that is? Last night, when I left here, I acted out of shock, but since then, I've had time to think. What happened is between me and Gary, no one else, and I want you packed and out of my house before he gets home from work. I'll go downstairs and make myself some tea. Give you some space to get rid of all this.' She gestures at the books, the rug, the pictures. 'Oh, and I'd be grateful if you'd put the chest of drawers back in the place you found it.'

Catherine had expected Lisa to move out of her way, but the girl stands her ground. 'I'm not going anywhere and you're wrong about the photographs. The reason—'

'I don't want to hear it.' She folds her arms, hoping it will give her an air of confidence she doesn't feel. 'And I haven't time to play your games. It might interest you to know that this morning I paid your parents a visit. Or should I say Gary's dad and step-mum. I don't expect it will be a surprise for you to hear that they've never heard of you. I was going to tell them about the awful things you've done. Breaking into my files to change Jake's coursework, then telling Ellen it was me who'd done it. Trying to take over my job. I've no idea who you are, Lisa, but you need some serious counselling. Someone who will help you through whatever it is you're going through.' She waves her hand at the room. 'Whatever *this* is, because believe me—'

Lisa's face stiffens. 'Have you finished?'

The rest of what Catherine had been going to say, freezes in her mouth. The interruption, the clipped and brittle tone Lisa has used, is worse than any of the lairy comments made by her students.

Catherine's never seen her like this before and the truth is a bitter pill. Gary had been right all the time. The awful things happening recently only started after Lisa joined the school.

Maybe the photographs of her brother are the clue. What if there's some link to Aled that she doesn't know about?

'Did you ever meet my brother?' Catherine moves closer to Lisa, waves the photographs in her face. 'Tell me the truth. What do you know about him? What have you heard?'

'Your brother is dead.' Lisa's voice is defensive. She blinks behind her glasses. 'It was years ago... You told me yourself. What makes you think I'd ever have met him?'

Catherine pushes fingers deep into her hair. She has no idea. But now she knows that the girl lied about being Gary's half-sister, anything seems possible. She doesn't trust her. Doesn't trust anyone anymore.

'Who are you, Lisa? Why are you in my home? You said it was because you were related to Gary, but that was a lie. Everything you told us is a lie.'

She can't think straight; too many thoughts are racing through her head.

Lisa is standing by the chest of drawers, watching her. She looks tired, her face pale, but even so, there's a natural beauty to her. A glow to her skin that Catherine can only achieve with expensive serums, a shine to her hair that she no longer has.

It's only now a terrible thought comes to her and she presses a hand to her chest.

'Oh, my God. Is it Gary you've been after all this time? Did you worm your way into the house to seduce him?' Her mind is working overtime. When she'd seen them through the window, she'd thought the argument they were having had been because Gary didn't like his sister being there... that Lisa being in their house was too much of a reminder of his father. But what if it had been a lovers' tiff?

'Have you been sleeping with my husband?'

Lisa steps back, the shock on her face genuine.

'Of course not.'

Then what? There was the money she'd seen Gary give her. The money that Lisa had transferred from her bag to her holdall, along with Aled's photographs.

'Maybe not now,' she continues. 'But what about before? Were you blackmailing Gary?'

Feeling dizzy, Catherine puts her hand out to the wall to steady herself. Because nothing adds up. Nothing makes sense anymore.

'I've never slept with your husband.' There's a note of disgust in Lisa's voice. '*Never*. You've got it wrong. So, so wrong.'

'Have I?' Catherine folds her arms. 'Tell me, Lisa, why should I believe this when everything else you've told me has been a lie?'

'Because it's true.'

Catherine's head snaps round. It's not Lisa who's spoken but Gary's voice she's heard. He's standing in the doorway, his face pale. Tense. She hadn't heard the front door. Hadn't realised he was home.

She looks accusingly at her husband.

'Why would I believe you wouldn't want to sleep with her?' She points to Lisa. 'Look at her. She's gorgeous. Don't tell me you haven't noticed. Haven't thought about it.'

Gary's face slackens, making him look older. 'I tried to tell you, but you hung up on me. Blocked my calls. What you're thinking is way off the mark.'

'And what *is* the mark, Gary? You've always liked your women younger. Enjoyed dominating them... that feeling of control. Power. What's changed?'

Gary looks pained, her barb hitting its mark.

'What's changed,' he says, his voice full of resentment. 'Is that Lisa wasn't lying when she said she was related to me.'

'What?' Catherine stares from one to the other. 'What do you mean?'

His face is grim.

'Lisa thinks she's my daughter.'

THIRTY-SIX

Catherine leans back against the wall. Afraid she's going to faint or be sick – maybe both. It's too much to take in. Too absurd.

'It's not true, Cath.' Gary had been waiting for her to respond, but now he looks at her beseechingly. 'You know it isn't.'

There's a wicker chair in the bedroom and Lisa has moved to it. Her legs are tucked under her and she's watching the two of them as though seeing how things will play out.

Catherine turns on her. 'Why are you lying? Tell me, Lisa. What can you possibly gain from all this?'

Gary answers for her. 'It's because she's desperate.' He points a finger at his temple. 'Crazy! She doesn't know what she's talking about. All this time, the girl's been blackmailing me. The money you saw me give her wasn't a bribe to get her out of the house as I told you. It was to stop her doing what she threatened to do... tell you the truth.' He shoots Lisa a dark look. 'Or what she *believes* is the truth. The girl's nothing but a fantasist.'

Catherine's voice is tight.

'If that's so... why didn't you simply tell me? What the hell made you play along with the charade that she was your sister?'

'Because I was desperate. I didn't know what else to do. When I came to pick you up that evening and Lisa said I was her half-brother, I didn't know what was going on. I hadn't seen Anne since she was a kid and presumed she'd changed her name for some reason, but when Ellen called you out of the classroom, Lisa dumped it on me... who she really was. She said she'd tell you the truth unless I went along with her story and I didn't know if you'd believe me if I told you she wasn't my daughter. I had no choice but to pretend.'

'But why you?' Nothing's making any sense. 'If it was to make money, there were other people Lisa could have chosen. You hadn't even met her until the day she asked if she could move in.'

Gary shifts uncomfortably. 'It's because I knew her mother.'

Catherine's whole world comes crashing down. 'Are you serious?'

'It was a long time ago, Cath. It didn't mean anything.'

Her voice is cold. 'Then why don't you tell me.'

'We worked at the same school and I'd already been there a few years when she joined.'

'Her name was Dawn, Gary.' Lisa points an accusing finger at him. 'My mother's name was Dawn.'

'Yes, I'm sorry. Dawn. I was asked to show her the ropes.' His neck has reddened and he rubs at it. 'It wasn't as if we were properly seeing each other, I suppose you'd call it a fling. Anyway, it hadn't been going on very long when she just upped and left the school.' He chews at his lip, the memory clearly painful to him. 'No one knew why she'd gone or where. I didn't know she was pregnant. No one knew.'

Catherine looks at Lisa, then back at her husband.

'Why in all the years we've been together have you never told me this?'

He shrugs. 'What's to tell? Like I say it was something and nothing and if it hadn't been for this kid turning up here, forcing her way into our family, I *still* wouldn't have known.'

'How old was she, Gaz?'

'What?'

'Lisa's mother. How old?'

'I don't know.' He scuffs at the bed leg with the tip of his shoe. 'Nineteen? Twenty? She was a student. Doing her second-year placement.'

'And you? How old were *you*?'

'What has that to do with anything?'

Catherine shakes her head to rid herself of the image. 'A lot. Jesus, Gary. The girl was a teenager... not long out of school herself. You should have been helping her, not preying on her.'

'For God's sake. It wasn't preying! We were both consenting adults. She knew what she was doing.'

'Then why would she leave the school so suddenly?' It's not adding up and from Gary's expression she can see there's more. Something he isn't telling her. 'If she knew about the baby before she handed in her notice, why didn't she tell you?'

'Because the baby wasn't mine. Lisa *isn't* my daughter. We hadn't had sex for weeks.'

There's something off about him. A nervous shifting of his eyes that she's seen in her students' when they're trying to get out of something. The protestations too strong. Too emphatic. *The lady doth protest too much.* Except this is no scene from Hamlet – it's her life and the person protesting is her husband.

'Now who's the liar?' Lisa is out of her chair. She'd been so quiet they'd forgotten about her. 'Are you saying you don't want me?'

'I'm saying you're not my daughter. That you're mistaken.' He turns to Catherine. 'Ask Ross. He'll tell you. We were sharing a flat back then. You've always accused us of being in each other's pockets... well, it was no different back then. We were both on the local football team, were training most nights after school, and there was no time for women. In fact, that's why I put an end to it with Dawn.' He stops, satisfied. Clearly pleased with what he's come up with. 'So there's nothing more to say on the matter. The whole thing is stupid.'

'I think there *is* more to say.' Catherine's attention is on Lisa now. 'You went to so much trouble, Lisa. Not just to get into my house but to make sure you got rid of me. Why would you do that?' She folds her arms, fights to keep the sarcasm out of her voice. 'Please do tell me. I'd love to know.'

'Do what, Catherine? I never did anything.'

'Don't make me laugh. The car fire. The writing on my windscreen. The way you broke into the school's system and altered Jake's coursework. God, the list is so long I barely know where to begin.'

Lisa shakes her head sadly. 'The only crime I committed is accepting Gary's money. It was foolish of me to take his bribe when the threat of telling you the truth, that I was his daughter not his half-sister, would have been enough for him to let me stay here. He was terrified of you knowing.'

'It was blackmail, Cath! You have to believe me.'

'Shut up, Gary.' She turns back to Lisa. 'But why do it at all? Why did you want to live here in our house?'

'Because I thought that living close to my dad would help us bond.'

'But that's just the point.' Gary's face is red. 'I'm not your bloody dad.'

Catherine holds up her hand. Glares at him. 'Let her finish.'

Lisa folds her arms. 'Like I said, I thought Gary and I would bond and that, when the time was right, when you were used to me being here, we'd be able to tell you who I really was. But as I've got to know him better, I've started to see a side of Gary I don't like. The sexist jokes he made to Ross when he came round, but the worst thing was hearing Gary tell Ross that they were both bloody lucky they'd never had kids to cramp their style.' Lisa pulls a tissue out of her pocket and blows her nose. 'The father I'd created in my head... he wouldn't have said those things. He'd be the one I could go to if I was struggling. The person I could turn to when I was down. Gary wasn't that person and I'm glad you know because I don't think I even want him to be now.'

Gary's pacing the room.

'She's making it all up, Cath. Trying to get you to feel sorry for her. Of course it was her who did all those things. She wanted to scare you. To drive you out of the house and out of your job. Get rid of you to punish me because she knew I didn't want her as my daughter.' He stops in front of Lisa. Folds his arms. 'Don't want a daughter at all. She knew that if I lost you, Cath, I'd be losing the only thing that mattered to me.'

'Lies.' Lisa's face remains deadpan. 'All lies.'

Catherine offers up the palms of her hands in confusion. 'But you were the only one capable of changing Jake's course-work. The only one with the means. Why deny it?'

Lisa shakes her head sadly. 'Because what's the point?' She takes off her glasses and wipes them on a corner of her cardigan. 'Even though you access the school computer all the time when you're at home, and it's pretty likely Gary knows your password, you've already made up your mind to believe him over me.'

Catherine looks at her suspiciously. 'You keep saying that he's your father, but how do you know for sure? What if we go and talk to your mother together? Get this mess sorted out.'

'My mother's dead.' The unemotional way Lisa says it, shocks Catherine.

'Dead?'

'Yes, when I was three. She took her own life. With no father's name on my birth certificate and no other family, I was brought up in foster care.'

'I'm sorry, Lisa. That's incredibly sad, but it still doesn't explain how you know about Gary.'

'Let's just say I did a lot of research. Rang the school where my mum did her teacher training and found there were still a few members of staff who had been around when she was there as a student. I waited outside the school at the end of the day and, eventually, one came out who I recognised from her photo on the website. When I explained who I was, she was happy to talk to me.' She looks at Gary. 'Okay no one knew exactly what had gone on between the two of you, but there had been gossip. Hearsay. Your name had been mentioned—'

'For God's sake. I've heard enough. You, young lady,' – Gary's face has darkened – 'can get the fuck out of my house. When you first told me your little story I was shocked, but I had no choice but to let you stay. Now though...' He takes a step towards her. 'Catherine knows the truth and you've tried my patience enough. I'm going out to calm down, and when I get back, I expect you to have slung your hook.' He walks over to Catherine. Puts an arm around her shoulder. 'My wife and I have a lot to talk about.'

The weight of his arm on her shoulder feels oppressive. She looks up at him, seeing a man she's not sure she likes... not entirely sure she trusts. She shrugs his arm away.

'Don't think this changes anything, Gary. These last few days your loyalty has been tested and you've failed miserably.'

She picks up her bag, goes to move past him, but he catches her arm. 'Please, Cath. There's no reason for you not to move back here. None of this is true, you know. She's a scheming cow. Can't you see she's making it all up?'

Catherine shakes her head sadly. 'What I can see is what a weak man you are. I've always suspected it but loved you too much to delve deeper. I'm going back to Ross's tonight. When I've decided what I'm going to do after that, I'll let you know.'

Shock settles on his face. 'Ross's?'

'Yes, where did you think I've been staying?' There's a certain satisfaction in saying it. 'He's my friend too, you know.'

She pushes past him and this time he makes no move to stop her. A part of her wants to look back to see what Lisa is doing, but what's the point? She hasn't a clue what to make of the things the girl's said... or the things she's left unsaid. All she knows is she can't live in this house with Gary anymore. Needs space and time to work out what's going on. What's real and what isn't.

As she passes the hall table, she sees Lisa's name badge and key card. It makes Catherine remember Lynne's outstretched hand. Her words, *Your lanyard, Cath. I have to take it. I'm sorry*, and it makes her anger rise again. Without thinking, she snatches the card from the table with the idea of slipping it into her bag but then she stops herself. Places it back on the table.

She gets into her car and pulls away and as she reaches the junction, a glance in her rear-view mirror shows Gary striding down the road in the other direction. He's walking fast and she knows he'll go and have too much to drink at The Crown. She shouldn't care, but despite everything, a part of her hopes Lisa will use her common sense and leave before he gets back.

Because Gary, when he's feeling wronged, is not someone you'd want to encounter after he's had a few drinks.

THIRTY-SEVEN

Ross puts down his box of folders. Pulls off his tie with a grimace.

'Jesus, I fucking hate wearing these things. No wonder the kids take them off as soon as they're out of the school gate.' He slips off his jacket and hangs it over the back of the chair. Sees the despair on Catherine's face and goes over to her. 'I'm sorry, Cath. Listen to me harping on about ties when you must be feeling dreadful.' He puts a hand on her shoulder. 'Do you want to talk about it?'

Catherine appreciates his concern. She should tell him the real reason for her misery, but the bombshell of Lisa announcing she's Gary's daughter isn't something she's ready to discuss with him. Not yet anyway. Not when she hasn't had time to take it in herself. But that's not the only reason. The truth is, she's scared of sharing because if Ross were to take Gary's side in this, it would be like she was losing him as well. And that's the last thing she wants when she's in desperate need of a friend.

No, it's better to stay on safer ground. Keep to herself the shock of finding out Gary might have a daughter. That Lisa has been lying to her... Gary too, most likely. And who is she to believe when they've both accused the other of terrible things – Gary of bribery and Lisa of blackmail.

Catherine sinks her head into her hands. Tired of it all. The different threads slipping through her grasp the more she tries to keep hold of them and make sense of them.

'Cath?' There's concern in Ross's voice.

She lowers her hands. Turns teary eyes to him. The need to share her worries too strong now to ignore. 'I know it sounds mad, Ross, but I think it was Lisa who changed Jake's coursework. She not only had the means but also the motive.'

Ross frowns. 'The motive? Has something happened to make you come to that conclusion?'

'It doesn't matter.' Catherine breathes in deeply. Her reference to a motive had slipped out and now she doesn't know what to do with it. 'Forget I said anything.'

But Ross isn't going to let it go.

'Come on, Cath. Let me in. What possible motive could the girl have? She's Gary's half-sister. You're her mentor. What would she have to gain by setting you up like that?'

Catherine sees from the look on Ross's face that it's too late to backtrack. Maybe once he knows everything, he'll be able to help. It would feel good to have someone to talk to, and trust, again.

She fights to control her voice. 'Gary thinks she's trying to ruin our perfect marriage.'

'Gary thinks that? Well, clearly she's succeeded, but that still doesn't explain why.'

She pauses a moment. Preparing herself. Hating what she's about to say.

'Because Gary might be her father.'

'What?' His confusion turns to shock and he leans forward, fingers steepled against his nose. 'Fuck.'

'Exactly.' Despite her reservation, she'd been right to share it with him as, immediately, it's as if a weight has been lifted from her shoulders. 'Gary thinks she's a fantasist. She'd lost her mum when she was very young, too young to remember, and thought that if she was living in our house, she'd be able to get closer to Gary. Bond with him. Even though he'd never heard of her.'

'But why pretend she was his sister?'

'She says she thought I wouldn't let her stay if I knew she was his daughter. Was biding her time before dropping the bombshell on me, thinking we'd all play happy families and live happily ever after once it was out in the open. What I can't believe is that as well as going along with it, Gary actually gave her money to ensure she'd keep it quiet.'

Ross turns worried eyes to her. 'And Gary? Has he admitted to it? To being her father, I mean?'

Catherine shakes her head. 'No. Quite the opposite. He told her she was talking nonsense, refused to believe a word of it. So now the fairy tale is broken. No happy ending for Lisa, or me come to that, because his rejection of her has made things a hundred times worse. She's out to punish him and I'm the fall-out. Breaking up his family as good a way as any of paying him back for not having been there for her when she was a child. For rejecting her a second time.'

Ross is quiet, his face solemn, and Catherine wonders what he's thinking.

'Please say something, Ross. Your best friend has been accused of having fathered a child he says he knew nothing about. Doesn't that mean anything to you?'

'Of course it does.' His voice is tight. 'But Lisa can't be his daughter. It's nonsense. She doesn't even look like him.'

Catherine's heart sinks. It's what she'd been afraid of... Ross choosing sides.

'A lot of kids don't look like their parents. That doesn't mean anything.'

'You're right, I suppose, but all this doesn't explain why you're here. Now Lisa has been rumbled, I'd have thought you'd be straight back home patching things up with Gaz.'

Guilt settles on her. She'd had her suspicions about Gary, but they hadn't been right.

'I know. It's what the old Catherine would do.'

And yet there's something that's stopping her... the knowledge that he's no longer the man she'd married.

Before she can say more, her mobile rings. She takes it out of her pocket and sees it's Lynne from reception. Knows she has to answer it. It might be something to do with Jake.

'Hello, Lynne.'

'Hi, Cath. This is a courtesy call because you asked that I let you know as soon as I heard anything about Jake. Well, I have now. The hospital called the school this afternoon to let us know he's out of his coma.' She lowers her voice. 'I shouldn't really be passing this information on, but you did ask and, well, you *are* my friend. I'd be grateful if you'd keep it confidential, though.'

'Of course.' Catherine gets up from the settee. Walks over to the window on the other side of the room where Ross won't overhear. 'Has he said anything yet? Does he know who did this to him?'

'No. He's not spoken... is still very sleepy. But they're hoping he might be well enough for the police to interview in the next day or so. I just wanted you to know in case you were worrying.'

Guilt floods through her. With everything else, Jake hasn't been uppermost in her mind.

'Thanks. It was good of you to stick your neck out for me.'

'It was no trouble. Take care of yourself, Cath.'

'You too.'

She ends the call. Sees Ross has got up and has poured himself a scotch.

'I hope you're okay with me drinking this.' He taps at the glass with his fingernail. 'It's been quite a day.'

'Go ahead. It's your home, Ross.' At this moment in time, there's nothing Catherine would like more than a large glass of wine, but she resists the urge.

'Ta... and I meant what I said. While you're here, you must think of this as your home too.'

Catherine parts the curtain at the window and looks out. The unfamiliar street with its line of parked cars, its houses that would once have been grand but are now divided into flats, makes her feel lonely.

'I can't stay here forever, though. At some point, I'll have to go back and sort this mess out with Gary.'

Ross raises his glass to his lips. 'You think you'll go back to him?'

'I don't know.' A well of sadness opens up within her. Last night she'd lain in her bed, the mattress too hard for her to get comfortable, and thought about all that she'd lost. Remembering the good times she and Gary had shared in the early days. The laughs. The fun. She turns from the window. Leans her back against the radiator and looks at Ross. Willing him to understand. 'Whatever he's done, I still love him. He's let me down, but I don't know whether I'm ready, or strong enough, to end it.'

'Even though he's lied to you? Has fathered a child he won't admit to and accused the girl of making it up?'

'We don't know for sure if Lisa's his daughter, even though he admitted he knew her birth mother.'

'He did?' He looks troubled.

'Yes, she was a student teacher at the school he was teaching at, but he was adamant whatever they'd had together was over and that they hadn't made love in the weeks leading up to her leaving the school. That means the timings wouldn't have been right for the pregnancy, and if he's telling the truth, then Lisa can't be his. She would have—'

She stops. There's something about Ross's expression she doesn't like.

'What is it, Ross?'

He doesn't answer. Continues to look at her.

'Is something wrong?' Catherine crosses the room. Stands over him. 'Do you know something?'

'You forget I worked there too.'

'Of course... and shared a flat.' How could she have forgotten. He'd have known everything that had been going on. 'Please, Ross. If you've any information about this, you have to tell me.'

Ross turns his head away from her. The muscles of his jaw tight. 'I can't.'

'You must.' Catherine's insides twist unpleasantly. 'I know you're his best friend, but you're mine too. Please, Ross. This is important.'

'Okay.' His voice is weary. He still can't meet her eye. 'But if I do, you must swear you won't hold it against me. I did what I did because I was young. Stupid. I thought protecting my best friend was my job.'

The twisting sensation in Catherine's stomach worsens. 'Protecting him from what? What did Gary do, Ross?' She's scared now. Terrified of what the truth might be.

'I was an idiot. I gave him an alibi.' Ross's voice falters. He covers his face with his hands. 'When he said he hadn't made love to the girl in weeks, he was telling the truth.'

'I don't understand. So, what's the problem?'

'Oh, Jesus!' He rubs a hand over his short hair. 'Can't you see? He didn't make love to Lisa's mother because love didn't come into it. It was purely sex. What Gary didn't tell you was that on the night before Dawn handed in her notice, he went into her classroom after school – after the other teachers on their floor had left. She'd told him she didn't want him around anymore, but he didn't believe it. He was an arrogant sod back then and thought he'd be able to persuade her to start things up with him again. When she said she wasn't interested, it didn't go down well. You know Gary, how sometimes he won't take no for an answer, well he was worse when he was younger. Felt entitled, if you know what I mean.'

He stops, his face reflecting his pain. But he doesn't need to say anything more. The rest of the story is only too obvious.

Catherine sinks to her haunches, the enormity, the shock, of what Ross has just told her too weighty for her body and mind to take.

She was right all along: she can't trust her husband.

THIRTY-EIGHT

'Tell me everything.' Catherine's emotions are running wild. Everything she's known, everything she's believed, turned on its head. 'We're not discussing a drunken night out with the lads after football or a fumble at the office Christmas party. You're saying that Gary raped this girl. Raped Dawn.'

The simple act of saying her name makes it real. Makes it so much worse. She feels sick. Can hardly look at him. That he'd *known* it. Said nothing.

'Yes.' He sounds wretched. 'Don't hate me, Cath. I'm only the messenger.'

Anger flashes. 'Maybe. But you lied for him, Ross. Covered it up.'

He shakes his head. 'I didn't lie... not about that anyway. I didn't need to because no one knew. She never told anyone what happened.'

'I don't understand. Then how...'

'I'd have been just as in the dark as everyone else if Gary hadn't told me.'

'Oh my God. He actually *told* you?' She can hardly believe it.

'Yes. It was about a week later and he'd gone on a bender. Had taken time off work, saying it was flu, although he'd been fine the day before. He shut himself in his room and wouldn't let me in. I didn't know it then, but he was scared, Cath. Terrified by what he'd done and the consequences if people found out. After the third day, I began to get really worried. He hadn't eaten. Hadn't showered. So I didn't bother knocking. Just went straight in and found him in bed, dressed in the same clothes he'd been wearing the last time I'd seen him. His breath, the room, stank of booze. It was vile.' He presses the tips of two fingers to the space between his brows and circles them. Remembering. 'I got him some food. Stayed with him until he'd eaten something and had started to sober up. And when he was halfway human again, I made him tell me what the hell was going on.'

Catherine's face is slack with shock. 'And he admitted it?'

'Eventually. Like I say, he was terrified. You should have seen him... like a kid with nowhere to run.'

'*He* was terrified?' She can hardly believe what she's hearing. 'What about the poor girl? What about Dawn? Alone with him in that classroom. Not knowing what he was going to do until it was too late.'

Even though she fights against it, Catherine's transported back to the public toilets again. The click of the lighter. The smoke from the burning rag drifting under the door. Unable to guess who it was out there. Terrified of what they might do.

This is how Dawn must have felt in those moments when Gary had been in the classroom with her all those years ago. Uncertain. Nervous of having said and done the wrong thing. Aware, too late, that she was dealing with fire.

'I know. I know. I should have said something.' Ross throws himself back onto the settee. Screws his eyes tight. 'I had nightmares about it for weeks after. Came close to telling the police on more than one occasion.'

Catherine shoots him a look. 'Then what stopped you?'

He opens his eyes again. Locks them with hers. 'I don't know. That I was a fool probably and because Gary was my best mate. For some idiotic reason, that mattered to me more at that time. You have to understand, Cath, that we'd spent the whole of our school and university years together. Had been through good times and bad, always knowing we had each other's backs. We'd gone on to do our teacher training at different colleges, but when we ended up working at the same school together, it was back to how it had always been. Like old times. Like we'd never been apart. And it was a bloody good laugh – hanging out together in the staffroom after the bell rang and at football coaching.'

He looks out of the window and Catherine wonders whether it's not his street he's seeing but a playing field in a school long ago. Him overseeing the training drills. Gary on the touchline blowing his whistle and shouting orders to the goalie. Striving to recapture the heady time they'd spent together before it had all gone wrong.

'When he handed in his notice,' he continues, 'decided to do supply teaching instead, it wasn't the same there. I lost my passion for teaching. It's why I changed schools. Applied to Greenfield Comp in the hope I could rekindle the flame.'

'You think that's why Gary finally left teaching? Because of what he did?'

He'd told her it was because the money was crap. Because he was fed up with the paperwork that dogged his life. Couldn't hack it anymore.

'I think so, yes. But, the strange thing was, about a week after it happened, when Dawn had upped and left but he was still teaching there, he retracted what he'd told me. Said I should ignore what he'd said as he'd been off his head at the time and it had just been a load of nonsense. Yes, he'd had sex with Dawn that evening in the classroom, but she'd been a willing participant. He'd never forced her.'

'And you believed him?'

'God, how I wanted to.' He rakes fingers through his hair. 'I'd known Gary for such a long time he was like a brother to me. So, as time went by and he continued to act like everything was okay, I told myself his second version of events was the one I should trust. If what he'd told me originally had been true, he'd never have been able to teach classes as if nothing had happened. Days went by and it became easier to believe him.' His fingers are worrying at the material at the knees of his trousers. He looks down at them, then back at Catherine. 'But you know the saying *what soberness conceals, drunkenness reveals*?'

Catherine nods. She's heard of it.

'Well, I couldn't get it out of my head. Because, deep down, I think I knew the truth. No one in their right minds would confess to something as awful as that unless it had happened.'

'And Dawn never made a complaint? Never went to the police?'

He shakes his head. 'No. She can't have, otherwise they'd have been straight over to our flat, or to the school, to question him. I really have no idea why she didn't.'

Catherine looks away from him, knowing the answer. Dawn hadn't told them for fear of making things worse. Making it real. And when she'd found out she was pregnant, she'd no doubt wanted to distance herself further from what had happened. Because loving her baby unconditionally could only be done if the spectre of her violent conception wasn't hanging over them.

Catherine had been pacing, but now she stands in front of Ross. 'You haven't explained the alibi thing. Why he needed one?'

'That's easy. News got round that Dawn was pregnant and Gary panicked. The story he spun to me was that he didn't want people thinking the kid was his as he'd never wanted children and didn't want anything to do with the pregnancy. But I reckon it was because he was scared Dawn might change her mind and tell the police the truth. He begged me to say I'd been with him the evening it had happened. Tell anyone who asked that we'd been in his classroom discussing the interschool five-a-side match we'd helped the PE department organise for the Year 12s. Stupidly, I agreed.'

'So, what about Lisa?'

'Lisa?' He looks confused. 'What *about* her?'

'Surely, she has the right to know the truth.'

'Maybe. But if Dawn had wanted it to be made known, don't you think her pregnancy would have been the catalyst for her doing something about it? Going to the police? The fact she didn't must account for something.'

Catherine sinks down onto the settee next to him. She'd come to the same conclusion herself. That Dawn, for reasons of her own, had wanted the truth of her baby's conception to remain hidden.

He looks sideways at her. 'You can't go back home, Cath. If Gary finds out I've told you...'

There's a hollow pain in her chest. How could she go back anyway... knowing what she now knows? Yet, it doesn't feel right doing nothing. If Gary had been capable of something like this when he was a younger man, wasn't it possible he could do it again? Might already have.

The thought is a terrible one and it occurs to her that for all the years they've been together, she might never have known Gary at all.

THIRTY-NINE

'You're safe here.' Ross puts his arm around Catherine. 'I know I was Gary's friend before yours, but I care about you, Cath. I always have, I'd never let anything happen to you.'

Catherine's breath catches at the back of her throat. 'What do you think Gary would do if he found out I know everything?'

'He *doesn't* know and we have to keep it that way. Your greatest hope is to believe he's changed. That he'd never do anything like that again.'

She leans her head on his shoulder. 'Do *you* believe that?'

'I have to because to think otherwise is too terrible to contemplate.'

Tears leak from her eyes. Run down her cheek and chin, dampening the neck of her top. 'I can't believe this is all happening. I wish we could go back to how we were before.'

'You're crying?' Ross tucks a strand of damp hair behind her ear. 'Please don't.'

Catherine looks up at him. Glad that he's there. That he hasn't chosen Gary over her. For then she'd have no one.

'I can't help it.'

'God, I'd do anything to make you feel better.'

To Catherine's surprise, Ross dips his head to hers and she feels his lips on her own, the warmth and gentle pressure of them giving her comfort. It happens so quickly that she has no time to think or decide what to make of it and, for a second or two, she forgets herself. Her lips moving against his, her body responding.

But then she remembers where she is, who she's with, and pulls away. Shocked at what's just happened.

'Oh, God. I'm sorry, Ross, but I can't do this.'

She puts a hand to his cheek. Feels the warm flush of it under her palm.

'No, I'm the one who should be sorry.' He moves away, his face stoical. 'It's too soon. I'm an idiot.'

'You're not. You're my very dear friend. But you're right. It *is* too soon.'

Ross runs a hand down his face. 'And, despite everything, you're still in love with your husband. I wasn't thinking.' He pauses. Shakes his head. 'It's just that you looked so lovely sitting there with your beautiful sad eyes that I couldn't help myself.'

Catherine takes his hand. 'Don't beat yourself up about it. I'm flattered, really I am. It's not often a man gives me as much as a second look these days. More often than not I feel invisible.'

'And Gary makes you feel that way?'

She nods. 'Sometimes.'

'Then he's more of an idiot than me.'

Catherine takes in Ross's close-cropped hair. The longish sideburns that he tells her he's had since the days when Paul Weller was in the charts. He's still a good-looking man and a lot of women would give their right arm for a date with him. She thinks of Karen. Wonders why it ended.

'We can't be anything more than friends. You know that, Ross. Don't you? It would spoil everything.'

'Yes. I know.' He smiles ruefully. Gives her a brotherly hug. 'Please. Forget it ever happened. I have.'

Catherine's relieved. 'And we're all good?'

''Course we are. I'll go and start supper, yeah?'

'Need a hand?'

'Nah. This is the guy who teaches Shakespeare for a living. The instructions on the oven chips bag are not going to defeat me.'

Despite the shock of everything that's happened, she forces a laugh. 'If you're sure.'

'I'm sure.'

'Okay then.' Catherine picks up the TV controller and points it at the screen. Flicks through the channels until she finds something mind-numbing. She's just watching an estate agent show a couple round a house in Spain, is listening to the soothing background sound of Ross opening kitchen cupboards and clattering pans in the next room, when her phone pings.

Without thinking, she opens it. Reads the message.

I know the truth about your brother.

It pings again and a second message pops up.

She stares at it, blood roaring in her ears.

'Your dinner is served, madame.'

Ross puts a plate of breaded cod and chips on the table. Draws cutlery from his pocket and holds them out to her. When Catherine doesn't respond, he frowns.

'What's up? Don't you like fish?' He wipes his hands on his trousers. 'I caught it myself… not.'

Catherine looks up at him, knowing she has to say something. He's seen her face. She'd not been able to hide it from him.

'Someone's sent me a text.'

'Yeah? What does it say?'

She reads aloud the first message, then puts the phone back in her pocket.

'*I know the truth about your brother*. What the hell is that supposed to mean?'

She looks away. 'When Aled was a teenager he had problems...' She stops. Sees his face. 'You know, don't you? Bloody hell, what *hasn't* my husband told you?'

Ross holds up his hands. 'You're right, it's true. He told me a long time ago – before you were working at Greenfield, in fact. But he only did it because he was worried about you. Said your brother had broken into your classroom one night at the old school and had died in the fire. Mentioned his death had affected you badly and that you needed a fresh start.'

'Is that why you got me the job at your school? Because you felt sorry for me?' She'd thought she'd won the position on merit. Because, despite everything, she was a good teacher. 'Jesus, Ross. All this time and you never said.'

He rubs a hand around his neck. 'I didn't want you to feel bad about it.'

'Well, you didn't make a very good job of it. How do you think I'm feeling now?'

'I know, I know and I'm sorry.' He taps at the phone. 'But *this* is what you should be worrying about now. This message. Who do you think sent it?'

'Whoever it is, I wish they'd said what they know about Aled.'

He looks at her strangely. 'What else *is* there to know? The guy's been dead for years.'

A creeping chill has enfolded Catherine. She hasn't told Ross about the second message. The one with only a single word written on the screen. *Murderer*. It's the same word that had been scrawled on the windscreen of her car and the truth screams at her. Someone knows what happened and it isn't hard to guess who.

It's Lisa... it has to be.

While they'd all been living under the same roof, she'd found out she'd been snooping... had caught her, red-handed, with photographs of Aled in her bag. Now she wishes she'd pressed her more for a reason. Had she been digging for information? Had she found out the truth?

'I have to know, once and for all, what this is about. I can't go on like this.'

Ross takes her hands in his. 'Don't do anything rash, Cath.'

'But I have to know.' Catherine looks at him earnestly. 'I'm sick of it all, Ross. Tomorrow I'm going to go back to the house. Talk to them both. I don't trust either of them.'

'Don't do that. There's something not right about all this.'

'I have to.'

Ross sighs. 'Then I'll come with you. But you must promise me one thing... that you'll leave it until the morning. Sleep on it. We can talk again when things aren't so raw and decide the best thing to do. It might well be something best left to the police.'

Catherine nods. But, whatever he thinks, she's not going to let Ross come with her. She's also not going to involve the police. For if they find out she was responsible for her brother's death... her life will be over.

FORTY

Catherine wakes suddenly. There's a glow on the bedside table. Her phone lighting up the space around it with another message. She reaches out a hand and pulls her mobile towards her, her insides knitted tight. It's the same number as before and she rolls over and switches on the bedside light, wondering whether to open it. But when she looks closer, it's not a message, it's a video.

Catherine's breathing becomes shallow. She knows that no good will come from not looking. Bracing herself, she taps on the screen, stifling a cry with her hand at the sight of the flame that dances in front of her eyes. No person there. No face to show who holds the lighter that slides into view, then away again.

It's night-time on the screen, the sky black, and now the phone is moving, taking her through a gate and up a driveway. Making her feel as if she's there too... at the front door of a house.

But it's not any old house.

Her heart hammers in her ears as she realises it's *her* house – not the one she's in now of course, not Ross's flat, but the one she left a couple of days ago. A house where, upstairs, her husband will be sleeping. Maybe Lisa, too, if she refused to leave. The girl's childish books still on the shelf above the bed. Her only link to a childhood she wishes she could rewrite.

The phone moves nearer to the door, the screen brightening as the security light comes on. It hones in on the letterbox. On the rag that's stuffed in it, the protruding end dark with the liquid it's been soaked in. Then, as she watches, her fear gathering and growing, the flame passes in front of the rag. Not quite close enough to set it alight. The warning of what could come next, enough to stop her breath.

'No!'

Catherine drops the phone onto the bed, but the video has already ended. She stares at the screen terrified at what she's just seen. Jumping when the phone pings. Not another video, this time, but a message.

With shaking fingers, she opens it. Reads the words.

Does this bring back memories?

Catherine stares at the words, her heart beating wildly. She has to keep the writer engaged. Mustn't give them cause to touch the flame to the rag in her letterbox. Quickly she taps her own message back.

Just tell me what you want.

To speak to you. I know the truth.

She's filled with a sick rush of adrenaline and her thumbs tap across the letters on her screen.

Please don't do it. I don't live there anymore. It's only Gary who's there. Only my husband.

As the image of the flame and the rag stuffed into the letterbox comes back to her, she types faster.

Who is this? If it's you, Lisa, this isn't a joke.

She can see they're writing.

I'm your conscience. Do you know what it's like to have the flesh seared from your bones? The smell, Cath, is one that never leaves you. Even after you're dead.

She stares at the words. Bile rising. Thank God they don't know where she is... that she's in Ross's flat.

But Gary isn't. He's inside the house, probably pissed out of his head. Dead to the world. Alone. Because the more Catherine thinks about it, the more certain she is that there's no way Gary would have let Lisa stay in the house another night. Not now her real identity is in the open.

It has to be her who's outside their house. She must have found out what Gary did to her mother, how she was conceived. Must be bent on wreaking this terrible revenge. Finding out the truth would have been devastating for her, but whatever he's done, Gary doesn't deserve *this*. Is Lisa capable of carrying it through?

Despite everything, her husband is not a total monster. She couldn't have survived without him, back when they met. Because, even though she hadn't been physically hurt in the fire at her old school, the awfulness of it had remained with her. Destroying her confidence. Contributing to the breakdown that had left her unable to teach effectively. Unable to live a normal life.

Gary had saved her and now she has to save *him*.

Catherine waits. Her heart almost forgetting to beat.

Wondering what they're thinking. What it would take to flick the lighter and touch the flame to the rag. She could phone the police, but by the time they got there, it would be too late. The arsonist is already at her front door... a click of the lighter away from burning down the house with Gary inside. She's the only one who can stop them and she needs to succeed where she failed before.

Quickly, she types.

Are you there? Please say something.

Seconds go by. Then the reply.

Meet me.

The two words give her hope.

Where?

Your classroom in an hour.

Catherine doesn't like the thought of it. The dark empty corridors. The echoing classrooms with their blank windows looking out onto an empty playground. Whoever's holding the phone is playing with her – knows she'll be remembering the heat and the smoke and the stench of her old classroom in flames. But what choice does she have?

I know it's you, Lisa. Just tell me you won't do it. That you'll get away from our house.

But there's no reassurance. Just a final warning.

If you tell the police, you know what will happen.

A flame emoji appears, then they're gone.

Catherine looks at the time on her phone. Sees it is two thirty. With anxiety building inside her, she throws back the duvet and gets out of bed then, without turning on the light, she pulls on her clothes. Giving herself no time to think for fear of changing her mind.

She picks up her bag, digs inside it for her lanyard with the key card before remembering she'd given it back to Lynne. Damn. She thinks of the high fence. The automatic door to get into the school. How will she get in?

Stepping out onto the landing, she stands and listens. There's no sound from Ross's room and a thought occurs to her. She can take *his* card. Put it back again when she gets back home.

But where is it?

Catherine closes her eyes as she tries to remember if she'd seen him take it off. Seen him put it somewhere. Unable to remember, she takes a wild guess. By now her eyes have adjusted to the dark and she can see his large plastic box on the floor by the door, ready to take into school later. She hurries over to it, but a quick search reveals no lanyard. It's not on the side table either, and when she goes into the kitchen, she can't see it on the breakfast bar or any of the worktops.

She's standing in the living room, having searched everywhere she can think of, when she has a sobering thought. The lanyard must be in Ross's bedroom. He might not have taken it off at all when he came in but slipped it off when he got ready for bed. And now she's had the idea, she can picture it clearly – the way it had swung from his neck as he'd wrestled with his tie. She's going to have to go into his room to see, but if she wakes him, how will she explain what she's doing?

Time is not on her side and not knowing what else to do, Catherine goes back onto the landing. Listens at Ross's bedroom door. Hearing nothing, she presses down on the handle and opens it a crack. The room is dark, but the digital clock on Ross's bedside table gives enough light to see that he's lying on his front. His head turned away from her. One arm stretched across the other pillow.

His breathing is regular; he's sleeping soundly.

Slowly, Catherine picks her way across the room to the chair where he's thrown his clothes. With a quick look over her shoulder to make sure he's still asleep, she lifts his work trousers, biting her lip in apprehension when the buckle of his swinging belt makes contact with the chest of drawers. But Ross doesn't stir.

Knowing she needs to act quickly, she lifts his jumper, his shirt, feeling under them with her free hand. And as her fingers catch the sharp edge of the plastic key card, she allows herself a slow breath out.

Catherine puts the clothes back on the chair as she'd found them and makes to leave, but she hasn't even reached the open door when Ross moans. Turns over. One arm shoving back the duvet to reveal his bare chest, the hairs on it just a dark shadow, and the pale arc of his hip below his tan line.

She freezes, the lanyard clutched in her hand. Waiting for the moment when he'll open his eyes and ask her why she's in his room. But he doesn't. Instead, his breathing becomes heavier again and she forces her eyes away from his body. Hurries out of the door while she's got the chance.

As she closes the door behind her, her heart is racing. Her mind too. It's already past three and she'll need to hurry if she's to get to the school in time. And there's a reason she wants to get there first. There's something else she wants to do while she's there. Something very important.

FORTY-ONE

Catherine leaves her car in a side road. She locks the door and, staying in the shadows at the side of the pavement, hurries towards the red-brick building in the distance.

At this hour, the streets are empty and she's thankful; she doesn't want anyone to know she's here. Doesn't want to give anyone a reason to call the police when she lets herself onto the site.

When she reaches the metal fence, she stops, her eyes lifting to the security camera next to it. Not moving any closer, she pulls the hood of her sweatshirt over her head and carries on to a smaller gate around the side of the building. She presses Ross's name badge to the keypad and slips through as it opens. Then she waits in the shadow of the building, forcing her mind to remember the position of the cameras inside the school. Writing herself a mental map. When she hears the click of the gate that signals it's closed again, she ducks her head and runs across the open space towards a side door in the building. An emergency exit from the school's theatre wing. One that isn't monitored.

Her heart in her mouth, Catherine lets herself into the dark atrium and stands for a minute allowing her eyes to adjust. When she's happy she can see enough, she crosses the space between the chairs and the stage to the other side of the auditorium where there's a door leading into the main school building. The corridor beyond has no natural light, but she doesn't flick the light switch on the wall. Although it's unlikely any residents living near the school will be awake at this hour, she's not taking any chances.

As Catherine feels her way down the corridor, her fingers trailing the cold doors of the lockers, the familiar smell of the school follows her: the pine scent of the cleaning fluid used to wash the floors, the distinct sharp odour of the dry-erase markers they use on the boards, even the faint whiff of yesterday's canteen offering. And the emotion it creates, a terrible, gnawing sadness at all she's lost, vies for space with the apprehension of what's to come.

Lisa did this to me. She can't get the thought out of her head. *She's the one who forced me out of the school and out of my home. She's the one who's ruined my life.*

But even as she's thinking it, she knows that she can't blame her entirely. Gary played his part in it. A major part.

As she moves through the building, avoiding the main corridors and common areas where she knows she could be caught by the CCTV cameras on the wall, Catherine thinks of everything Ross told her about the terrible circumstances of Lisa's conception and Gary's involvement. She wants to forgive her, but how can she after everything she did?

And she's still not sure of her link to Aled. How could she know he'd died in the classroom?

Pushing open the double doors at the end of the corridor, she takes the lesser used back stairs to the first floor where her classroom is but a look at her watch shows her she's too early. Much too early. So, instead of turning right, she turns left towards Ellen's office.

She stops outside the door, the recent interview she'd had with the police coming back to her... but she can't worry about that. Opening the door, she goes in and moves quickly to the computer on Ellen's desk. Turning it on, she searches the home screen until she finds what she's looking for, then logs onto the school's network using the login details Lisa shared with her when she became her mentor. It doesn't take long to navigate to the place where the coursework folders are kept and when she finds the one belonging to Jake, she clicks through to the document history. Searching for the work she was supposed to have changed and finding the most recent modification.

Catherine stares at the screen, reading it a second time, unable to believe what she's seeing. She'd expected the changes to have come from Lisa's login, but they haven't. She squints at the screen still thinking that, even though it's right there in front of her eyes, she's made a mistake. But she hasn't. She sits heavily in Ellen's swivel chair trying to process it. Not understanding. Because the login details for that final modification to Jake's work aren't Lisa's.

They're Karen's.

The truth leaves her breathless. What could have made her do such a thing when she'd thought they were friends? And why the hell hadn't Ellen checked?

Knowing there's nothing she can do about it now, she takes a screenshot of the evidence, then reaches across the desk and switches on the small reading lamp. Maybe there's something else she's missed. Next to the computer, there's a two-tiered plastic filing tray half-full of letters and documents. The top one has an orange Post-it note attached to it. Reaching for it, Catherine reads the words scrawled in black marker. *Ring hospital about Jake.* A telephone number is written underneath it.

Catherine runs a finger over the words, remembering Lynne's phone call earlier telling her Jake had woken. That the police would be questioning him soon. She looks at her watch. Lisa will be here in twenty minutes, but she needs to know what happened to him. Who it was who attacked him.

The telephone is cool to the touch when she picks it up, but now it's in her hand, she's unsure what to do. She'd had the idea she could ring the hospital, pretend to be Ellen, but it's the middle of the night and the head teacher of Greenfield Comprehensive would hardly be ringing at this hour. Whoever answered the call would be suspicious. Might even call the police.

The police. That's it! She can't believe she hadn't thought of it before.

Catherine punches in the number on the Post-it and presses the phone to her ear. And as she waits, heart racing, for someone to answer, she searches her memory for the sound of PC Olds' voice. Wondering if she can replicate it.

'Greenfield General. How can I help you?'

Catherine clears her throat. Hopes for the best. 'It's PC Olds from Crowther Road Police Station. I know it's late, but I'm calling in relation to Jake Lloyd, the boy who was attacked outside Greenfield Comprehensive. The fact is, some new information has recently come in which I'd like to follow up on...' She stops, needing to regulate her uneven breathing before she continues. A part of her not wanting to hear the answer to what she's about to ask. 'So anything he's said, anything he's remembered about the attack, I'd like to hear it.'

'PC Olds you say?'

'Yes.'

There's a pause. 'If you could hold on a minute, I'll see what I can do.'

The phone goes silent and Catherine waits in Ellen's dark office. Terrified she's been found out. It isn't long, though, before the voice comes on again.

'I've spoken to the ward sister and you're in luck. Jake's

awake again and sitting up. He's also given her a pretty decent description of the person in question. The one who assaulted him.'

'Thank you for that.' Catherine fights to keep herself calm. 'If you could tell me exactly what the ward sister said to you, I'd be very grateful. It will give us a place to start once we come in to see him.'

'Yes, that's no problem. Jake didn't get a good look at their face because of the balaclava-style mask they had on, but they were wearing jeans and a black sweatshirt with a Motorhead logo on the front.'

Catherine goes cold. 'And did they say anything to Jake?'

'Indeed they did. Their exact words were, "*That will teach you, you little shit.*"' She gives an embarrassed laugh. 'Excuse my language. Anyway, from his voice Jake put him at around his forties.'

The room is spinning. Catherine can't move. Can't speak. Her lips and tongue unable to form any words.

'PC Olds. Are you still there?'

She forces her lips to move. The words to come out. 'Yes... yes. I'm still here.'

'Did you need me to repeat any of that?'

'No. That won't be necessary.'

Because she's already said too much, and because of it, the world is no longer making sense to her. How can it when the man Jake described is Gary? The Motorhead sweatshirt he was wearing, a Christmas present she'd bought him in their early days together – an ironic present after he'd told her he liked them.

'And that's exactly the description he gave? You're certain there's been no mistake?' The edge of the phone is pressing into Catherine's temple, but she needs the pain to centre herself. To concentrate on what the woman is saying.

'Yes, I'm certain. So, when exactly were you thinking of

coming in to speak to Jake? You should know that the lad's very tired and needs to rest. In fact, the ward sister doesn't recommend anyone interviewing him until at least tomorrow after the doctor's done his rounds.'

'That won't be a problem. I'll let my colleagues know... and thank you.'

'You're welcome.'

Catherine replaces the phone and rests her elbows on Ellen's desk, fingers scraping through the hair at her temples. Unable to believe what she's heard. She'd thought it was one of the boys from Greenfield who'd followed Jake to the school in the small hours and beaten him so severely he'd been hospitalised. Never in her wildest dreams had she imagined it to be Gary.

She shakes her head, trying to remove the terrible image. It's all her fault. Gary had been jealous of Jake and the hours she'd spent with him. Considered the boy a rival for his time. And because of it, he'd beaten Jake up. To teach him a lesson.

Catherine feels sick. Had the same thought been in her husband's mind when he'd forced himself on Lisa's mother, Dawn? Had he wanted to teach *her* a lesson too? It's a question she can't answer, might never know, but there's something she *does* know about her husband. By being here tonight, she's saved Gary's life. In agreeing to meet Lisa at the school, she's stopped her house ending up the same way as her car, or the classroom she'd once taught in.

A burnt-out shell.

Catherine pushes herself up from Ellen's chair. Walks slowly to her classroom. And as she goes in and closes the door behind her, she can't help wondering. She might have saved his life, but after everything he's done, does her husband deserves it?

FORTY-TWO

Catherine sits back in her chair and looks at her phone. It's four fifteen.

Without the children in it, the lights off, her classroom feels strange. The cupboards, the tables and chairs, dark shapes in the gloom. Every sound amplified: the creak of her chair as she swivels it, the wind that rattles the windows, the thump of her heartbeat in her ears.

She wishes she'd never come. It's only now she's in the school that it occurs to her how vulnerable she is. No one knows she's here. Why had she been so stupid? She should have left Ross a message or, better still, woken him and told him of her plan. But it's too late now. She's heard something.

Catherine's on her feet. She rushes to the door and, with trepidation, opens it and peers into the dark, empty corridor. Seeing nothing, she tries to persuade herself she'd imagined the bang, but when it comes again, it's no longer possible to pretend it's not happening. The sound had been closer this time – one of the doors at the far end of the corridor. Lisa is on her floor, and the reality is that, just as in the past, she has no idea what the girl wants from her.

Her fingers as they clutch at the door handle are clammy. She should never have come here alone. But her common sense, her self-preservation, has kicked in too late. There are footsteps now. Echoing, confident footsteps. The person they belong to not bothering with stealth, not needing it, as the only other person in the building, the only one to hear them, is her.

And then a terrible understanding comes to her. One that makes her step back from the door. The footsteps are too loud for a woman. Too spaced apart. Fear tightens its hold. It's not Lisa who's in the building. It's a man.

'Aled?' His name has come to her lips unbidden and she sees it now. How the burnt-out car, the lighter left on her doorstep, the video of the petrol-rag in her letterbox, all have the stamp of his hallmark. His calling card.

But Aled is dead. His charred remains found in her burnt-out classroom. Yet how can she be so sure when those same remains had been impossible for the police to identify? Her brother had been sleeping there, yes, but that doesn't mean it was him. What if he'd invited another homeless person to take refuge there with him? What if it had been someone else altogether who'd died?

Catherine pictures her brother as he'd been the last time she'd seen him. The sunken cheeks. The desperate eyes. The arm he'd stretched out to her, as he'd pleaded for money, covered with scabs and bruising.

It can't be him. Even if he'd lived, too many years have gone by for him to be seeking her out now. But that's not the only reason she knows. Aled would have no means to get into the building. Only someone with a lanyard would be able to get through the security. It has to be someone who works at the school.

For one wonderful moment, she imagines it is Ross's feet that stride down the corridor. Her friend come to find her. To tell her it was a bloody stupid idea to have come here and to persuade her to come back home with him. But it isn't him either because the awful truth is she did the unthinkable. Crept out of the house in the dead of night without telling him where she was going. Or that she was even going at all.

Catherine's fingers touch the lanyard that hangs around her neck. And even if a miracle had happened and he *had* woken as the front door had closed, if he'd guessed where she was going, Ross would not have got into the school because she has his key card.

So, who is it who's striding towards her with heavy, urgent steps?

Catherine looks around wildly. There's no place to hide. Nowhere she can run without being seen. If only she'd taken Lisa's key card instead of Ross's, then she might at least have had a chance.

A picture of Lisa's card on its lanyard comes into her head, and she feels again the hard edges of it pressing into the palm of her hand as she'd picked it up from the hall table. But wait... there's something else coming to her. She remembers the eyes that had been on her as she'd put the card down again. Gary's eyes. The man who'd failed to stand by her when she'd needed him. The man who had raped Lisa's mother and beaten up Jake.

The next thought comes at her hard and fast, leaving her breathless. What if Gary had taken Lisa's key card without her knowing and used it tonight to let himself into the school. The same way she'd used Ross's?

But how could he have known she'd be coming here?

The truth doesn't come at once but in pieces... fragments of memory. The flicker of the lighter flame in the darkness. The ping of the first message. Gary would know where she was if *he* had been the one who had held that lighter. The phone. If *he* had been the one behind everything.

The shock is visceral and Catherine clutches at the door

frame to steady herself. She's never been scared of her husband before, but she is now. Because, since she found out what he did, he's no longer the person she'd thought he was. No longer the man she married but a stranger.

What a fool she's been. Everything – the fire under her car, the person who'd followed her into the public toilets, the videos she'd been sent and the attack on Jake – it had all been him. Had it been his way of controlling her? Had he believed her fear of the past would make her leave her job? Make her more reliant on him?

Slamming the classroom door shut, Catherine runs back to her desk and heaves at it. It's heavy but panic makes her manage to drag it a few feet. When she can't pull it anymore, she runs behind it, and using every ounce of strength she has, succeeds in pushing it further still with her hip so she's barricaded in.

The footsteps stop and Catherine sinks to the floor. Crawls under the desk. She doesn't see the press of the door handle, but she hears the kicks that threaten to jar the door from its hinges. Feels the jolt of the table leg as the door makes contact with it.

She curls herself into a ball and draws her knees up to her chest, making herself as small as she can. Arms crossed over her head. Lips wordlessly praying the desk is strong enough to keep him out. Knowing she should call the police but too scared to move.

Glass shatters, sending shards splintering across the top of one of the students' tables to Catherine's right. The shock of it making her press her hands to her ears in horror.

The windows between the classroom and the corridor are large, only thin strips of wood separating each pane. Gary's striking the glass with something hard, something heavy – the fire extinguisher attached to the wall beside the noticeboard most likely – and the irony of it isn't lost on her.

Any second now and he'll be climbing through the jagged broken teeth of the window. Jumping from the table where she's hiding, onto the carpeted floor. Splinters of glass crushing under the heavy soles of his shoes.

He's in front of her now, grabbing her arm and hauling her up. He shoves her back against the wooden cabinet with its rows of blue plastic drawers and the sharp pain she feels as her side makes contact with the edge, forces her to take an inward breath. It's only then she looks at him properly.

He's standing with his arms folded. The Motorhead logo on his black sweatshirt – the same one he'd worn the night he'd attacked Jake – just visible above them. If only she could predict what he was thinking, what he was planning to do, but it's impossible. There's no way she can read his expression when, in the dark classroom, the whites of his eyes are the only thing showing through the slits in his balaclava.

'What do you want?' Catherine's voice wavers. 'Why did you ask me to come here?'

He doesn't answer, just looks at her, his lack of words bringing on another wave of panic. Forcing her to make up her own answer to the question: Gary's here because he suspects Ross has told her about Dawn. And Gary would calculate there was every chance she would have believed what he'd told her was true. Not just because Ross is her friend, but because, unlike Gary, he'd been there for her in her time of need. Had offered her his flat as a refuge, his shoulder for her to cry on. A loyalty that should have been to *him* not to her.

How Ross's betrayal must have hurt Gary.

Had he pictured his friend and his wife in Ross's apartment? The two of them discussing him, sharing their disgust at the way in which Lisa had been conceived. And had he imagined the way her face would have changed as the scales had fallen from her eyes and she'd finally seen him for who he really was? A man who believed he had the right to take what he wanted even when it wasn't his for the taking.

A monster.

She'd once asked Gary if you could love someone too much. Now she thinks of all the times she'd turned away from the glimpses she'd seen of the real Gary: when his eyes had lingered too long on a pretty young face, when his thumb had left a bruise on her wrist after love making... and knows that you can. It's not that difficult.

And the fallout from that is standing before her in this dark classroom. The black balaclava that covers his face dehumanising the man she'd once believed had saved her. The fabric of it obliterating everything that had ever bound her to him. And it comes to her now, the reason he's tricked her into coming here tonight. It's to silence her. To make sure she'll never be able to tell anyone else the truth.

She watches as his hand slips into the pocket of his jeans, her pupils widening as she sees the lighter he draws out. The click as his thumb flicks at it, making the flame dance in front of his face. Making her skin creep.

'I won't tell anyone, Gary. I promise.' Desperation makes her throat constrict, her voice come out strained. She gestures to the glass-covered floor with shaking fingers. 'Not about this or about Dawn. You have my word. No one will believe Lisa when she says you're her father. Without a paternity test, she'll never be able to prove it.' She's babbling. Saying anything that might make him change his mind. Make him let her leave the classroom. 'And even if she does, there are no witnesses to what happened that night because Dawn's dead. You misunderstood the signals and made a stupid mistake.' She takes a step forward, her hand outstretched. 'You, me and Ross. We'll make a pact. Stick together and make sure that no one ever finds out. It's what best friends do, isn't it? Look out for each other? It's what we've always done.'

She stops, the hopelessness of it all descending on her. Because, after all the years they've lived together, why would Gary believe an iota of what she's just said? He'll know that it's desperation that's brought those words to her lips rather than her belief in them. Or her love for him.

The certainty of it makes her try another tack.

'And Ross isn't exactly whiter than white, is he? You know better than anyone what he's like after he's had a few and it's not as if he's managed to keep a woman for more than a couple of dates without it falling through. Karen, for instance. He said he was the one who ended it, but who knows the reason. Calling you out on what you did might be his jealousy talking... a way of making you look bad because you've never had a problem keeping a woman. Okay, I admit I believed him when he first told me about Dawn, but now I'm away from him, I can see it for what it is... lies.'

The words stall in her throat because he's already taken the few steps towards her. His hand slamming up against the wall beside her face.

'Shut the fuck up.' His words echo in the empty classroom. It's the first time he's spoken.

She shrinks away from him. 'I'm sorry.'

Lifting his free hand to her face, he presses the cold metal edge of the lighter against her cheekbone. 'You will be.'

'Stop it. Please stop it.' Catherine hears the click of the lighter. Her attempt to move her head away from the scorch of the flame blocked by his arm.

'You think you're so clever, don't you?'

'No, I don't. Of course I don't.' She's close to tears. Scared that anything she says will provoke him further.

But despite the fear that's making it hard for her to comprehend, she knows something's amiss. It's the smell of his breath. His voice too. There's something about them that's not right.

It's not Gary in front of her.

FORTY-THREE

Below the black material of the balaclava, a tendon in his neck bulges. Catherine stares at it, trying to make sense of what he's saying. Shock and anger colliding as she realises how stupid she's been. How naive. She grabs at the balaclava that covers his face. Wrestles it off.

'Fuck you!' Ross's contempt for her, now his face is no longer obscured by the black fabric, is evident, not just in his words, but in the steel of his eyes. The set of his jaw.

'How did you get in?' She'd taken his key card. It was impossible.

His eyelids lower a fraction, as though disbelieving that she can be so stupid.

'Karen, of course. Fucking the designated emergency coordinator has its perks. I always knew a copy of the master key would have its uses one day.' He fishes it out of his pocket and holds it up for her to see. 'It seems that day came sooner than I thought. It never occurred to me they'd ask you to give back your lanyard and that you'd take mine.'

Catherine stares at him, uncomprehending. 'But why are

you doing this? If what you've told me about Gary is true. What he did to Dawn...'

Ross takes a step towards her and she shrinks back, her fingers gripping the edge of the cabinet of plastic drawers. The lighter is still in his hand and, as he reaches for her, the heat from the flame scorches her cheek. In the tray on her desk are worksheets and the students' essays waiting to be marked. Behind her, pinned to the noticeboard, are posters and examples of work – all would go up in a second if Ross touched the lighter to them. She stops speaking, reminded of the seriousness of her plight... of what happened before.

'What he did to Dawn?' His breath makes the flame shiver. 'You really don't get it, do you?'

'I don't understand.'

The laugh Ross gives is not one she's heard from him before. It's mirthless, devoid of emotion, and it frightens her.

'Gary's a coward... always has been. He'd never have had the nerve to have done anything to her. But don't let anyone tell you he wouldn't have been thinking about it... when he was alone in that classroom with her. When she'd told him he was wrong and that she hadn't changed her mind about ending it between them.' He rubs two fingers up and down his sideburn. 'But he didn't act on it. Why would he need to when he could have anyone he wanted? Could step out of those school gates, click his fingers and have them all come fucking running. Like *you* did.'

Catherine folds her arms across her body to stop the shivering and stares at the balaclava that lies on the floor between them. Scared of what he's saying. Not understanding.

'I didn't even know him then.'

'So what? He only approached you after he'd shown me a photo of you on the school website and I told him I thought you were hot. Saw it as a challenge. That he stuck it out with you so long is what surprises me. He used to be so much fun.'

Catherine recoils from his words. Her grip on reality loosening. 'So Gary isn't Lisa's father?'

He leans back against the desk. Grins. 'No. That stupid bitch Lisa got *that* wrong. Her prig of a mother had told him where to go.' His smile slips. 'I thought it was because she wanted me. Gave me all the signals. You know, a smile when Gary wasn't looking. A brush of her arm.' He pauses. 'A bit like *you* really.'

'Then if Gary isn't the father. Who...?' She stops, and the air seems to shift around her as the realisation shapes itself.

'Yes. It was a surprise to me too. Not that the woman had got pregnant, had a kid, but that the girl would one day turn up at Greenfield Comp looking for her father. When you told me what had happened, that she'd been on a mission to find her happy ever after with her daddy, it was almost impossible to stop myself from laughing. Not because she'd pointed the finger at the wrong guy – Jesus, I honestly had no idea – but because she was the icing on the cake. I'd put in the work to make you feel threatened, vulnerable, now here was this girl muscling her way into your family.' Ross's tone is conversational, as though they're back at his flat, sharing a whiskey and a cup of tea on his settee. Not alone in this dark classroom. 'You know, Cath, she more or less handed you to me on a plate and there was I waiting with open arms to console you. To commiserate with you. Biding my time. Knowing that, sooner or later, you'd see this for what it is... that we're meant to be together.'

Catherine's world is shaken. Everything changed. Ross is staring into space as though watching a film she can't see. Their future together panning out before his eyes – a future of his own making. Not hers.

And she sees that he believes every word he's said. Every delusion.

In front of her stands the person she believed to be her friend. But *he's* the monster, not Gary. Not Lisa. She can barely

look at him. The thought that she had kissed those lips making
her sick to the stomach.

'It was you who raped Dawn.' Catherine can barely get the
words out. '*You* not Gary.'

'That's a bit harsh, Cath.' He looks hurt.

'Are you saying it was consensual?'

Ross gives a slight shrug of his shoulders. Pushes himself up
onto one of the tables, his legs swinging. As though it's a normal
day at school. As though nothing terrible has happened. But
Catherine's not fooled. There's blood on her arm where a shard
of glass from the broken window cut it. The hateful balaclava
just inches away from her. He's as dangerous now as he had
been when he'd lured her here.

He doesn't look at her but idly flicks at the lighter that's still
in his hand. 'She'd been coming on to me all week, then on the
evening Gaz had gone into her classroom, when he'd given her a
hard time because he didn't want to accept it was over, I had the
luck to be walking past.' He laughs to himself. 'She'd basically
told him to fuck off and I reckoned it was my chance. Knew
she'd done it because of me.' His face turns darker. 'Only the
bitch pushed me away.'

Ross's eyes meet hers now and he doesn't need to say what
he's thinking because she can read it in them.

Like you did.

Catherine feels a sudden coldness as though the tempera-
ture in the room has dropped. The inevitability of what
happened next in Dawn's classroom draining her of every
emotion except one. Disgust.

'Does Gary know?'

'Gary?' He looks confused. 'Does he know what?'

'What you did after he left.'

His scorn is clear from the narrowing of his eyes. 'Did he
hell. The only person Gary is interested in is himself. He

wouldn't have given Dawn another thought once he'd left the building.'

Her relief at his words, at the fact that her husband hadn't known, is intense. But it's short-lived because Ross is on his feet again. Pacing between the tables.

'I wasn't lying when I told you he was worried, though – shitting himself that the girl would point the finger at him and say the kid was his, when it became obvious she was pregnant, because a baby was the last thing he wanted. What Gary said about not having slept with her for weeks was true and he knew she must have slept with someone else after him. But, after the way he'd treated her that evening, he didn't trust her not to accuse him of being the father.' Ross laughs to himself. 'He hadn't a bloody clue what had happened after he'd left... didn't even know I'd still been in the school. He begged me to be his alibi. To say he'd been with me all evening. And, when I agreed, it was like a gift from heaven because by giving him an alibi, your precious husband had ensured I had one too. Oh, the irony!' He stops when he reaches her. Looks thoughtful. 'Not that I needed one. Dawn never told a soul what happened in that classroom. I've always wondered why.'

Outside the window, the sky is lightening. Still too early for the morning cleaners. Too early for this nightmare to end.

Catherine wraps her arms around her. 'She said nothing because it would have been her word against the two of yours and she knew there was a danger she wouldn't be believed. You're evil, Ross, pure evil, and I can't believe I never saw through you.'

A sudden pain shoots through her jaw as Ross reaches out and grabs hold of her chin. Spits the words into her face. 'I played the fucking waiting game for you, playing the best friend card, laughing at your bloody awful jokes and letting you believe I enjoyed playing your stupid games. Christ... as if I fucking cared who got into school first.' His fingers dig deeper into her skin. Making her catch her breath. 'And for what? To be screwed over just like before. By a tease. A fucking little tease. Well, just remember that I asked nicely once and it won't happen again. In this world, if you want something, you have to take it.'

It's not this classroom he's seeing in his head but another one, and a terrible realisation comes to her – the reason he'd lured her to the school when he could have easily forced himself upon her in the flat. It was because in a classroom, many years ago, he'd got away with one of the worst crimes a man can commit. It had made him feel invincible, powerful.

And he needs the adrenaline that comes with that power, to commit the deed again.

Catherine struggles, kicks out at his shin, but it's hopeless. He's too strong for her, the weight of him pushing her back into the rack of drawers. His hand covering her mouth, extinguishing her screams. But she knows she has to fight. She bites down hard on Ross's finger. Tastes blood. The shock and pain enough to make him snatch his hand away. Take a step back.

'Fuck!'

But she can see how his eyes have darkened. Recognises the raw anger there – that she's dared to stop him. And she knows that things will only get worse. Much worse.

He lifts the lighter, flicks it until the flame ignites. His voice a snarl. 'No one will want you after I've finished with you. No one.'

Before, it had been a threat, but now he means it.

'Please, Ross, don't,' she begs. 'Think what—'

But she doesn't have a chance to finish. A sharp, pressurised hiss breaks her sentence and before she can see what's happening, Ross is enveloped in a jet of dry powder.

'What the hell?' He staggers back, rubbing at his eyes. His face. 'I can't see. I can't fucking see.'

Catherine can, though. Enough to know that it's Lisa who

stands a few feet away, the nozzle of the fire extinguisher still directed at Ross's face.

The dense white cloud envelops them all now. She can hear Ross coughing. Struggling to breathe. Feels, rather than sees, Lisa's hand as it grabs at hers.

'Run, Catherine. Go now!'

'I'm not leaving you.' She's coughing too. Choking on the chemicals.

But Lisa's not listening. She pulls away and, through the white haze, Catherine sees her lift the extinguisher above her head. Hears the impact as the girl throws it with all her strength at Ross.

'That's for my mother, you bastard,' she screams through her tears. 'That's for Mum.'

The extinguisher rolls away across the classroom. Ross is on the floor clutching his leg. His eyes screwed up tight against the chemicals that have temporarily stolen his sight.

'Come on.'

Lisa grabs Catherine's hand again and drags her to the broken window their feet crunching on the broken glass. They climb through and then they're running. Flicking on every light switch as they pass. Waving their hands at every security camera. Hoping, praying, that someone will know they're there. Not daring to stop and call the police on Lisa's phone until they're out of the building. Far enough away from the man who has ruined both their lives to feel safe.

To breathe again.

And when they hear the first siren, they turn to each other. Knowing that, after this, neither of them will be the same again.

FORTY-FOUR

Gary sits at the dining table, his forehead pressed against the heels of his hands.

'I can't believe it. All these years we've been friends. How could I not have seen it? How could I not have known?'

Catherine pulls out a chair. Sits opposite him.

'Ross fooled us all.' Her fingers trace the bruising around her chin. 'It's what men like him do.'

'And all this time...' Gary lowers his hands. Looks at her. 'All this time he was lusting after you. Planning a way of taking you from me.'

Catherine nods, remembering how it had been Ross she'd seen putting out the blaze in the school car park, knowing it would make him a hero in her eyes. A fire he'd been the one to light, and to film using the basic timer on the burner phone he'd propped up on the wall that separated the car park from the road. Guessing, correctly, that the fear he'd instilled in her, a reminder of what had happened all those years ago, would make her feel vulnerable. A vulnerability she wouldn't be able to share with her husband. And when Gary had made it impossible for her to remain in her house, he'd been waiting to lure her in, like a fish on the end of a line. Biding his time. Knowing it would be worth the wait. Except she'd rejected him as Dawn had.

'You made it easy for him, Gaz. He knew you too well – knew you were terrified of me having another breakdown. By playing on my guilt and messing with my head, it wasn't hard for him to drive a wedge between us. Have me running to him.' Catherine shakes her head at her stupidity. 'Then when Lisa pushed her way into our home, upsetting the equilibrium and giving me the final push to leave you, he must have thought all his birthdays had come at once.'

Gary swallows. 'I should never have told him about Aled. Not because I couldn't trust him, but because I promised you I wouldn't.' His eyes are pained. 'But Ross and I told each other everything, always did... or rather I *thought* we did.'

He stops, not needing to say more as he can see from Catherine's face that she's thinking the same – Ross's biggest secret, the terrible thing he'd done to Dawn, was one neither he nor Catherine had known.

She feels the warmth of Gary's palm as it covers hers. The graze of his thumb as it strokes the skin of her knuckles. He knows he's let her down. Knows he might lose her.

'I'm so sorry, Cath. I wish to God I'd never told him about your brother or the fire in your classroom. If I hadn't, then none of this would have happened.' Gary looks sideways at her. 'It was evil of him to use that knowledge for his own ends, but you should never have felt guilty. The fire at your school wasn't your fault.'

'Wasn't it?' Her voice catches.

Years ago, when she'd told him Aled had been in the classroom the night of the fire, she'd stopped short of the whole truth. She'd said Aled had broken into the classroom, but it was a lie. The night it had happened, she'd stayed late after classes, allowing her brother to slip in unnoticed with his sleeping bag –

a small concession because she'd refused to give him money. She'd put his needs above the welfare of the children she taught. Above their safety.

It's been her strong belief that, rather than it being an accident, Aled had started the fire that destroyed the classroom and seriously damaged the one next door. To get back at her for not doing more. And the guilt that had lodged in the deepest part of her heart when she'd stood in the playground, seen the aftermath, is something she's had to live with ever since.

Ross had guessed the truth even though Gary hadn't.

Murderer.

She looks at her husband. Maybe she'll never tell him the truth.

Catherine slides her hand out from under his. 'But even if you hadn't told Ross, he'd have found another way. If it hadn't been me, then it would have been someone else. That line he gave me about you having everything, leaving him no option but to take what he wanted, was bullshit. It was an excuse, that's all. Someone to blame for the sick fantasies in his head.'

'I didn't know what he was like, I swear. Didn't know about Dawn.' Gary's voice has an urgency to it. 'If I had, I'd have told someone. I know what you're thinking, but I'd never have kept a secret like that. Never. He set me up. Wanted you to believe I was the one behind everything.' He pinches the space between his eyes. 'I can't believe he framed me for the attack on Jake. I gave him that sweatshirt after we'd been to the pub. It was pissing with rain and I thought the bugger would catch his death if he walked home in nothing but his shirtsleeves. Now I wish to hell I never had.' He shifts his eyes over to her. 'I was wondering... did the police say why he beat up the lad?'

She shakes her head. 'No. Maybe he thought Jake was getting too close to me.'

'That's what I thought too.' Gary slumps back in his chair.

'I'm glad the boy's leaving hospital soon. That he's doing well. And us, Cath... are we good?'

She rubs a hand down her face, winces as her fingers reach her chin. She doesn't want to answer his question.

Sensing what she's thinking, Gary reaches over and takes her hand again.

'Please, Cath. I can't lose you too.'

She looks down at his hand, at the wedding ring that's all that's left of their marriage. *Lose you too*. Those words, so carelessly said, tell her everything she needs to know. She'd always taken second place to Ross. And whilst Gary never did anything wrong, she can't deny that the trust they had is broken.

Catherine stands. 'I need to see Lisa. Find out how she is.'

The last time she'd seen her was two days ago outside the school, a blanket around her shoulders. Her shocked, white face luminous in the glare of the police car's headlights. If it hadn't been for the girl's bravery, things might have ended very differently.

'I made her leave the house.' Gary's voice is plaintive. 'You didn't think I stood up for you, but I did. When I got back from the pub, she'd packed her things and gone. If I hadn't done that, she wouldn't have even been in the school. She wouldn't have—'

'Give it a rest, Gary.' She's heard enough. 'Are you expecting me to thank you?'

But, despite her tone, she knows it's true. With nowhere else to go, Lisa had gone back to sleeping in the classroom. The smash of the classroom window had woken her and she'd heard everything Ross had said. Knew everything he'd done. Poor girl... what a terrible way to find out. They'd both made their statements to the police and now she needs to go to her. Make sure she's okay.

She picks up her coat.

'So you'll be back later then?' She hears the desperation in Gary's voice despite his attempt to hide it.

Catherine looks at him. Tries to remember the reason she married him. She'd thought it was because he saved her, but now she wonders if in fact it was *she* who'd saved *him*. Gary's clever, good-looking, has always had what he wanted, but deep down, he fears being on his own. It's a fear that had weakened him. Ross had seen it and now she sees it too.

This is not about Gary, though – it's about her and Lisa. Others too, like poor foolish Karen who will most likely lose her job. And Jake... beaten up by a man wearing her husband's sweatshirt, whose future has been put in jeopardy by the fallout.

It's about everyone who's been affected by her and Gary's toxic friendship with Ross.

'I'll see you when I see you.'

Catherine closes the front door and gets out her phone. Hopes she'll pick up. She's treated Lisa badly. Accused her of things she hadn't done and she needs to make amends.

EPILOGUE

Catherine stands at the window of her classroom and looks down, watching the students leave the building. When the last of the stragglers has filed through the green metal gates, she folds her arms and smiles. It's been a good day. A really good day.

There's a knock on the door and she turns. Sees Ellen Swanson standing there, a bunch of files in her hands.

'How was the class from hell today?' she asks. 'In particular Dean.'

Catherine's eyes move to the table he'd been sitting at fifteen minutes earlier. 'Oh, you know Dean. You can never be certain what's going to come out of his mouth at any one moment.'

Ellen smiles. 'All of them... they seem to have settled down in the last few months.'

'They have. I was wrong, you know, Ellen. I see that now. The different way I viewed the kids in the school. In my own way I was discriminating between Jake and the rest of them because my unresolved issues around my brother had skewed the way I looked at things. All the kids needed my time, needed my effort and input equally, and I'm just so grateful you didn't hold it against me.'

Ellen shifts the files in her arms. 'What? And lose one of my most valued members of staff? I don't think so. But I will, of course, be needing to find a new English teacher.'

She doesn't need to say anymore because they both know she's talking about Ross. The school's CCTV footage had given the police everything they needed to know and after he'd been taken into custody the truth had come out. The video he'd taken on the night he'd lured her to the school, of the lighter and the rag stuffed into the letterbox of her house, was one he'd recorded the evening before. Something to use if ever there was a danger that Catherine might go back home to Gary. And when that time had come sooner than he'd expected, his plan had worked well. Catherine would never suspect him of being the one to send it when he was asleep in the bedroom across the hallway.

Except he hadn't been asleep. He'd been planning the next steps. Writing the messages to her in his darkened bedroom. Messages he knew she'd presume were from Lisa.

Ellen coughs, forcing Catherine's thoughts back to the present.

'Anyway, let's move on to something cheerier, guaranteed to put a smile on all our faces... the forthcoming Ofsted. I presume our new Head of English is up for the challenge. Any cunning ideas to make the inspection go smoothly, Cath?'

'Not yet, but don't you worry. I'll think of something. Lisa said she'd help me.'

She expects Ellen to laugh, but she doesn't, and when she looks at her, blotches of red are creeping up her neck.

'To think I was a day away from telling Ross he'd got the job instead of you. He made me promise I wouldn't tell you he was also after it.' Ellen shakes her head in disbelief. 'I'm ashamed,

Cath. Utterly ashamed. You're an amazing English teacher – the proof is in Jake Lloyd's A level results.'

Catherine nods. Jake's results had been the first ones she'd checked. 'I'm proud of him. He did really well despite what happened.'

'And thank the Lord for that.' Ellen purses her lips. 'I still can't believe Ross had that much influence over Karen that she'd do his dirty work. Risk losing her job over him. It was a cruel thing she did to you, changing Jake's script and making it look as if you'd been the one to do it. She'll have to live with that every day... as will I.'

Catherine puts a hand on her arm. 'Everyone makes mistakes.'

'Not ones that could ruin a colleague's reputation. End a career. I should have checked the files more carefully... not jumped to conclusions.'

'We're only human, Ellen. It makes us fallible.'

She thinks of Karen. Wondering, not for the first time, if she should go and see her. But it's unlikely she will... Some bridges are too broken to mend. She'd heard that after losing her job at Greenfield Comprehensive, she'd left the teaching profession altogether and it saddens her. Karen had loved her job almost as much as *she* had.

'Ross took us *all* in, me more than anyone, and what were you supposed to do? Believing I'd falsified Jake's coursework left you no choice but to suspend me. I would have done the same thing if I'd been head.' She looks down at her feet. 'And you weren't the only one to lay a false blame. I thought it was Lisa who had framed me and that's something I'll have to live with as well. That girl did nothing wrong.'

Ellen nods. 'Despite her rocky start, I think she's going to be a good teacher. Having you as her mentor certainly helped.'

'That's good to hear. Speaking of which, I'd better go.' She delves into her bag and brings out a set of keys. She's been rubbing along beside Gary in their house since Ross was arrested. Lisa has been sleeping in the spare room in Lynne's house. Neither has been ideal.

'First night in the new flat and I've still got a few things to move from the house.'

'I'll let you go then... and I wish you luck in your new home.'

'Thanks. I appreciate it.'

Catherine follows Ellen out of the classroom, turning off the lights as she goes. They walk together down the corridor, and when they reach Ellen's office, Catherine says her goodbyes and carries on. At Lisa's door, she stops and pokes her head round.

'Ready yet? Or do you need more time?'

Lisa smiles. Gestures to the books on her desk. 'I'm ready if you are. I can take these home with me.'

'I like the way you're calling it home before we've even spent a night there. It's a good start.' The door to the resource cupboard is open and Catherine spots the sleeping bag Lisa had once slept in. The pillow. She hadn't wanted to take it to Lynne's as there wouldn't have been space for it in their small spare bedroom.

Catherine points to it. 'You won't be needing that... not unless you're planning on going camping.'

Lisa pulls a face. 'Definitely not.' She stands and pushes her chair in. Looks at the sleeping bag. 'Thanks for not saying anything to Ellen about me sleeping here that time.'

'No worries. It was the least I could do after...' She stops. The memory still painful. 'Anyway, if you hadn't, things would have ended very differently.'

They both stand quietly, remembering.

It's Lisa who breaks the silence.

'It's also kind of you to let me stay in your new flat. I really appreciate it, Cath... especially after I was such a cow. Barging into your life like that.'

Catherine takes the sleeping bag out of the cupboard and slips the carrying string over her shoulder. Tucks the pillow under her arm. 'You needed to know who your family was. I understand that. This is a fresh start, Lisa. For both of us.'

'And you're not having second thoughts?' She looks doubtful. 'About the move, I mean.'

'None at all.'

Lisa picks up the books. Places them two at a time into her box, then lifts it. She walks to the door, then stops. Looks back at Catherine.

'I thought, after we've eaten tonight, that you could tell me a bit more about your brother, about Aled... only if you want to, of course.'

Catherine smiles. 'I'd like that. Gary never wanted to talk about him. Thought it would set me off.' She draws quote marks in the air. 'My brother was a good lad underneath it all. Clever. Thought out of the box. He reminded me of Jake in a lot of ways.'

She thinks of the phone call she'd had from Jake's mum the day he'd got his results. Heard the pride and relief in her voice. Jake was thinking of taking a job, then applying to university the following year to study English. She'd thanked Catherine for her help and support... support that her brother Aled had never had.

'I'm sorry I took his photographs. I shouldn't have. I wanted to find out more about him. Thought that if I knew more, I could—'

'There's no need to apologise. I understand.'

They carry on walking, and as they reach the door, Catherine's phone rings. Gary's name flashing up on the screen. He'd been shocked when she'd told him she was leaving. Had begged her not to, but she'd stayed firm. Since then, he's been ringing every day, twice sometimes, but she just can't get over everything that's happened.

There's another reason too.

She'd been packing her clothes into her suitcase, ready for the move, when a strange feeling had come over her. In her hand was a beach cover up she hadn't worn for years and as she'd let the chiffon fabric slip between her fingers, a memory had come back to her. She'd been standing in the bedroom of a Spanish villa, packing to go home from their holiday, and Gary was out on the balcony. The sliding doors partly open. His voice easy to hear.

Of course I won't fucking tell anyone, Ross. He'd sounded agitated. His phone pressed to his ear. *I'm your best friend. Why would I after all this time?*

It hadn't meant anything to her then. But it does now.

'Let's go, Lisa.'

Lisa points to the phone in her hand. 'Aren't you going to answer it?'

Catherine shakes her head. 'No. It's not someone I want to talk to.'

She'll never know for sure what Gary was talking about, but she has her suspicions. Had he guessed what Ross had done to Dawn in that classroom and confronted him? Had he agreed to be his alibi if he needed one? She could ask him, of course, but he'd only deny it and she wouldn't be able to live with the uncertainty if he did.

But there's something else she can do.

Tomorrow she'll give PC Olds a ring. Tell her that not everything makes sense. Because the night Gary had lent Ross his Motorhead sweatshirt, had been after the attack on Jake not before as he'd told the police in his statement.

Gary had viewed her career, and the success she was making of it, as a threat and her guess is, he'd acted on it. Justice must be allowed to take its course. Maybe when the police question him, other things will come out. She hopes so.

The only question left unanswered is why Ross lied when

he said Gary hadn't known about him and Dawn. It was as though the two men had an understanding. Perhaps it was simply a case of what happens in school stays in school.

Catherine puts her phone back into her bag and steps out onto the playground. With Lisa beside her, she passes through the school gates and heads for her car. When she gets there, she glances at the blackened ground where her car had burnt before looking away.

Sometimes, you *can* love someone too much...

A LETTER FROM WENDY

I want to say a huge thank you for choosing to read *Make Yourself at Home*. If you enjoyed it and want to keep up-to-date with all my latest releases, just sign up at the following link. Your email address will never be shared and you can unsubscribe at any time.

www.bookouture.com/Wendy-Clarke

I come from a family of teachers and some of you may know that before I was an author, I was a teacher too. It seems a long time ago now (I've written nine novels since then) but teaching was once a big part of my life. Unlike Catherine in my novel, I worked in a primary school, but despite teaching a younger age group, I experienced the same comradery with my fellow teachers, the same staffroom politics as my protagonist.

A small part of me misses those days in the classroom, but nothing compares to making up stories for a living. It was a lot of fun drawing on those memories to create a setting for my thriller that readers would recognise. Those long dark corridors when night fell were just asking for the sound of echoing footsteps!

I hope you loved *Make Yourself at Home* and if you did, I would be very grateful if you could write a review. I'd love to hear what you think, and it makes such a difference helping new readers to discover one of my books for the first time.

I love hearing from my readers – you can get in touch on my

Facebook page, through X, Goodreads, Instagram or my website.

Thanks,

Wendy

www.wendyclarke.uk

facebook.com/WendyClarkeAuthor

x.com/WendyClarke99

instagram.com/WendyClarke99

bsky.app/profile/wendyclarke.bsky.social

ACKNOWLEDGEMENTS

Thank you to my wonderful editor, Jennifer Hunt, whose insight, talent and dedication to making a book the best it can be, has enabled *Make Yourself at Home* to be in your hands today. She has championed me from the start and, nine books later, is still guiding and encouraging me with her words of wisdom.

My grateful thanks also to the rest of the Bookouture team who work so hard behind the scenes, before and after publication, and to the book bloggers and reviewers whose thoughtful reviews and passion for sharing stories are instrumental in connecting my books with a wider audience.

Thank you to my friends for their continued support of my writing – especially my lovely writing buddy, Tracy Fells, who has been by my side since this crazy journey started. Sharing the good times and the not so good with cups of tea, sympathy and a lot of laughs. My Bookouture sister, Liz Eeles, also needs a mention for the sea walks we share when we need to put the world to rights. And I haven't forgotten my 'Friday Girls': Carol, Linda, Helen, Barbara and Jill, who remind me life isn't all about writing!

My family are always there in the background cheering me on and for this book, I must give a special acknowledgement to my stepdaughter, Emma, who allowed me to take a peep into her life as a secondary school teacher and patiently answered my many questions.

Finally, as always, the biggest thank you goes to Ian, whose ability to thrash out tricky plot problems is second to none and whose patience is just what I need when I'm pulling my hair out.

Before I go, I'd just like to say that without readers there would be no books, so a huge thank you to everyone who has bought and read mine... especially you!

PUBLISHING TEAM

Turning a manuscript into a book requires the efforts of many people. The publishing team at Bookouture would like to acknowledge everyone who contributed to this publication.

Audio
Alba Proko
Sinead O'Connor
Melissa Tran

Commercial
Lauren Morrissette
Jil Thielen
Imogen Allport

Cover design
Aaron Munday

Data and analysis
Mark Alder
Mohamed Bussuri

Editorial
Jennifer Hunt
Sinead O'Connor

Printed in Great Britain
by Amazon

58955190R00169